CRUISING WITH MOM AND DAD

CRUISING

WITH

MOM AND DAD

From Hong Kong to Athens:
Thirty-five days of adventures,
destinations and reflections
on Oceania's Nautica

by Jack Hovenier

To obtain additional copies, please e-mail nautica@gumball.com

Cover design by Davin K. Knight
Edited by Sukey Rosenbaum
All photos by Jack Hovenier

To Mom and Dad

CONTENTS

FOREWORD

When I took a 35-day cruise on Oceania's Nautica with my mom and dad in the spring of 2007, I began to post online about our experiences.

I expected that future travelers would appreciate information about the ports, the ship—all the things I appreciated and learned from reading other passengers' experience online.

A funny thing happened. The story had a mind of its own, and as I wrote, the focus shifted from the ship and exotic ports of call to spending time with my mom and dad. While I don't feel it, at 44 I am middle-aged now, and this book has the reflections of a man in the prime of life crossing the globe with his parents in their later years.

Most of this book was originally posted on the Oceania discussion board on Cruise Critic (cruisecritic.com), an online forum for cruise-ship enthusiasts. The 75 contributors who encouraged and wrote online during the trip are part of the story. They come from Australia, Canada, the Canary Islands, Germany, Mexico, New Zealand, the U.K. and the U.S.A. The majority of their questions and comments are included.

The original posts were edited for grammar and consistency, and a few factual corrections were made. No one is responsible for errors.

"Honor thy father and thy mother: that thy days may be long upon the land which the LORD thy God giveth thee."

—Exodus 20:12

Chapter 1

HONG KONG

JackfromWA   *April 1, 2007 10:34 a.m.*
NAUTICA IMPRESSIONS: HONG KONG TO ATHENS

As our cab turned the corner at Hong Kong's Ocean Terminal, I captured my first glimpse of Oceania's Nautica. There is nothing like the anticipation of boarding a luxury cruise line for the first time. Sometimes the ship exceeds my expectations—Radisson (now Regent) Seven Seas Mariner springs to mind—or, in the case of the Royal Suite of Celebrity's Summit, my expectations weren't met. I have enjoyed every cruise—some just much more than others.

Before I share my initial observations, some of my background may be helpful. I am a 43-year-old gay male in a long-term relationship. I have been on many cruise lines—once each on Holland America and Silversea, and many times on Royal Caribbean, Celebrity, Princess and Radisson (now Regent). Overall, my favorite is Regent. I particularly like their cabins and ship size. Silversea has equally good, sometimes better, cuisine and service, but I prefer Regent's larger ships and slightly more casual passengers.

Given the buzz about Oceania, I couldn't wait to get onboard. I carefully read the reviews on Cruise Critic, purchased Lonely Planet guides to our destinations (Hong Kong, Vietnam, Thailand, Singapore, India, Oman, Egypt, Jordan and Greece) and gleaned tips in the message boards.

I am traveling with my retired parents (my partner of seven years couldn't get six weeks off…imagine that!) and paid a single supplement for my own outside cabin. My parents are experienced cruisers too. We are all optimistic that we'll enjoy this itinerary and, more important, the chance to spend time together. My dad is 75 and a cancer survivor. My mom is 69. I realize if I want to do things like this with them I can't procrastinate any longer. Rather than pay for balcony cabins, I elected to reserve a cabana on Deck 11 for all 35 days of the cruise.

As we exited the cab, the baggage handlers grabbed our luggage and less than five minutes later we were literally onboard the ship where the actual check-in occurred. Immediately upon boarding Nautica, I grasped why Oceania ships are often described as reminiscent of an English manor. The decorative paneling, crown molding, color scheme and warm ambience immediately evoke a luxurious English bed and breakfast or country estate.

Check-in took less than 10 minutes, and my dad and I sat in stately, overstuffed green chairs on Deck 5 while my mom went up to Deck 10 to reserve the two specialty restaurants. My birthday is April 4th, and we wanted to celebrate at the Polo Grill. We successfully reserved both days we wanted. We were advised to book both Polo Grill and Toscana early in the itinerary in case we want to eat there again. According to the ship staff, on most cruises standard (*i.e.*, non-suite or non-concierge-level) passengers are guaranteed only one reservation to each of the specialty restaurants, but owing to the length of our cruise we could likely eat there several times if we chose.

Our cabins wouldn't be ready until three o'clock, so we wandered around and I continued to enjoy the many little spaces to comfortably relax, the excellent library and the computer room. Finally it was announced that all the staterooms were ready for occupation. I knew this was only a 165-square-foot stateroom, but when I entered it I was disappointed for the first time since boarding. It has been many years since I have had a standard room without a veranda. Admittedly, I decided to purchase a less expensive stateroom and I received what I paid for, but I didn't like the size. The bathroom is extremely small and the shower is tiny. In all fairness, I am 270 pounds and 6 feet tall (I am watching my diet on the cruise—the goal is: Don't gain any weight), but I felt pretty cramped in both the bathroom and stateroom. After being used to walk-in closets and decent-size bathrooms on Regent, this was a real step down. As I settled in, I grew more accustomed to the cabin size, and since I am traveling alone I am certain it will be fine. I don't know that I would want to share this cabin for 35 days, but it would be fine for two on a seven-to-15-day trip. The bedding is excellent, and the closet space and layout are intelligently designed for maximum efficiency.

My cabana, on the other hand, absolutely exceeded my expectations. Each cabana is named after a famous port of call, and I was assigned "Saint Bart's." There are eight cabanas total, they stretch completely across the most forward section of Deck 11, and they have the same expansive view as the bridge. On my trip, all but one are sold for the entire cruise, but on most cruises they are available for daily rental of $50 on port days and $100 on sea days. Although they include amenities such as fruit skewers, ice towels, chair massages and meal service from the Waves grill, the real reason I wanted it was to enjoy the large outdoor Balinese daybed-for-two while reading several long-due-to-read novels and laying in the sun. Having a reserved private outdoor space was particularly appealing to me and, by choosing this instead of a veranda, the cost was less. I am sympathetic to those passengers who complain that the sale of cabanas takes away some of the best viewing areas on the ship, but I doubt Oceania will remove them since the extra revenue for the ship is significant (I paid $1,500 for 35 days' exclusive use).

I checked the Internet speed, and it wasn't quite as slow as I feared. The download speed today was 118k and upload was 85k. This will get worse on days when the satellites are occluded, but it is tolerable for e-mail. I had planned to purchase a 500-minute access package for $300, but beginning tomorrow Nautica is also offering 800 minutes for $400 and 1,200 minutes for $480. Unfortunately, I have to stay in touch with work or I couldn't have come on the cruise, so I am buying the mack-daddy 1,200-minute access. It costs as much as a year of broadband at home!

Dinner last night was good. Not exceptional but certainly on par with some of my meals on Regent and Silversea. Even the best cruise line cuisine won't please everyone; some passengers will always rave about the buffets on Carnival while others will always complain about Silversea. Judging solely from the first two days, I haven't noticed any significant enhancement or deficiency comparing Oceania's cuisine to my dining experiences on other luxury cruise lines. Overall, I expect the food will be great.

3

Several other things are wonderful about Nautica. The ship size feels "just right" to me. Oceania ships are large enough to feel bigger than an overblown yacht but small enough to get from one end of the ship to the other in less than five minutes. The crew is exceptional and couldn't be more helpful. So far the service on board is equal to or better than any ship I have sailed on.

I have been to Hong Kong several times in the past few years to attend trade shows, and the city never ceases to impress me with its vitality, commerce and unique blend of East and West. This is my parents' first trip, so today we took the double-decker public bus from Kowloon to Stanley Market. This roughly hour-long ride is a superbargain at $13 HK (less than $2 US). We had a great tour of Hong Kong from our second-story perspective atop the bus. I purchased four pair of genuine Tommy Bahama shorts and three shirts for less than $100 US. My mom found five silk shirts she loved and paid about the same. All in all, the shopping was great and we were a little sorry to see Victoria Harbor disappear as Nautica set sail for Da Nang, Vietnam.

If anyone has any questions about the ship, please post and let me know. I am off to Vietnam!

*****

Lane40   *April 1st, 2007, 11:05 AM*
Thanks for the great first post regarding your cruise. I look forward to reading more of your impressions regarding the cruise and the Nautica in the coming days.

LHT28   *April 1st, 2007, 11:05 AM*
We spent 32 days in the C1 cabins and found them fine, but we have not sailed RSSC so have not had the experience of bigger bathrooms, closets etc.
Maybe I would be spoiled if we sailed in the larger suites.

orchestrapal   *April 1st, 2007, 02:06 PM*
Glad you are enjoying the cruise so far. Loved your first report and the new Internet-package information. Continue to have a great trip, and keep us all posted.

4

shesgoneagain   *April 1st, 2007, 07:23 PM*
Appreciate the fine details!

Wonderful narrative and great detail. I am booking this trip for next April and appreciate all the information. Thank you so much for the time and effort in sharing your trip with us. I'll be checking often for updates. BTW, how is the weather? Have a grand time with your parents. I took my parents on a 40th-anniversary cruise to Alaska. That trip has since become one of my most treasured memories since they are both deceased. ENJOY!!

Elizabeth

meow!   *April 1st, 2007, 08:33 PM*

Thank you so much for such an informative, detailed and candid account of your trip—I agree with your description of the cabin, the food and the comparison with other lines. I look forward to reading the rest of the report, which I am sure will be very lengthy. Having written long reports in parts on this Oceania and the Silversea columns of this Cruise Critic board, I can appreciate the effort and amount of work required!

Aussie Gal   *April 1st, 2007, 09:18 PM*
JackfromWA,

First of all, happy birthday for Wednesday. It is a special day for us too, our 43rd wedding anniversary, so you may have been born on our wedding day, 4/4/64. If so, you are a very lucky man as it is a wonderful date.

Thanks so much for posting your cruise thoughts and diary. We have booked the same cruise for next April, and I was hoping someone would let us know how it pans out.

Also any little bits of info regarding the ship are very helpful. Particularly giving us the prices of the Internet package was fantastic.

Enjoy your time on board, and we hope to hear your next installment soon. Please tell us also about your shore excursions in each port.

Jennie

merryecho   *April 1st, 2007, 11:12 PM*
Good luck with keeping to your weight goals on the trip—one meal at a time...

*****

JackfromWA   ***April 3rd, 2007, 03:25 AM***

Thanks for all the replies. I wasn't expecting so much activity! Before my next installment I wanted to reply to everyone:

shesgoneagain: The weather is muggy, hot (80s) and until today sunny. I don't think anyone will need a jacket outdoors this cruise, but some find the ship's air conditioning in public rooms too cold. I keep my room about 68 so it doesn't bother me. Almost 10 years ago, my siblings and I went with my parents on their 40th anniversary to Alaska. It was wonderful. I find cruises to be the best choice for multi-generational vacations. We are hoping to do it again for their 50th in August 2008. It will be 19 people if all the in-laws, grandkids and my partner Ty make it.

Aussie Gal: Happy anniversary. 4 APR 64 is special for me too.... It was my first birthday, and I have a photo of that not-remembered occasion where I proudly sit in front my large chocolate elephant cake. My mother refers to that photo as the first of my dad's many unsuccessful efforts to turn me into a Republican (the elephant is the symbol for the Republican political party in the U.S.A.).

merryecho: I am doing pretty well. Last night I did break down and had the Maine lobster with a little prime rib, but it was the Captain's Gala welcome-aboard dinner. Actually, the oatmeal in the dining room is good, and fresh, sweet fruit is plentiful.

6

Chapter 2

FIRST SEA DAY
AND DA NANG, VIETNAM...
SECOND DAY AT SEA

JackfromWA　　　*April 3rd, 2007, 03:25 AM*

At 6:30 a.m. the Sun Deck was unexpectedly bustling with passengers. Since most guests are North Americans, we are struggling with various stages of jet lag. I observed this firsthand when I woke up about 6 a.m. and unsuspectingly decided to enjoy a quiet morning and a cup of coffee on the deck. It was as bustling as Central Park at lunchtime. I am sure as the days move forward, people will get up later, but for now this is an early-to-bed, early-to-rise crowd. Ben Franklin would be proud.

One of the differences between Nautica and some of the other luxury lines is that Nautica occasionally feels a bit more crowded. Not uncomfortably so, but just enough to notice a difference. Doing the math reveals why. For example, Regent's Seven Seas Mariner (my favorite ship) has about 750 passengers and weighs about 50,000 tons. Nautica has about 700 passengers and weighs about 30,000 tons. Much of that space savings is in the different standard stateroom size (165 square feet vs. 250 square feet) but sometimes it is apparent there is less room per passenger on the Pool Deck, in the lounges and when embarking. I don't find it a problem; in fact, I admire it as another way that Oceania management has reduced expenses and passed on savings to customers while achieving a minimal reduction of guest luxury-cruise experience. Oceania is very adept at this—they cut corners all over the ship, but they cut the right corners, and as a result the experience is still perfectly acceptable to most passengers comparing Oceania to her competitors.

After my dreams of a solitary deck were dashed, I joined the expanding crowd and walked along to the beat of my iPod, forming the little meaningless circles that cruise-ship joggers and walkers perform on ships' jogging tracks the world over.

Despite my comments about awareness of less space and more passengers, deck chairs were consistently available throughout the day. I carefully watched and saw at least 10% of the shaded chairs and 20% of the exposed-to-the-tropical-sun chairs available. This is another area in which Oceania excels. They combine a reasonable number of chairs along with an enforced "after 30 minutes of abandonment, your towel, book or whatever else you use to hog the chair you aren't sitting in will be removed." I don't know where the stuff goes, but it certainly isn't overboard, so the hogging passenger will probably get to retrieve his or her belongings from a friendly Indonesian deck attendant. Personally, I think if they actually lost their books, hats, etc., the policy would be better followed, but Oceania is too nice for that.

Our safety drill was held indoors at 10:30. Attendance was mandatory, and roll was taken. The whole process was very civilized, and we were finished in 15 minutes. Because of high winds and wet decks, we were not taken from our muster stations to the lifeboats.

The ship staff emphasized that anyone caught smoking anywhere but the two or three designated public smoking areas would be put ashore at the next port. According to the ship staff, this has happened and will continue to happen. If you are a chronic smoker challenged by authority figures, Oceania is not the cruise line for you.

Immediately following the drill, we held a small Cruise Critic gathering. Screen name "seasoned" (Sukey) had wisely suggested meeting in the forward portside of the Horizons lounge immediately after the drill. I met her, Lulu (Louisa) and her husband Mike, Steamboat Sista (Chris), Jancruz1 (Jan; her husband Stu had a cold) and several friends of Jan and Stu's. We visited for about an hour. Among other topics, we shared our experiences of procuring visas. Our combined anecdotal experience is that everyone but Louisa and I had taken Oceania's visa package. Although the service was slow, expensive and apparently not well documented, it got the job done with minimal stress.

Louisa and I procured our visas independently—she is from Montreal and was able to get the visas locally—and I don't like relying on other people for things I sometimes mistakenly think I can do better myself. My work takes me to China at least every two years, and since I was getting Chinese visas for a work-related trip prior to the cruise, I decided to get the other visas for my parents and me as well. I am on a first-name basis with one of the agents for Travel Document Systems based in San Francisco, and she advised me that all but Vietnam were easy to independently obtain.

Vietnam has arcane bureaucratic requirements such as no use of Federal Express, DHL or UPS, two money orders for each visa instead of just one totaling the full price, and other similar nonsense. Petty bureaucracy notwithstanding, I trudged forward. Between mid-January and late February I obtained our visas for China (which was not necessary for the cruise), India, Vietnam and Egypt. Since I still had a month before leaving and I don't like waiting in lines, I decided to obtain our visas for Jordan even though I knew I could get the visas at the port upon arrival. While I had no experience to indicate whether this would result in actually saving time in Jordan, I figured it couldn't hurt and might just get me on shore half an hour quicker than other passengers.

I started to get concerned after seven days when the Jordanian visas hadn't arrived back at my office. I called the embassy, and they said not to worry, that visa processing takes at least five business days. Since the embassy is open daily only from 10 a.m. to 2 p.m., I figured they move at a snail's pace. Finally the self-addressed envelope arrived back, and I breathed a sigh of relief when I saw my own handwriting identifying this as the U.S. Postal Service Express Mail envelope (no FedEx for the Jordanian embassy either) from the Embassy of Jordan.

I had commented earlier to my co-worker Eric how ironic it would be if after getting all the other visas I needed that getting the Jordanian visas I really didn't need resulted in losing my passport, so I was really happy the envelope arrived safely. As he laid the envelope on my desk, Eric looked concerned.

"Uh, Jack, there was nothing inside in the envelope," Eric said. "I opened it since it looked like a check from a customer, but it was completely empty."

"C'mon, Eric. Give me the passports. I don't have time for this. I have too much going on trying to get ready for this trip." He continued to swear that the envelope really was empty, and it slowly dawned on me he wasn't kidding—the envelope from the Jordanian embassy really didn't contain our passports! My worst travel nightmare had come true. The passports were lost, there wasn't time to replace them, and even if we could get them replaced by a completely overwhelmed U.S. State Department Passport Division, there wasn't enough time to get all the visas again.

After several frantic calls to the Jordanian embassy, our three passports were found amid the clutter of someone's desk. No one at the embassy knew why our envelope had been sent empty. They apologized and said they would ship them the next day on my Federal Express account. I tracked that FedEx envelope on the Internet from the moment it left Washington, D.C. until it was out for delivery in Bellingham, Washington. Mom and Dad were blissfully unaware their irreplaceable passports were lost, so when I told them the whole story later it didn't have the impact it had on me. Although I would still get my own visas necessary to board the ship (Vietnam, India, Egypt), I would risk waiting a half-hour in line and obtain the Jordan and Oman visas along with all the other passengers on arrival. Needless to say, I did not send our passports to the Oman embassy for visas. We will wait in line like everyone else.

This morning I woke around 6 a.m. and due to the lack of motion thought the ship was already docked in Da Nang, but when I opened the curtain to check the weather through the window, I quickly realized we were still at sea. I assumed we would be docking soon, but as 7 a.m. passed with no land in sight and as our scheduled 8 a.m. arrival time loomed large and the ship still showed no sign of docking, I knew something was wrong. We were not going to be docked on time. A loud sound intruded in my stateroom: DING-DONG! DING-DONG!

"Good morning, ladies and gentleman from the bridge. This is Ray, your cruise director, speaking. We regret to inform you that the port of Da Nang is closed due to high winds and low visibility. We will keep you informed throughout the morning of the ship's plans."

The Nautica team sprang into action, and within an hour each stateroom received a revised schedule, which includes a stop in Nha Trang tomorrow from 8 a.m. to 5 p.m. and many additional shipboard activities today. My father plays bridge; since my primary goal in taking this trip is spending time with him and my mom, I am attending a last-minute beginners' bridge class with him this morning.

I feel very badly for the Vietnam veterans aboard who wanted to visit Da Nang. I personally wanted to visit Hoi An, but these things happen. I was impressed with how quickly the cruise staff made alternative plans. They clearly are a well-oiled machine. I am just glad we didn't cancel Saigon, as I am scheduled to visit an orphanage and take photos of some children already assigned U.S. families but waiting for final adoption.

Two days at sea in a row isn't a bad thing, but I will be ready to go ashore in Nha Trang tomorrow. Next stop: Vietnam.

*****

Aussie Gal   *April 3rd, 2007, 03:38 AM*
JackfromWA,
     Thanks so much for the next installment. I am printing them out so that I can go back and reread them at a later date. I can hardly wait until the 8th April next year when we board the Nautica. A big thank-you for spending the time in posting such an informative diary.
                                                                   Jennie

shesgoneagain   *April 3rd, 2007, 11:45 AM*
The saga continues...
Jack—
     I feel like I am reading a wonderful travel novella—and anxiously await the next chapter. I will be traveling with my sister next April. We are considering the cabana for our trip. Will your parents be able to join you in the cabana? Is it spacious enough to

11

have a few guests? Nice to know that Oceania can respond so quickly to unanticipated weather. I have rock and rolled all over the seas and have always had a wonderful time despite changes in ports/excursions/time, etc. Sail on—

Elizabeth

merryecho   ***April 3rd, 2007, 04:00 PM***

While wading through paperwork it is great to take a break and join you and your folks on your journey, Jack. Thank you, and please keep us all posted.

BTW, have you ever tried Atkins? It works great for helping me avoid temptation on cruises, but of course isn't for everybody.

Merryecho
Former Bellinghampster
Fairhaven College, '70-'73

Fetchpeople   ***April 3rd, 2007, 05:46 PM***
I'm frantic with worry

Please dispel my fears; I'm losing sleep; I'm close to a nervous breakdown waiting for the critical news:

Tell me that the berry supply is better, more varied, and fresher than ever.

Tell me that the cheese course is saturated with a worldwide supply of the best that cows and sheep can provide.

Tell me that the casino manager is so friendly that dealers are instructed to hit on 17.

Tell me that you were able to get shrimp cocktail in the GDR and not have to resort to an alternate dining arrangement.

Help! Don't make me wait any longer for this information. Perhaps you could skip a tour to post the information. After all, inquiring minds want to know...

Lagunaman   ***April 4th, 2007, 01:10 AM***
Jack's great reports from Nautica

Really enjoying your excellent travelogue, especially as my brother and wife from L.A. are sailing with you!

I am very excited about seeing them when you dock here in Phuket. Also it will amaze them that I am so well informed as to how their first two weeks have been onboard.

Personally, not tried Oceania, so far Crystal, Holland, QE2, with HAL being my preference.

12

Looking forward to your next installment with report on Vietnam, one S.E. Asian country I have not yet visited.

However, any info needed on Phuket or Bangkok, will be glad to provide you with my local knowledge

John

Jancruz1   **April 4th, 2007, 03:25 AM**

Hi, all,

Jack is posting such a wonderful review that I won't attempt to embellish it except to say...Jack is charming and it is fun getting to know him...we have also had dinner with Kendra and Peter from Australia and as all CC people they are wonderful...Nha Trang was a nice port to visit...and tomorrow on to Saigon...we have been there before so Stu and I will get a massage at the Rex Hotel and shop...

Regards to all...

Jan
CruzUnlimited

*****

JackfromWA   **April 4th, 2007, 09:37 AM**

A FEW RESPONSES

Aussie Gal: Happy 43rd anniversary today!

shesgoneagain: The cabanas are fine for two, but there isn't really room for three. The ship was initially resistant to letting me share with my parents since it is supposed to be one cabin = one cabana, but they relented and also provided my dad and mom a "cabana card" (it shows staff you are authorized to be in the cabana) when I pointed out that I had paid a 200% single supplement but I could have been sharing a cabin with them—not that any of us would have had much of a vacation! We tend to use the cabana in shifts, and sharing hasn't been a problem but it hasn't been simultaneous.

merryecho: I lived in Stack III at Fairhaven College in 1980 while attending WWU. I bet you had fun there! We'll have to chat sometime.

13

<u>Fetchpeople:</u> To stave off your breakdown I am posting today even though I intended to wait a few days and do a better job proofing my writing—too many editing errors yesterday. To put you at ease, here you go:

1. Berries are abundant. I have personally seen raspberries and strawberries, and today a ripe blueberry sprayed my dad's new shirt while he ate breakfast. The berries are sweet, plump and delicious.

2. My friend Sukey loves the cheese course. I prefer hard Dutch and Italian cheeses and these are mostly soft cheeses, but she was in a state of bliss and passed on all sugar to have the cheese plate for dessert night before last. She made small audible pleasurable moans between bites, so I think the cheese course passes.

3. Casino manager was friendly to me. They stand on 17. I went in with $200, now I have $300, and since I am up 50% I am hoping to stay the hell out of the casino.

4. The shrimp cocktail in the Grand Dining Room may be a problem. We were discussing availability of special requests in the dining room last night. Since Princess, Celebrity and RCI can do it, I believe Oceania will furnish off-menu shrimp cocktails, but I need to discuss it with a headwaiter. I did order a Caesar salad off-menu and that was no problem.

<u>Lagunaman:</u> Thanks for the hospitality offer in Phuket. Tell your brother that you heard the Italian guitarist, Warsaw String Quartet and Gypsy violinist were excellent. Also, the bridge instructor, Jean Joseph from the Midwest, is phenomenal. In Phuket, I arranged for a day room and massages at the Banyan Tree. I wish we had another day there.

Chapter 3

NHA TRANG, VIETNAM

JackfromWA   *April 4th, 2007, 09:37 AM*

Claiming I have traveled to Vietnam, Thailand, Singapore, India, Jordan and Egypt based on my short stay in each port is like saying I am a 1970s music devotee because I bought Casey Kasem's *Best of the '70s* CD and really enjoyed it. Cruises are greatest hits. To really delve into a city like Nha Trang, I need at least three or four days there. I can't claim the Beatles' *Abbey Road* is my favorite record if the only song I've ever heard on it is "Here Comes the Sun."

I hesitate writing anything about a town I merely set foot in for four hours, but since it is of interest to people taking this cruise next year I will. Hopefully, the 2008 Hong Kong-to-Athens itinerary will include Da Nang and Hoi An again. Hoi An is of much greater interest to me than Nha Trang.

My first impression of Nha Trang was that it is foreign, crowded, dirty, hot, friendly, pushy and different from any place I had ever been. The markets have numerous touts who vigorously attempt to take you to their shop, and though I have never been anywhere exactly like Nha Trang, I have been many places that resemble its high-pressure shopping, and I don't feel like hanging out in the town markets again.

Nha Trang has beautiful beaches, high-end resorts, mid-end resorts and young backpacker meccas scattered throughout the town center and the surrounding countryside. Coming back on the ship's shuttle, I overheard numerous passengers complain that Nha Trang reminded them too much of Mexico (think Mazatlán). But I think even Mazatlán is wonderful if I am doing something I enjoy.

Tonight is my 44th birthday, and my parents, Sukey and I are having dinner at the Polo Grill. The menu looks great, but the

15

combination of the heat, a few days eating business dinners in mainland China before the cruise and a few other personal body-related conditions that out of sensitivity for the reader will remain nameless, have diminished my enthusiasm for a jumbo prawn cocktail/French onion soup/tableside-prepared Caesar salad/steak-and-lobster dinner followed by coffee and crème brulée for dessert. I'll eat what I can, but I would much rather feel good than eat for sport, so I may end up just ordering salad, soup and prawns. God forbid they ordered a birthday cake. I can't think of anything more useless than a birthday cake on a fine-dining, all-expenses-paid cruise ship. I would rather choose my dessert than have to eat a cake I don't want anyway.

One of the new and liberating feelings I am enjoying is the length of this cruise. My mother pointed out last night that if this were an Alaska seven-day cruise we'd be going home the day after tomorrow. I am just beginning to adapt to the motion of the ship, the rhythm of the crew and to enjoy the ships facilities. I love knowing there are more than 30 days remaining on this trip.

Expectations determine whether I really enjoy a cruise. Since I primarily take cruise vacations because ships provide a great space to interact and have intimacy with people I love, I am rarely disappointed with mediocre itineraries and slightly disappointing food. Of course, exciting itineraries like this one, great food and excellent service such as Nautica's enhance the whole experience.

*****

bdmagee   *April 4th, 2007, 10:00 AM*
Thank you
Just wanted to thank you for taking the time to write this review. As I am looking forward to my first Oceania cruise in 13 days (who is counting?), it's great to hear both the positives and negatives of your great journey.

Once again, thanks for your humorous and detailed writing. And please do not concern yourself with any possible typos you may have had. I can promise you no one here cares. Just want more updates!!!

shesgoneagain　　　*April 4th, 2007, 10:03 AM*
Happy birthday, Jack!!

> *Wishing you many more grand voyages.*
>
> > *Elizabeth*

aneka　　　*April 4th, 2007, 10:17 AM*

> *Happy birthday Jack from WA!*
>
> *I am enjoying reading your travel diary. My husband and I sailed on Nautica in Oct. '06, Istanbul to Athens. We enjoyed the ship and the people we met through CC. I hope you are well enough to enjoy your birthday dinner in the Polo Grill. Our dinners there were a highlight of our cruise.*
>
> *Thank you for taking the time to report on this wonderful adventure as it is happening. I feel like I am there with you.*
>
> *Have a great trip.*
>
> > *Annette*

scdreamer　　　*April 4th, 2007, 10:35 AM*
Great report—thank you!

> *Thank you for the wonderfully detailed trip report! Even though it will probably be years before my husband and I make it to that part of the world, it is definitely on our list, so I am enjoying the opportunity to vicariously visit the ports and experience the ship with you.*
>
> *Sending wishes for the happiest of birthdays—hope you are feeling well and will continue to post!*
>
> > *Leslie & Wayne*

Hibiscuss　　　*April 4th, 2007, 02:09 PM*
Happy birthday, Jack

> *We also send out our "Best Wishes" for your good health with wonderful memories as you share your cruise with all of us. We are booked for next year, so it is so nice to have you give us your impressions of what to look forward to. We appreciate the opportunity to follow in your wake.*
>
> > *Sandy & Ray*

Aussie Gal　　　*April 4th, 2007, 06:05 PM*
Jack,

> *I have just printed out Part 3 of your travel diary. I hope your birthday yesterday was as great a day as our anniversary. We had*

blue skies and a temp of 22C, a perfect day. We went out and had a lovely French lunch with not too much food.

Nothing is worse than overeating, and I hope your birthday dinner was to your liking.

Jennie

Jancruz1   **April 4th, 2007, 09:28 PM**
Good morning, all…

It is 8:20 a.m. and we are about 1.5 hours from Ho Chi Minh City…it is very warm and humid…we have a speaker on board talking about many facets of Vietnam, and it is very interesting.

Stu and I had a wonderful time in Nha Trang yesterday, and tho I haven't been to Da Nang…appreciated the fact that we were only 10 minutes from the beautiful beach and town, we were not looking forward to the almost two-hour drive to Hoi An so for us it was a perfect switch…Last night dinner in the GDR was excellent and afterward we went to see the classical guitarist in the Nautica lounge, he was excellent…I am afraid Jack will be disappointed, I know for a fact they will NOT bring shrimp cocktail from Polo into GDR…and for good reasons…if they do it for one they will have to do it for all!!

Happy birthday, Jack…I am trying to find you…if I don't, can you contact me in 8049…

Regards all…

Jan
CruzUnlimited

Lagunaman   **April 5th, 2007, 03:06 AM**
Phuket call

Hi, Jack,

Chosen well, my home backs onto the Banyan Tree Golf course and it is my favorite hotel on the Laguna Complex; also all homeowners get use of the facilities, a nice bonus!

If time permits, a short taxi from there is the new Trisara Hotel, apart from being nice to see, the route is scenically the best on the Island.

You may find the following site useful in describing all that the chaotic and fascinating BK offers:
www.bangkok.com/attractions/index.html

Continue with your excellent reporting and belated "Happy Birthday."

KIWP   *April 5th, 2007, 02:54 PM*

My husband and I have circumnavigated the globe numerous times (land and sea) and the "O" ships are our favorites. We took this trip in 2006 (the inaugural), and it was FANTASTIC. Even though we've been to all the places numerous times, we're going to take this cruise again in 2009. It gets better every day. But next time you book, try a Penthouse. Not for snobbery, but just plain comfort and space.

Your descriptions are spot on, but please do try all the eating venues because overall, the food is the best at sea. I usually leave the ship having lost weight (because I don't eat much and exercise daily), but I have sampled on the many cruises we have taken with them.

Hopefully you'll go to Agra. To see the Taj at sunrise and sunset (no, I won't break into song) is one of life's special moments. The other one is going to Petra. The Treasury wall at Petra (along with the Library wall at Ephesus) is a must see for anyone who truly enjoys discovering the world.

Sorry to hear about Da Nang, because it is wonderful, but the rest is just as special and you will enjoy Vietnam immensely. What you describe about the way the ship's staff reacted to the change of itinerary is how they always do things. The manager of Destination Services on the Nautica, Cinthya Pavan, is a jewel and one of Oceania's best.

I hope the weather gets better. Great log so far. Thanks again for sharing.

Enjoy and do keep up the report. I'd love to hear your further impressions.

merryecho   *April 5th, 2007, 07:44 PM*

Happy birthday, Jack! You mentioned there were some Vietnam vets onboard—have you had a chance to talk with them? How interesting it would be if Oceania hosted an informal chat, to hear their feelings on going back. I guess you were too young to remember any of that, though.

How funny that you were a Fairhavener too. I was there the second year it opened—was Ryan Drum still teaching during your time?

Patty Cruiser   *April 5th, 2007, 11:18 PM*

This is my first time on this web page so hope you get my message...your intake is great, but when you get to Petra, do the Petra and Bedouin tour. One of the highlights of the cruise. We did it last year and loved every minute. Know what you mean re: cabins. We took a 10-day Caribbean and opted for cheap...never again. Our cabin was O.K., but not what we like.

JanCruz1   *April 6th, 2007, 03:36 AM*

Yesterday had a fabulous day on our own...took shuttle from ship to Rex Hotel at $5 per person round trip...went into the Rex...asked them to suggest lunch place they did (Lemon Grass) and it was delicious...also made a reservation for a car and driver for today...(we have been here to Ho Chi Minh City before...) seven-passenger air-conditioned new Toyota with a driver and wonderful guide who spoke perfect English (I have his e-mail) for $10 per hour for the car...not per person...

After making our 2nd-day arrangements, we continued on to Ben Thanh market and shopped until we dropped...then went off to lunch...after lunch about 2:30 we went back to the Rex and went to their spa...Stu and I had the MOST fabulous massage for one hour each and it was $5 a person...we each tipped $5 because I couldn't believe the price...after our massage took the shuttle back to ship for a nap and dressed, had dinner in Tapas and joined the cruise tour for a special show at the top of the Rex...show was wonderful and we had a beer (included,) and at 10 p.m. returned to ship for the night...Food in Tapas was wonderful...tho we didn't eat too much we were so warm, even after showers...

More about today later...time to do our last bit of shopping on the pier!!

Please feel free to ask any questions while we are on board...

              Jan
              CruzUnlimited

bdmagee   *April 6th, 2007, 11:35 AM*

The Rex has an unorthodox history: It used to be a French garage, was expanded by the Vietnamese, and then was used by the United States Information Agency (and some say the CIA) from 1962 to 1970. The hotel was transformed in a massive renovation and opened in 1990 as the kitschy, atmospheric government-run place it is today.

Chapter 4

SAIGON (HO CHI MINH CITY)

JackfromWA   *April 6th, 2007, 11:48 AM*

In 20 minutes Nautica will pull away from Pier M1 at Saigon's Nha Rong port and magically transform back from a five-star downtown hotel to a luxury cruise ship. I love the overnights in port, especially in places like Hong Kong and Saigon where we are docked in the heart of the city. Last night I left the ship at 9:30 p.m. and didn't return till close to midnight. The crew also seems to love these overnights. They flock to the discos, restaurants, shops and markets and while ashore are tourists like the rest of us. On cruise ships there are two distinct classes: those serving and those being served. I enjoy meeting a favorite waiter or purser in the market and chatting as equals in a way it is difficult to genuinely do onboard.

Saigon is a great port. The locals refer to the downtown core as Saigon and the surrounding area as Ho Chi Minh City. On our first day in port, I didn't take any of the ship excursions as I had previously arranged to visit an orphanage and take photos of children who are already assigned to families in the U.S.A. but can't leave the country until all the Vietnamese and U.S. paperwork is complete. The orphanage was extremely clean, and the children were clearly well adjusted and well treated. I brought some small gifts, took lots of photos and just enjoyed being around all the life that accompanies several hundred under-the-age-of-five children. My parents decided to come along, and we all enjoyed the unique glimpse into Vietnam society this visit gave us. It is sometimes said a society can be judged by how it treats its prisoners and orphans, and by at least half that standard, Vietnam looks very good. The orphans appear to be better looked after than many of the kids I saw on the streets.

The whole orphanage visit ended up taking the better part of the day, so afterward we returned to the ship and ate dinner at Tapas on the Terrace. Even though Nautica's dress code is always "country-club casual," sometimes it is nice to just stay in shorts and sandals. Since it was at least 90 degrees with about 90% humidity, we didn't want to change, and Tapas has a come-as-you-are policy. The eggplant parmigiana was excellent, as was the fresh sushi and sashimi. Tapas always serves a pasta of the day, fresh sushi, buffet-style entrees, starters, desserts and salads. Service was excellent as it has been in every dining venue on board. While I prefer the Grand Dining Room for overall food quality, presentation and ambience, Tapas offers a perfect alternative nicely positioned between room service and the other dining rooms. I suspect I'll eat there at least once or twice again.

On April 4th we celebrated my 44th birthday, and I am feeling better. Polo Grill is excellent, and I have nothing but good things to say—the shrimp cocktail is the largest I've ever had on any ship, the garlic mashed potatoes were exquisite, and the service was superior. Although the meat was excellent, the tenderloin I enjoyed in the Grand Dining Room was truly as good as the tenderloin served in the Polo Grill. While I think the Polo Grill is better than the Grand Dining Room, it is only incrementally better. It is nothing like the quantum difference between the fine dining restaurant—the SS United States—on Celebrity's Infinity and her regular dining room. I would be disappointed if I hadn't eaten there, I intend to eat there again, but I won't sit in the Grand Dining Room thinking: Gee, I sure wish I could eat at the Polo Grill again instead of this dump! The deciding factor on any given night for me would be the menu selection in the Grand Dining Room (Polo Grill is always the same), what sort of ambience I want (Polo Grill is steakhouse club, intimate and easy to have conversation—the Grand Dining Room can be hard to hear in), and whether or not Polo Grill can accommodate me. Unless you are vegetarian, it would be a mistake to go on the ship without trying Polo Grill, but the meals served in the Grand Dining Room can usually hold their own against the meals in Polo Grill.

After dinner we went to the Ben Thanh night market. The night market skirts around the edges of the day market, and I estimate there are about half as many vendors at night as there are in the daytime. We had to be very careful walking through, as unlike any other night market I have shopped in Asia, this one allows motorbikes. Everywhere. It was a little scary to step out of a booth

22

and quickly look both directions to make sure a moped didn't immediately knock me into a pile of imitation Prada, Louis Vuitton, Gucci and Polo, and fake Rolexes. Although the quality of most of the replicas wasn't as good as Hong Kong or Shenzhen, China, the prices were less than half. Opening price for negotiation of a T-shirt purchase was $3. Price of a cab back to the ship: $4. Vietnam is really cheap and a great place to stock up on extra shirts if you don't need anything bigger than a U.S. size large.

Today we visited some typical tourist attractions. First stop was the War Remnants Museum. Since this is about cruising, I won't say too much about my feelings over the Iraq War except that I oppose it, I opposed it from the beginning and I expect to continue to oppose it. Seeing the photo images neatly hung on stark whitewashed concrete bunker walls depicting American soldiers killing Vietnamese woman and children was painful. I know this is a one-sided view of history, but I love the U.S.A., I want to be proud of my country, and this exhibit made that very difficult.

I also felt old. I am a veteran, and when I was barely 17 years old I volunteered for the Army National Guard and was assigned to U.S. Army boot camp at Fort Jackson, South Carolina in the summer of 1980—five years after the end of the Vietnam War. I remember marching down Tank Hill, firing M-16s (680 rounds a minute in rock-and-roll or automatic mode), firing M-60 machine guns, throwing grenades and hearing stories from our drill sergeant of what it was like to fight, defend and kill in Vietnam. Back then, all the pop-up target silhouettes at the rifle training ranges were painted in communist soldier colors—we were Eleven Bravo infantry, training to shoot commies. Today, 27 years later, I saw an M-16 and an M-60 behind clear acrylic in the museum. They looked like antiques. I remember using those weapons (soldiers don't call them guns) like it was yesterday, and I remember eating left over C rations and training on equipment left over from the Vietnam War. I didn't expect any personal connection from my visit to the museum today. I am not a Vietnam War veteran; I am a veteran who thankfully served only in peacetime. Seeing my old weapons and looking at pictures of GIs dressed in the same Army-issue olive-drab fatigues I wore brought back many memories. After an hour I was ready to leave.

Next stop was the National Museum. Most of the exhibits were under construction but the renowned water puppets were performing. We decided to go to the 11 o'clock show, but when we arrived we were told the performance must have five paid admissions to proceed. Since there were three of us, my dad bought two extra tickets and we enjoyed a command performance. I don't know why no one else was there. The show is unique and lots of fun—I was wishing I had some of the orphans with us from the day before. The intimate outdoor theatre would have been filled with raucous applause and loud, high-pitched peals of laughter. The show is well worth seeing, but don't be surprised if a few drops of water leap from the dragon's mouth to you!

We left the museum and returned to the Ben Thanh day market, and then my parents and I split up. They are shopping their way across the Far East, and I wanted to have lunch onboard Nautica to avoid any further health issues. My dad loves to bargain, and sometimes I think he shops simply to enjoy the negotiations. The shopkeepers always congratulate his bargaining ability—he rarely pays more than half of the initial offer—often much less. My parents' shopping pattern is that my mom identifies and my dad procures. Despite his prowess, he did get himself into a bit of a bind in Nha Trang.

We were walking down the street near where the ship shuttle dropped us off, and my dad spotted a tailor sign. He had a pair of shorts that needed altering. He and my mom went to the tailor, while I bought a SIM card for my phone. When I returned, my mother was standing in the street waiting for me.

"They took your father to a different tailor, so I waited here so you could find us," she said.

We walked a little way to the associate of the first tailor. When I arrived, I immediately noticed my dad was no longer wearing his shorts. A short, craggy-faced Vietnamese woman was intently removing stitches and attempting to tighten the waist of his pants but there were too many pockets. My dad was wearing a large pair of ill-fitting, possibly early-communist-era brown slacks I'd never seen before. "Dad, where did you get those?" I asked, cringing with fear that he liked and bought them and desperately hoping they were only temporary.

"They belong to the shop," he replied. "I am just wearing them until mine are fixed."

Internally, I breathed a sigh of relief. "How much did it cost to alter your shorts?" I asked, sure that he had negotiated a great price.

A look of concern flashed across his face as it instantly dawned on him he was standing in a back-alley tailor shop in an unfamiliar city in Vietnam, wearing someone else's old pants—and he hadn't set a price for the repair. He quickly recovered and said, "I am sure they'll give me a good deal." He knew he had lost this one—he was in a strange foreign city in someone else's out-of-fashion pants—and even though they offered to let us walk around and enjoy the unappealing immediate surrounding shops he waited a half-hour for his pants and paid the $15 US they asked for without complaint. My dad is an excellent bargainer, but he knows when he has been outwitted playing the timeless art-of-the-deal game.

The shops in the Ben Thanh day market were similar to the night markets, but in addition the day market has copious quantities of unappetizing meat innards, unidentifiable seafood parts, delicious looking exotic fruits, and fragrant, fresh flowers. The combined competing odor of the fragrant food and flowers was pungent and at times repelling but at the same time strangely attractive and unique. It reminded me of the smell of a similar market in Cuzco, Peru, half a world away.

My parents and I split up; I went back to Nautica for lunch on the Terrace, my mom bought a white purse. The previous night Jan told us about the best bang-for-the-buck shore excursion on the entire voyage: a $5 massage at the Rex Hotel in downtown Saigon. Finding the Rex Hotel is easy since a shuttle runs between Nautica and the Rex every half hour from about 7 a.m. to 10 p.m.

I decided to take the ship shuttle to the Rex and enjoy a massage. The health club is a little tricky to find, but after trying three different elevators and asking several staff I finally arrived. I paid my 80,000 dong ($5) and went to the men's changing area. I was assigned a locker and given a key to wear. Since there is no assurance there isn't a second key lurking about, I elected to leave my clothes in the locker and bring my wallet to the treatment room. I was given a little T-shirt-weight half-robe and shorts to wear, and I followed my guide to the room.

The massage that followed was good—great for $5! Apparently the women who work there start at 10 a.m. and end their day at 11 p.m. Their wages come from tips from happy customers. Jan suggested leaving $3 to $5, which I intended to do. Apparently the desire for satisfied customers to leave large tips encourages a little of the world's oldest profession. Midway through my massage the young attractive woman attentively rubbing my body brushed her hand on my groin and asked, "Do you want this?"

I politely declined and neither of us seemed to take any offense. This is why I usually limit myself in Asia to a foot massage—it keeps things simpler. Often the foot massages for men are performed by men in a semi-public setting. In my limited experience, most foot massages are focused on health and relaxation. Body massages can move into other territories if boundaries aren't clear. I had kept my underpants on, which is likely why I wasn't at the receiving end of a more assertive offer. I mentioned the whole experience to my mom and dad. My mom, of course, had no extra offers and my dad was a little vague about whether he was propositioned or not—I am not sure if he was avoiding the topic for the sake of my mom, or if he was simply embarrassed that at age 44 I was propositioned and at 75 he was presumed not to be interested. Either way, he didn't directly answer and I didn't press the question. I have traveled a bit in Asia and know that even in expensive hotels there are always outlets for randy foreign travelers. I have been told that in the major hotels in China many foreign guests won't stay there if "companionship" services aren't readily available.

I was also propositioned by the cab driver who took me back to the ship. He generously offered to introduce a "very sexy lady" to me. It was my lucky day. All this leads me to think you don't have to look very hard in Vietnam to find the world's oldest profession—in fact, odds are that if you are a male by yourself, you won't be able to entirely avoid it.

26

Tomorrow is another sea day; then we are off to Bangkok.

*****

herenthere   *April 6th, 2007, 12:10 PM*
Yesterday I was reading your live messages from the Nautica. Then I went to cruise calendar to check out the number of ships in the ports when we cruise in May on Nautica. There was a webcam column with the link "ship," so I finally decided to see what it was all about. Sure enough, there was a live webcam from your ship in Ho Chi Minh City. I knew it was live because I had just read your thread! So, where are you writing your emails...and is it costing a bundle?
Sounds like a great trip! I'm enjoying reading about it.

KIWP   *April 6th, 2007, 12:29 PM*
Happy belated birthday, and I hope you feel better. You are having much too much fun to be uncomfortable. Besides, I'm sure I speak for all who are reading your reports, that they are wonderful and we're loving your narrative.
Try Toscana too. Very different from Polo, and most enjoyable.

meow!   *April 6th, 2007, 06:58 PM*
We usually take taxi tours in the cities we visit. It is convenient, private, comfortable and flexible, that is, as long as you can easily get one. The prices ranged from 60 euros per hour in Monaco to 50 euros in France to 30 euros in Italy (200+ euros for the whole day) a few years ago. In Australia and New Zealand, it was A$50 and NZ$50 respectively. Even in Mexico, it was US$30 per hour. So the price of US$10 per hour in Vietnam is amazing. There is the question of safety though. In some countries, it just may not be safe to haul down a taxi and ride in it. There is the chance of your being taken to some back alley and robbed, or worse. Is there any such concern in the countries of your voyage?
Another thing is the local food. Is it safe to eat, as sanitary standards are not the same as ours? Of course, you should take the necessary shots before you leave home. Consideration of safety and security is one reason that for the more exotic destinations, taking a cruise may be more desirable than a land trip. You can always eat on the ship, take bottled water from the ship with you when you land,

27

and if necessary follow the ship's tour. Indeed, several postings in the past recommended just that for St. Petersburg, for example. How about the Southeast Asian ports?

This narrative has been very interesting, no less than reading The Adventures of Tom Sawyer. *I am sure it is very helpful to those planning on trips to that area of the world. Thank you kindly for your effort.*

JanCruz1   ***April 7th, 2007, 12:02 AM***
Jack...glad you liked the massage...I didn't get a guy doing that to me...LOL...I love reading your reports...I compare them to my experiences...Yesterday we took a car, driver and guide...the guide works at the Rex part time and goes to college part time to learn the hospitality industry...We had a short day as it was so hot and Stu tends to get tired...Andy (guide) took us to the lacquer factory at our request and we spent hours there picking out gifts...they have the most beautiful things all hand made...Next we went to the flower market...I think we were the only Americans to ever set foot there...and Stu and I bought two dozen red roses in a beautiful arrangement for $2...the prices are absolutely amazing. I love Vietnam and hope to get back again some day for a longer time! Today is at sea and the laundry room is a zoo...so I guess I will wait for a day or two...Today there is a brunch from 10 a.m. to 1 p.m. with pancakes, waffles, etc. since I am TRYING to watch my weight we will pass...Stu is at a cooking demonstration that our friend Wolfgang is giving...so I am sure he will try it out on me when we return home!! I am off to the pool area to read...hi to all...

Mike, say hi to Carol for me and I look forward to seeing you on our return to the desert...

> *Jan*
> *CruzUnlimited*

Jancruz1   ***April 8th, 2007, 07:13 AM***
What a day today...it is 6 p.m. and I am in the business center of the Shangri La Hotel...last night and this a.m. no Internet onboard ship...At 9 a.m. had a driver (great guy named Nick) pick four of us up in a seven-passenger van...TV set, cooler with water, Cokes, iced tea, etc...two-hour drive from Laem Chebang to Bangkok and we went immediately to the weekend market...after being there two hours Nick picked us up, and as we crawled in the van prostrate from the heat he reached in his cooler and pulled out ice-cold

washcloths...what a dream he is...off to the Shangri La Hotel and went for lunch in their lovely restaurant... after a leisurely lunch of Thai food, Stu and I walked out and shopped on the street...bought a few more shirts and pants...then across the street was a wonderful place that gave one-hour foot massages for 200 baht and a change of polish for 150 baht...total 550 and that is about $14 for both of us...bring me to Thailand and Vietnam more often!!...

We are back at the hotel where we will sit out by the pool and have a drink for about an hour, and Nick will be here at 8 p.m. to take us back to the ship...(another two hours)

All in all a wonderful day...perfect for us...

Jan
CruzUnlimited

Fetchpeople   ***April 8th, 2007, 10:30 AM***
Best thread ever!

This is, by my reckoning, the best thread I've ever read on CC:

It brings back some fond memories of trips to S.E. Asia, especially to BKK. It has prompted me to book another O cruise. Jack and Jan are O's best sales representatives.

Now with tongue planted firmly in cheek, I ask that J & J adjust their daily schedules so we wait less for the next chapter in their wonderful serials!

Aussie Gal   ***April 8th, 2007, 06:33 PM***

I am loving reading both posts but also when they are being posted as for once they are in our time zone, more or less within two hours or so.

Jennie

Jancruz1   ***April 8th, 2007, 11:24 PM***

OK...I did it again, when we returned to the ship at 10 p.m., I went into the shop in the terminal...(yep, still open) and saw some copies of the Mary Frances purses...(ladies, I am sure you know the ones I mean). I talked myself out of it because it was $16, and now this a.m. I am kicking myself...and hoping I will see them again in Phuket...Today we are at sea and I think every woman on the ship is in the laundry room...so I will try after lunch!! By the way before I forget...the berries on Nautica are fabulous and since there was so much discussion about them...they are my breakfast every morning...

Have a great day...

29

Jan
CruzUnlimited
P.S. Glad you are enjoying my notes…my kids are also…

Aussie Gal   **April 9th, 2007, 02:22 AM**
Jan,
   I know exactly how you feel regarding the purse.
   I learnt a valuable lesson many years ago, way back in 1978, when we first visited the Philippines. I saw some beautiful pearls and couldn't decide whether to buy them or not. I didn't, and from the moment we left that country until this day I have always been sorry.
   I decided after that experience, that if I ever see something I really like when I am overseas, I will buy it, as you do not know when and if you will ever return that way again.
                                        Jennie

Chapter 5

TOSCANA AND BANGKOK (LAEM CHEBANG)

JackfromWA   *April 9th, 2007, 05:19 AM*

From the moment I set foot in Toscana, Nautica's Italian restaurant, I felt the warm enthusiasm of Italian hospitality. Paolo, the maître d', is a convivial host, and the Thai and Eastern European servers effectively transformed into authentic Italian waiters. Paolo explained there are two fat Italian chefs working in the kitchen and all our dishes would be prepared as we ordered them. Sukey graciously joined us for dinner, so with four at our table I was able to see and sample much of Toscana's cuisine.

My mom's shrimp-wrapped-in-prosciutto appetizer was the best-prepared giant prawn I have ever eaten. I am going back just to order my own. The buffalo mozzarella cheese and calamari were also excellent. The breads served are similar to those served in the other dining rooms but are prepared with more garlic and herbs. While I am sure butter is available, everyone has his or her own oil and balsamic vinegar bowl. There are six different olive oils and three different vinegars to choose from—selecting our individual concoctions was almost as much fun as trying to choose from the extensive menu.

We all enjoyed Caesar salad prepared tableside—with or without anchovy strips at your discretion—and my father sampled the Tuscany bean peasant soup. When the salad was prepared, I mentioned I liked Parmesan cheese. My salad had a perfect amount of aged slices and apparently another server overheard me and brought a dessert-size plate filled with large pieces of aged, fragrant, crumbly Parmesan carved from a massive cheese wheel on display as we entered. I have found little gestures like this ubiquitous on

Nautica. Staff genuinely discerns what you want and tries to accomplish it. This phenomenon is replicated in the dining rooms, public rooms, staterooms and guest services. Management has clearly ingrained this ethic into ship's staff.

The pasta course was so good I wanted to decline my osso bucco entrée and enjoy another pasta. I had the Tuscany trio, which included spaghetti carbonara, gnocchi in pesto, and a light risotto. All three were extraordinary. Although I have successfully eaten fairly healthy since boarding, all bets were off tonight—the food was too good and the opportunity too savory to resist. Admittedly when my osso bucco arrived I ate only half of it—even though it crumbled deliciously off the bone—as I wanted to have dessert and didn't want to leave the meal feeling uncomfortably full, something that would have been easy to do. My mom ordered the filet with mozzarella cheese, Sukey had the veal al limon, and my dad also tried the osso bucco. Everyone loved his or her entrée.

Dessert lived up to the promise of the previous courses. I enjoyed the chocolate lasagna. It was light, rich and sweet. My mother had the dessert sampler, which afforded the opportunity to try five or six small samples carefully selected from the dessert menu. I finally looked at my watch and realized more than 2½ hours had passed. Between the extraordinary meal and Sukey regaling us with her memorable shoreside experience in Vietnam, our time slipped into the night.

Wolfgang Maier, the ship's executive chef, came by our table just before dessert and visited for five or 10 minutes. He is from a small town in southern Austria, and my father speaks fluent German. They chatted a little, and we all enjoyed an interesting conversation with Wolfgang as he described his early days as a chef at sea serving on all four Silversea vessels. He proudly mentioned that every day Nautica serves more than 150 prepared-to-order menu items and that very few five-star land resorts offer this much variety.

My mother inquired about galley tours, and Wolfgang replied, "I will not do galley tours. I told them [meaning Oceania management] if they must have galley tours, they must hire a new chef. Several years ago there was an accident, and I will not ever take a chance with passengers in my galley again." We never did learn what ill fate befell the passenger injured touring the galley, as Wolfgang's pager beeped and he politely returned to work.

Toscana was as good as any experience dining I've had on any ship—including the Cordon Bleu restaurant on Regent, SS United States on Celebrity and specialty night on Silversea. To fully experience the cuisine, I think the meal must be served in Toscana. Having the same food delivered to a stateroom (which suite passengers can do on Oceania) wouldn't have the same impact. Something magical happens when superior service, intimate ambience and exquisitely prepared food combine. I highly recommend Toscana and enthusiastically look forward to dining there again.

BANGKOK (LAEM CHEBANG)

Nautica berths at a container-ship port, Laem Chebang, two hours from Bangkok. After discussing sightseeing options with Robert, the ship's knowledgeable concierge, my mom, dad and I purchased Bangkok-on-Your-Own tickets from the shore-excursion desk. Robert suggested we take a long boat from the Shangri-La Hotel along the Chao Phraya River to the Grand Palace, tour the palace and Temple of the Emerald Buddha, cross the river and tour Wat Arun, cross back over, shop a little and return to the Shangri-La Hotel, the drop-off and pick-up point for our bus by 5:30 p.m. We were scheduled to arrive in Bangkok at noon, so our itinerary was aggressive for a little over five hours, especially since none of us had ever visited Thailand.

Our tour tickets directed us to the Nautica lounge where we waited in line to receive our bus and guide assignments. One of my much-loved tricks on ship shore excursions is to get my bus assigned last, and then board the last bus first and sit toward the back. My goal is to have the seat next to me vacant. I asked the excursion staff if my bus was full, and to my delight learned it was not only 40% empty, but Oceania as a policy tries to leave between 10% and 20% of each tour bus vacant, especially on long tours. This is a great practice for passenger comfort and was reminiscent of Silversea shore-excursion policies. I boarded the bus, sat at the back and began to settle in.

Unfortunately a fellow passenger spotted me and came toward the back of the bus to join me. I had briefly met this man returning to the ship on the shuttle from the Rex Hotel in Vietnam. He noticed I had a good Nikon camera and a detachable lens (NikonD80 body and18mm to 200mm lens, for any camera buffs) and wanted to know how to use his brand-new Nikon camera. He had spent several thousand dollars on a Nikon body, lens, etc., and no one had taught him how to use it. The instruction book is horribly complicated; I bought a supplementary book just to help understand how to use mine. The camera salesman really laid him away—he should have been sold a good $300 fixed-lens digital Canon, Nikon or Olympus camera, since he didn't want to invest time in learning a more advanced model. I had politely offered to show him how to put everything on automatic but didn't want to become his camera technician for the cruise—and it felt like that was what he wanted.

Fortunately my mom recognized what was happening and as he approached said, "Why don't you sit by your father?" as she swapped seats with me, forcing him to sit out of earshot. I could have kissed her, as the prospect of two hours on the bus to Bangkok talking about digital cameras was as appealing as drinking tap water in Vietnam. Our bus left the port and our guide Ses gave a wonderful lecture on the history, future and current state of Thailand affairs. I didn't hear a word of it as I immediately turned on my iPod shuffle and listened to Neil Young, Coldplay, Pink Floyd and the Beatles. I love listening to music as the countryside rolls by the window.

Even though our tour was Bangkok-on-Your-Own, our guide showed us where to rent the long boat. For 1,200 Baht ($40) we had our own boat, which plied the main river and canals offering fleeting glimpses of daily life in Bangkok. Shortly after we departed, our boat slowed down and I noticed a smaller boat rowing out to meet us. A smiling young man had brought the floating-boat-store right to us. Despite his best efforts, we resisted the Buddhas, postcards, toys and figurines. He finally broke out a beer cooler, but I am a recovering addict active in a 12-step program, and my mom and dad are active Mormons, so he really struck out. He paid our pilot a small bottle of a foul-looking drink for stopping and off we went. We finally arrived, paid our tip and exited. Somehow it just didn't look right. Instead of gold-gilt imperial palaces I saw bad paintings of snakes and an advertisement for an alligator farm. After a minute or two, we realized we had been manipulated into a bad roadside attraction, Thai river style, and refused to pay entrance for the alligator and snake farm. We went back on our boat, our pilot smiled as if she had been caught, and off we went to our real destination.

I won't write much about the Thai Grand Palace as there are far better descriptions and books in print than what I can attempt here. Every vision I had as a child as to what Siam or Asia should look like is captured in the palace walls, buildings and grounds. It rivals Versailles or any of the great palaces I've ever seen. Although the heat and humidity were oppressive, we thoroughly enjoyed the overwhelming spectacle of gilt surfaces, traditional architecture and numerous strategically positioned large and small statues interspersed with radiant colors and intricate designs. The complex deserves hours or days to really appreciate the millions of tiny details. I left wanting to go back. I found it ironic that on Easter Sunday the closest we got to a church was visiting the Temple of the Emerald Buddha, arguably Thailand's holiest Buddhist site.

Wat Arun was similarly impressive, although the colors were muted. The gold of the palace was replaced with more subdued indigo blue, white and yellow ceramics. I sat alone for 15 or 20 minutes on a small ledge of Wat Arun trying to take in some of my holy surroundings. Occasionally an orange-robe-clad monk walked by, and I caught a glimpse of the peace and serenity that they find serving here.

When we arrived back at the Shangri-La we had 45 minutes before the bus departed, so we went shopping. Prior to our trip, I had purchased a new carry-on because of restrictions at London Heathrow Airport. My old carry-on bag was too large for the new British requirements, so I purchased a 20-inch Travelpro for $85. It was 50% off, and I encouraged my parents to get one. They bought one, but my dad decided it was too expensive and returned it. He carried a bag without wheels on our outbound flight to Hong Kong. I teased him every chance I got as I wheeled my Travelpro while he schlepped his bag. He told me he would find a better deal along our journey, and I replied, "Maybe, but I doubt it, and you certainly won't get a Travelpro."

Lo and behold, immediately outside the Shangri-La was a Thai luggage store and right up front was a beautiful 20-inch Travelpro carry-on. After the obligatory bargaining, Dad got his new luggage for about $30—a third of what I had paid at home. In all fairness I should have bought it for him, as I'd teased him rather mercilessly all during our travels. I was actually happy for him for proving me wrong, and he won't have to endure any more teasing.

On the bus back, the five empty back seats looked inviting. I was tired and briefly considered lying down. I told my dad, "That looks like a good place to take a nap."

"I did that once and got in trouble," he replied. I wondered where it had happened—maybe Germany where they get uptight if your feet touch the train cushions, I thought.

"Where did that happen?" I asked.

"I was coming to Uncle Jake's in California, and I was in Little Rock, Arkansas. I had just gotten off the Queen Mary, hadn't slept in four days, and those seats looked like a good place to take a nap," he said, pointing to the five empty seats along the last row of the bus.

My father was born in Holland in 1931. His mother's uncle, Jacob Dekker, had invited him to immigrate shortly after World War II ended. So, when he was 18, my dad took his first cruise, in steerage, six passengers to a cabin, bunks three high on each side, on the Queen Mary. Uncle Jake owned a large ranch in Malibu and had made a good living in the wholesale-flower business. After Uncle Jake got to know my father and realized he was intelligent, hard working and deserving of a hand up, he helped him. Between my dad's hard work and my Uncle Jake's help, my dad earned his education and eventually graduated with a Ph.D. from Stanford. I've always admired the discipline, responsibility and commitment it took for him to make the transition from non-English-speaking immigrant to university professor, with a doctorate from Stanford. I was born here and didn't make the commitment necessary to complete college. I was in my twenties before I realized what a difficult and noteworthy accomplishment my dad achieved, and what a great example he set for his children and grandchildren.

"The bus driver came back, shook me hard and said I was breaking the law. I couldn't figure out why sleeping on vacant bus seats broke the law, but I had only been in America a few days, my English wasn't very good and I didn't want to get in trouble.

"When the bus stopped and I was using the bathroom, I noticed people were staring at me funny. There was a sign on the door that said "COLORED" but as far as I knew that just meant lots of different colors. It was a long time later when my grasp of English improved that I realized I had tried to sit in the back of the bus in the South and I had used restrooms meant only for black people. The first black person I had ever seen was an American solider with the liberation forces in Holland, and I didn't understand the discrimination in the U.S."

My 75-year-old dad quietly reminiscing on a bus from Bangkok and sharing his experience with discrimination in the South as a teenage, newly landed immigrant to the U.S.A. is exactly why I took this vacation now—even though my business and other affairs at home would have been better served by choosing to stay home. For me, the best part of cruising is sharing new experiences with people I love, while increasing the intimacy and knowledge we have with each other—it is about the journey and who is there with you. The great meals, exotic ports and entertaining shows are frosting on the cake. Long after I've forgotten how delicious my osso bucco tasted in Toscana, I'll carry the vision of my father, a long way from home, scared, in a new country with little money, a poor grasp of English and trying to make sense of something that never would make sense no matter how well he understood it.

*****

ricktalcott   *April 9th, 2007, 01:09 PM*
Taking a shower
Hi Jack—
When you get tired of the tiny shower in your room, try the one in the spa. Either walk past the spa attendant, or use the last door on the left in the gym that will take you to the spa changing room. It is wonderful. About six showerheads.

Nancy and I were on last year's cruise from HK to Athens and enjoyed it immensely. Thanks for bringing back some of the memories.

Rick

dianancolin   **April 9th, 2007, 10:46 PM**
Happy belated birthday
JackfromWA—just found your articles and am highly impressed that another Aries—particularly one born on the same day (different year) as me and in a country many miles apart (I was born in England the same year as the war in Europe started) should produce such a wonderful travelogue. MANY thanks. The trip up the Chao Phraya River brought back happy memories to us. We stayed at the Peninsula, across the river from the Shangri-La and even know the luggage store your father patronized. Unfortunately the suitcase we purchased there (needed due to some excessive shopping by my better half—female side) only survived two air trips—down to Phuket and then back to Hong Kong. Such is the ability of Thai International to (mis)handle baggage gently!

Looking forward to your next episode.

Dianancolin
MCC (retired)

merryecho   **April 10th, 2007, 07:04 PM**
Jack—you really should consider offering your journal to the Bellingham Herald—they are too enjoyable for this little audience to keep to ourselves. I loved your delicate handling of your feelings about the U.S. involvement in Vietnam and elsewhere, and most of all your story about your growing appreciation of your dad. Should have gone to the snake farm though—I think every tourist boat stops at one—I too ended up there "by accident," and bought my favorite souvenir T-shirt of all time.

Jan—do you still plan to recommend the Rex hotel massages? Hope you mention the "rest of the story," in earshot of wives, if you do…

Jancruz1   **April 10th, 2007, 10:09 PM**
Hi, everyone…we woke up in Singapore and docked right next to us is a Japanese ship, Akura 2, which was the Crystal Harmony…she looks a little worse for wear and it was funny listening to all her

announcements in Japanese...we are just getting ready to disembark...will be back later with a full report...

Jan
CruzUnlimited

lahore   **April 11th, 2007, 04:06 AM**
Enjoying this
   Hi, I just discovered this thread and now will have to print off all the wonderful posts and read in bed at night. We are doing Rome to Singapore this year so am eagerly waiting to hear about the Indian and the Middle Eastern ports. Keep on having fun, everyone.

CruisingSerenity   **April 11th, 2007, 02:07 PM**
Amazing
JackfromWA:
   I was trying to wait until the end to say this but I cannot: With most sincerity, I hope you get paid to write. (I don't mean here, I mean in your life.) Your observations and descriptive narrative are brilliant. I get so lost in your posts and can picture the entire atmosphere.
   It's a thrill to me to read that written by someone who really knows how to write...your posts have been an absolute pleasure.
   I'm so glad you're on a long trip...that means we get more! (She says, greedily.)

TyrelJ   **April 11th, 2007, 09:29 PM**
Great posts
Jack, I am glad to hear you are having a good trip! LOVE your narratives, and wish I was there to experience with you!!!

Jancruz1   **April 12th, 2007, 12:36 AM**
   Singapore: In the morning it was pouring rain, so Stu and I stayed inside the terminal and wandered around...lots of security and checkpoints when you get off the ship...only port so far we had to pick up our passports and have them with us...
   After lunch it had stopped raining and we went off on the Raffles and Trishaw adventure from the ship...First stop was a Bumboat ride on the Singapore River...it is amazing all the land they are reclaiming from the sea...there are so many new buildings being built...even the Sands is building a casino here!!

Our guide told us 15,000 Singapores would fit in the USA…I found that really surprising…After a half-hour boat ride we were back on the bus to get our trishaws…they were really fun with the driver playing all American music on the radio and pedaling along…(with the weight we must have gained, I felt sorry for this skinny little guy)

On to Raffles Long Bar for the famous Singapore Sling…actually even having been in Singapore many times I had never had one…it was pretty good tho very sweet…I asked to have vodka instead of gin as gin gives me a horrible headache…Long Bar is really attractive with the old-time fans shaped like leaves going back and forth…Peanuts on each table and you must throw the shells on the floor…(according to custom)

Got back to the ship about 5 p.m. and was glad to get in the shower to cool off…it is really hot in each port…

I am delighted at the quality of the tours we have taken and have heard many people praising Destination Services and saying how much improved they are and I heartily agree!!!!

Jerry Blaine was the entertainment and since we have seen him before…we just stayed talking to some of the other guests…

Today we are at sea…and after a lovely rain this a.m. it is really a perfect day to sit at the pool…Tomorrow Phuket…

> *Jan*
> *CruzUnlimited*

*****

JackfromWA   **April 12th, 2007, 05:21 AM**

A FEW REPLIES:

meow!: I have felt safe everywhere. I have used common sense, however, and when out in Vietnam at night traveled in a group and left the expensive jewelry back in the ship safe. I haven't eaten on shore (I am sadly overly sensitive to foods from difference places, and I am trying to keep my system at 100%, if you know what I mean), but places like the Peninsula in Bangkok or almost anywhere in Singapore are probably fine.

merryecho: They did have a get together for veterans, and I have spoken to a few who fought in Vietnam. My partner Ty's father was a Marine during the Vietnam War, and I bought him an I-think-new-but-antique-appearing lighter inscribed with "The Marines Are a Pimple on the Ass of My Sanity." It was the only U.S. Marine item I could find, and I think he'll like it.

ricktalcott: Thank you! I loved the shower. Great tip to use the shower in Nautica's men's changing area. It is fabulous.

dianancolin: Happy birthday! Hope yours was as delightful as mine.

Jancruz1, meow!, Fetchpeople, merryecho, Aussie Gal, dianaancolin, lahore, CruisingSerenity, anyone I've left out, and most of all "Tyrel J," my partner—keeping everything together back home so I can be here: Thank you for your kind words, compliments and encouragement. I've never written this much consistently. In my profession (I run a small non-travel/non-cruise-related company) I write letters, and for five years kept a journal, but I have never carved the hours out of a day necessary to write this extensively. I've been enjoying it, but it is so much more encouraging to know that you are interested in reading what I write. Articles, blogs and books are like food—not everything appeals to everyone—but just knowing the little account I am writing actually has a few interested readers is a sensational feeling. So I thank each of you, sincerely, for offering that encouragement and taking time from your busy lives so we can meet on these pages.

41

Chapter 6

SINGAPORE

JackfromWA   *April 12th, 2007, 05:21 AM*

Nautica docked in the Singapore Cruise Center at about 8 a.m. Unfortunately, another ship, the Akura II—formerly the Crystal Harmony—arrived almost simultaneously. I made arrangements through a link on the Singapore Tourism Authority website to hire an air-conditioned seven-passenger Mercedes van for my mom, dad and me to take a six-hour tour. The price was US$160 for the tour. Our driver, Pharis Saleem, was scheduled to wait for us at 9:30 a.m. immediately past the immigration and customs exit.

We left the ship at 9:10 a.m. since we didn't want to be late. As we followed the long corridor toward immigration, we observed a large, unyielding crowd ahead. Apparently the surge of Japanese passengers from Akura II combined with the Nautica passengers overwhelmed the capacity of the Singapore cruise-terminal customs and immigration staff. Forty-five minutes and after listening to many disgruntled passengers and frenzied ship-excursion staff conversations later, we were officially allowed to enter Singapore. Our driver was right where we expected him to be, holding our name up on a large placard.

As we approached the van, the rain started. Quickly it became a torrential downpour. Pharis advised we look around downtown Singapore and do some indoor sightseeing until the rain lifted. We headed to the Raffles hotel and got our obligatory photographs. I spent a little too much in the gift store—it isn't cheap, but I wanted Raffles souvenirs for my partner Ty back home—and we wandered around Singapore's (perhaps Southeast Asia's) most famous accommodations.

After Raffles we drove through Little India, Arab Street and Chinatown and stopped to take photos of the Merlion. Singapore's mascot is a lion's head and torso attached to a mermaid's fins. I like the Venetian winged lion better (if I were inventing mythical beasts as symbols, I'd rather have a lion that could fly than a lion that could swim), but the Merlion is impressive and I'd never seen it before today.

The Merlion park is in the heart of town, directly across from five of Singapore's finest hotels, and it is a great place to take a few photos of the Merlion fountain. Singapore is building the world's largest Ferris wheel—although both my mom and I recall the London Eye as seeming larger—and it should be open next spring.

Our guide spoke impeccable English and had a great sense of humor. When we passed the Parkview Square office tower, I commented on how much I admired the building's intricate Art Deco design.

"Yes, it is just like Gotham City in Batman," Pharis said with a smile.

As we drove away from the city center, he explained that all Singapore males serve two years in the army, navy, air force, police or civil defense, from ages 18 to 20. Following two years of active duty, they train in the reserves for 10 more years. At age 40 they are released from all military commitment. I admired Singapore's cleanliness, friendliness, high standard of living and overall infrastructure. Unfortunately I am afraid it comes at a high price.

"In Singapore if you are charged with a crime you are guilty unless you can prove your innocence." Pharis told us. I was shocked.

"You mean if a policeman charges you with a crime you have to prove you are innocent or you will be convicted?" I incredulously asked.

"Oh, yes. In Singapore you have to prove you are innocent." It was clear from his tone that Pharis approved of his country's judicial system.

I abhorred the injustice of it. This is a country where my immigration entry card stated in large bold letters "DRUG SMUGGLING IS PUNISHABLE BY DEATH." Singapore has the highest per-capita capital-punishment rate in the world, and according to Pharis under their legal system a charge is a conviction unless the accused can prove his or her innocence. Not for me, thank you. As inequitable as the United States' justice may be at times, I fervently believe in the concept of innocent until proved guilty. I don't want a policemen deciding I am guilty and then I have to prove my innocence—I want a jury of my peers and a prosecutorial burden of proving I did it. I believe it is "better a guilty man goes free than an innocent man be convicted."

Out of politeness and deference to Pharis, I nodded my head as if Singapore's judicial system was the best invention since the telephone and continued to listen as Pharis shared other interesting facts and tidbits of information.

Eventually we made our way to Changi prison and toured the outstanding museum. All of us had read *King Rat*, and seeing the photos, mementos, letters from prisoners writing home and the physical layout of actual cells brought the book, and the horrendous reality of incarceration in Changi, to life.

Next we drove to the Kanji War Cemetery and memorial. If I understood correctly, the British maintain it. The main memorial is subtly reminiscent of a submarine's surfaced profile. It has been interesting going to these WWII sites with my father. He lived through the war as a young teenager in the Netherlands and has never talked much about that time. It was obvious, by the way he carefully read the descriptions of the photos and displays and captured the words inscribed on several large memorials with his camera so he could read them again later, that seeing all this was bringing back memories.

We drove through Changi village, passed through the agricultural and fish farm area where koi and other precious fish are raised for international export, saw orchid and palm farms and finally made our way back to town.

45

We stopped at a grocery store and purchased Diet Coke and water. A one-liter bottle of Evian on the ship is overpriced at $3.50. At the store it was $1.25. Diet Coke on the ship is $2, and we paid about the same at a Singapore grocery store as we would at home—about 40¢ a can. The rain began again; our excursion was sandwiched by torrential rain, and we returned to the ship.

We sadly said goodbye to Pharis. He was a superb, friendly, knowledgeable guide, and we boarded the ship about 4 p.m. Since we didn't depart until 8 p.m., I parted ways with my mom and dad, and we separately left the ship and shopped in the mall adjacent to where Nautica berthed for the day. The mall has a good international grocery store, drugstore and almost everything else you would find in a good mall in the U.S. I went to Starbucks for an hour and used some free, fast, wireless Internet access. My mom thoughtfully purchased *King Rat* for me (I haven't read it in 15 years or more), so I know what is next on my onboard reading list.

Singapore was a wonderful stop. It is a beautiful country, and I particularly admired how the Muslim, Chinese, English and Indian populations seem to peacefully coexist. There is an excellent social-services support system, and public housing is clean and readily available to all. Despite all that, something about the place bugged me. Singapore strikes me as too good to be true, and I believe if I really started scratching the surface all the wonderful social qualities Singapore has have come at a high price. I don't know what the value of free speech and the right to face and challenge accusers is worth, but I know it is priceless to me—and I know I wouldn't give them up to live in Singapore.

Tomorrow we arrive in Phuket. I have a day room at the Banyan Tree, and my mom, dad and I will get to enjoy one of the world's finest resorts and spas for the day.

*****

benfield   *April 12th, 2007, 03:30 PM*
Jack, I have never posted on these boards before. I have been reading them for the last few months as my husband and I are taking our first cruise on Regatta in the Med later this year.

Reading them has been an interesting experience for a NZer and, apart from the enormous amount of cruise information I have garnered that will make our cruise that much more enjoyable, I have been impressed by people's willingness to take the time to share their knowledge (and of course opinions).

But I had to write and tell you how much our family enjoyed in particular the portion on your father's early experiences in the U.S.A. Not really because of the story (which was excellent; my daughter has a Ph.D. in English lit and philosophy, she lectures at university here, and she said to tell you she gives you an A+ and wants to know why you are not writing a book) but because of the love and pride for your parents that shines through and illuminates what is often these days a sad world.

Aussie Gal   April 12th, 2007, 06:47 PM

Jack, I have now printed out Chapter 6 of your wonderful travelogue. It is such interesting reading, plus it will keep me going throughout this coming year when I will be wishing that our cruise was only a few weeks away instead of months!

Jennie

china addict   April 12th, 2007, 07:10 PM
Enjoyed your bulletin on Singapore

Jack, you are an incredibly talented writer, and we readers feel as though we are along on the cruise with you and your folks. My dad was a WWII vet and would have loved to read your messages. He was in the British Merchant Marine during the Relief of Singapore and said his supply ship evacuated literally thousands of women and children to safety. Back then it was a filthy, crime-ridden hellhole, but everything has changed. I am actually a fan of most of their social design and have never visited any other society where all races and religions meld so harmoniously. The government controls everything, there's very little private housing, and it's almost impossible for a private citizen to afford a car, yet there's "free" health care, schooling and other social benefits for everyone, and the citizens I met seemed genuinely happy. Unemployment and crime are virtually nonexistent. It was explained to me that because the government controls public housing, it can enforce the ideal mix of ethnicities in all apartment towers and schools. Because kids of all backgrounds live and play next to each other and attend the same schools, they fall in love and marry without regard to race or religion and there is no societal backlash about what we would call "mixed marriages." Ghettoes don't exist. From kindergarten up, all the kids are taught about every religion and celebrate every single one in entertaining ways, so Indian families turn out for the Santa Claus parade, the Chinese families are there for the Indian Festival of Lights, and so on. To me, the end result is a respectful diversity, but there are probably plenty of horror stories about how they achieved this and I know I couldn't handle being told where to live. One aspect of Singapore I did love was personal safety. It was amazing to know that day or night, I was not going to be robbed, mugged or worse. One of my travel companions had too many Singapore slings at Raffles (my version of the story, not hers!), then slipped on the marble staircase at our hotel. She was amazed at the high-quality free emergency-room treatment she received. We are blessed with a lot of things in America, but universal health care is not one of them, nor is public safety. One of the great benefits of travel is the exposure to different cultures and lifestyles and, Jack, I applaud you for digging under the surface in each of your destinations to get the local flavor. Your stories about the "extra services" with your massage and your dad's experience with the tailor were a hoot! Please keep the updates flowing in your own inimitable way, and tell your mom and dad how lucky we readers think they are to have a son such as you. We are eagerly awaiting the next installment of your travels.

lahore   **April 12th, 2007, 09:04 PM**
  I am fascinated to read the posts on Singapore. I lived there for quite a while and still teach there for several months each year and have very close friends there. The multicultural harmony is a little superficial—people will only tell you what they really think after they have known you for quite a long time. The stuff about "guilty until proved innocent" is also highly contestable—just ask one American academic who was sued by Lee Kuan Yew for alluding to something like that. But it has a kernel of truth. What visitors are told by taxi drivers, tour guides, etc., is one view, but it's not the entire reality, no more than it would be in America, Australia or anywhere else. In short, Singapore is a complex and fascinating place, and living there has its ups and downs like anywhere else. With all its difficulties, the people have a brilliant sense of humor. Visit www.mrbrown.com.sg for a taste of what they think about their society.

meow!   *April 12th, 2007, 10:47 PM*

From what I have read somewhere before, as a former British colony, Lee Kuan Yew has learnt the "rule by law" of Elizabeth I, not "rule of law" of Elizabeth II. From Confucius, he has learnt to legitimize dynastic autocracy. The merits of such a system is a contentious subject. Anyway, we are a cruise-travel forum, and as long as tourists are safe and happy, we may as well leave local politics alone!

monina01   *April 13th, 2007, 05:51 AM*

I am one of the many who have been reading this board extensively but have never posted. We have yet to go on our first cruise ever, and after a lot of reading, Oceania is my No. 1 preference.

I just have to say I love this thread. The descriptions of the ship itself, the ports, the excursions, the little tidbits of your life here and there…I am overjoyed that you are on a 35-day cruise; hopefully that means a lot more installments.

Also, I live in Holland (born an American in Boston, I have lived in Holland since 1978) and find the little anecdotes about your parents fun to read…

Please please keep on writing…if not for us, then for yourself. This will be a wonderful thing to have to remember your special cruise by.

*****

JackfromWA   *April 13th, 2007, 07:17 AM*

DISCLAIMER:

I am sorry if any of my comments on Singapore were inaccurate. To clarify, I am a first-time traveler to every port on this itinerary except Hong Kong, and these postings are nothing more than my perceptions, thoughts and feelings. If due to my ignorance I report something inaccurately, please feel free to correct my mistake. I won't, however, get into a debate—especially since I may not have my facts straight—I am simply passing along my reflections of this beautiful trip. As "meow!" said, the most important thing is that travelers are safe and happy, and for Singapore I would wholeheartedly say both are true. That being said, there will be times

49

my vision is colored by my biases, beliefs and values. I'll attempt to keep contentious subjects out of these reports (you won't get an abortion, legalization of marijuana or George W. debate from me here), as I hope the tone of this thread can be one of pleasure in discovering new places, not one of political or current-event debate.

A FEW REPLIES:

benfield and monina01: Congratulations on your first post! I have been a member here since 2001, but mostly I have just read posts (called lurking). It has been so helpful to me that I thought this time I would try to give something back to this wonderful online community. My study of other members' posts about various cruise lines and ports has vastly enhanced my vacations. "benfield," please tell your daughter I let my mom read your comments. It is a privilege to enjoy my parents' company for so long, in good health in this setting.

Aussie Gal: It tickles me that you are reading these in your bed at night. I hope it just isn't to go to sleep! Actually that is my favorite place to read, and I am humbled you deem these reports worthy of printing and late-night reading.

china addict: I told my parents how lucky they are ☺ and I am delighted to report things are much better in Singapore than when your father served in WWII.

lahore and meow!: Thanks for keeping me on task. The world is a big place, and I still have so much (and so little time) to learn.

Chapter 7

PHUKET

JackfromWA   *April 13th, 2007, 07:17 AM*

Our plan for our brief stay in Phuket was to enjoy a day at one of Asia's finest resorts, the Banyan Tree. Nautica's concierge, Robert, who lives part time in Phuket, heartily endorsed our plan and advised we could procure a taxi from the Phuket deep-sea terminal to the Banyan Tree for about $30. While I am sure his advice was accurate, the drivers working the pier today weren't interested. After three consecutive rejections, I increased our offer to $45 and got a ride.

The cab driver was everything you don't want from a foreign cabbie. His cab wasn't too clean and smelled of mildew and mold, he lied about distances, he claimed the Banyan Tree was closed, he attempted to wait (on his schedule) to take us back to the ship, he tried to stop at a jewelry store, he tried to stop at a massage parlor and spoke, at best, pidgin English. All in all I liked him—he was a character, but I booked the Banyan Tree's limousine for the return trip to the ship.

Since today is Songkran (Thai New Year's Day), the prices for cabs may be higher. I know in the U.S. most of us enjoy earning overtime on a holiday. The obvious sign of the holiday is water liberally splashed on tourists, passers-by, gangs of roaming teenagers, young adults and kids. Our Thai waitress from Toscana said that for her the real significance of the holiday was going home to honor her parents and adding jasmine to a small vessel of water and dousing her parent's hands. It certainly makes sense to me that teenagers and fun lovers of all ages would grab the idea of applying water to observe a time-honored family tradition and convert it into an all-out water fight and splashing extravaganza.

I woke up today feeling worried. Last night I learned that my partner, Ty, has some white spots on his tongue that his doctor is concerned about. They are performing a biopsy to rule out cancer. A few years ago my best friend and business partner was diagnosed with Stage III tonsil cancer. I walked with him all through the treatment—from the diagnosis, to the surgery, through the post-surgical recovery, through eight weeks of radiation and the stressful, time-consuming process of helping him return to work. He relied on me to sift through the facts, options and recommendations and to help him make difficult treatment decisions. A few months later, my dad developed prostate cancer and underwent a radical prostatectomy. About six months ago, Ty's dad was diagnosed with lung cancer, fortunately it was caught early—he is one of the rare victims of lung cancer who will probably survive it.

Once you have lived with cancer, whether as a caregiver or a patient, you never forget it—it stays with you. Somewhere inside you know how much pain, devastation and helplessness it can cause. All cancers are an emotional roller coaster. I hate cancer and, though I am stronger for having been a primary caregiver, I wish I hadn't encountered it. Since cancer entered my life, I've learned that, sadly, most people have a cancer story. The older you are, the more likely it is you have a tragic one. Whether the story originates with a mother, father, grandparent, brother, sister, best friend, child, spouse or yourself, it is a story indelibly imprinted in memory. For me, living life to the fullest is the best antidote, but when cancer threatened to rear its ugly, threatening head, the old stories and all the intense feelings, came slamming back. I know Ty will be fine and almost certainly doesn't have cancer—most cancer scares are just that, a scare—that his tests will likely come back benign. I know even if he has cancer it was discovered early and together we will survive it, but I am sad I am not home by his side, and I won't rest easy until the tests come back. I know you are reading this, Ty. I love you and it will be all right.

Our destination for the day, the Banyan Tree, is situated in a tropical lagoon along Bang Tao Bay, about 35 minutes north of the ship. The lobby is open-air, resplendent with beautiful woods, fine fragrances and attentive staff. The grounds feature lush landscaped gardens amidst traditional serene Thai architecture. All the villas are a sybaritic delight; the bed is divine (Nautica's bedding is good but nothing like this), the bath towels are so plush they feel like pillows, and even the toilet was decorated with a small orchid on the lid. I had booked the most basic villa since we could stay only six hours. It was more than satisfactory, but the villas with private pools must be sensational. All this doesn't come cheap, of course. Villas start at about US$500 and quickly go up from there.

Conde Nast has called Banyan Tree's spa treatments the best in the world. If they aren't, I haven't had any better. The treatment massage room is an open-air, meticulously decorated enclosed area measuring about 25 feet by 20 feet, completely encircled by a small two-foot wide moat filled with small, colorful tropical fish. Surrounded by the moat is a smooth, black-tiled island of tranquility featuring two relaxing chairs draped with fine, supple fabric facing the entrance and two massage tables behind them. The interior walls are adorned with tall, lush ferns and a variety of intricate, spiritual, eastern relief carvings. Two small fans rotate at the uppermost point of the high Thai ceiling, and birds casually chirp as they meander in and out. It is the most sublime setting for a massage imaginable. Every sense is engaged: Visually there are a myriad of intricate, rich surfaces, and parts of the ceiling are suffused with dappled, dancing light reflected from the moat—when I opened my eyes during the massage and peered down, a small green bowl containing a lotus flower symmetrically surrounded by red rose petals greeted me—the smell of jasmine, eucalyptus and beautiful native fragrances infuse everything from the welcoming cool towel to the soft oils and lotions. Tranquil music wafts quietly from hidden speakers, and when the massage is concluded a divine hot or cold lemongrass tea along with melon, pineapple and vegetable sticks is served. Touch is the focus of the massage, and suffice it to say only Thailand's best therapists serve at the Banyan Tree.

Far too quickly the time slipped away, and we left for the ship. Since it was Songkran we didn't want to risk being late. We departed the Banyan Tree in a Mercedes sedan (for the same price as the cab) about an hour earlier than we intended. My mom, dad and I all smelled wonderful from the massage oils, soaps and lotions. During the hour-long drive back to the ship, our car was doused with water and we watched all the excitement from the numerous water fights. Some participants stood by barrels filled with water, into which they quickly dipped bowls and immediately tossed the contents on any passers-by. There was a small compliment of air-powered water guns and garden hoses—one enterprising teenager commandeered a fire hose and sprayed everyone in shooting distance!

As we returned to the ship we noticed a very convenient temporary market set up alongside Nautica. Prices were good, selection of imitation Polo, Boss, Lacoste, Burberry and Diesel was plentiful—there were even two booths filled with Gucci, Prada and Louis Vuitton bags. After spending every last baht (Ty got two Burberry shirts; the sizes here don't fit me), I boarded Nautica.

Now we begin four sea days and then arrive in Goa.

*****

lahore   ***April 13th, 2007, 08:10 AM***
No disclaimer required here, Jack
Hey, Jack, I genuinely apologize if you thought my thread was censorious. It wasn't meant to be—it was just a reflection on things I have thought myself. It took me so long to get some idea of Singapore. It was just a musing, a thinking out loud, not a judgment, but now that I read it again I see it could be taken that way. I do enjoy the humor on the MrBrown website so I thought it might be worth sharing—but not for you, you have much more fun stuff to do! I had absolutely no intention of hijacking this wonderful thread onto "political" topics. Keep on enjoying, and sharing— we are all appreciating it so much.

Rob & Beckys mom   ***April 13th, 2007, 08:28 AM***
Thanks, Jack, for the wonderful posts. Ty is in my prayers.
                                 Jan

meow!   ***April 13th, 2007, 11:47 AM***
Jack: In fact I agree with your feelings about Singapore. I enjoy reading your posts and please keep posting. Good luck with the rest of your trip.

*****

JackfromWA   **April 13th, 2007, 11:55 AM**

lahore: Thanks for taking the time to clarify…. I wasn't totally
certain where your post was going—written communication isn't
always easy to decipher—but I deeply appreciate the quick
clarification, and the information you shared about Singapore. I look
forward to looking at the website you suggest when I return home
and broadband is free. Every once in a while some posts digress, and
I wanted this to just be a place for people interested in one
passenger's experience on Nautica. I just noticed your first cruise
was a couple of rubber dinghies—that was mine too! I tried to sink a
crab pot, and after throwing it overboard realized the weight from
pulling it out of the water would cause the dinghy to capsize.
Eventually I had to release and lose the crab pot. Anyway, thanks for
giving me the excuse for a short post…now it is off to bed!

Jack

*****

Decebal   **April 13th, 2007, 02:57 PM**
Great job, Jack
    *Hi, Jack. I've enjoyed your diary so much, it's become a daily
habit to read it at lunchtime.*
    *So sorry to hear about Ty, hope all turns out well. Man, that
sucks hearing such news on a long holiday.*
    *Wow! The Banyan Tree is something else, thanks for writing
about it. Was this property affected at all by the tsunami?*
    *What will you ever do with four long days at sea???? Cabana
time…can't wait to hear how you like it.*

lahore   **April 13th, 2007, 09:33 PM**
    *Tee hee, Jack—glad we share the same sense of humor. That
crab won the day, huh?*
    *By the time you get this you will be in India, so I can't wait to
read about that as I am anticipating with glee the bazaars and the
culture of Mumbai. But more especially I am keen to read your posts
on Oman and Egypt, as I am still a little conflicted about what we
will do in those ports. Whatever you do, I hope you have a totally*

55

fabulous time. At the moment I expect you are on deck soaking some rays. Ahhhhhh

merryecho   **April 14th, 2007, 12:00 PM**
Jack—we will all be waiting anxiously to hear how things go with Ty—I am sure extra prayers will be coming in from all over the place.

Just a thought—The airline magazines are always looking for good travel stories like yours. If you are interested you can find submittal info in writer's market. And they pay enough to buy an extra fake Burberry shirt or two!

Chapter 8

CELEBRITY AND TRIVIA

JackfromWA   *April 16th, 2007, 09:16 AM*

Our ship's resident celebrity is a former child star from the age of black-and-white, innocent, well-meaning family sitcoms—Lumpy from *Leave It to Beaver*. Although not as well known as the infamous, two-faced Eddie Haskell, or the Beav's saintlike dad, Ward Cleaver, Lumpy was a frequent "fun to make fun of" denizen of Beaver's world. Any fan of the show knew Beaver's older brother Wally's not-too-bright, not-too-nice-to-younger-kids friend Lumpy. Most kids with older siblings had someone like Lumpy over at their house, and the question was always: Why does my brother or sister hang out with such a dumb, mean, pathetic loser who isn't even nice to me? Lumpy represents an archetype that most of us who have older brothers or sisters immediately recognize.

Frank Bank played Lumpy, and he and his lovely wife Becka are passengers on the Nautica. I first learned Frank was Lumpy when I asked one of my trivia-team companions why the loud, complaining guy on the other team was so upset by losing.

"Oh, that's Frank. He was Lumpy on *Leave It to Beaver*, and he thinks he should win at everything," my teammate said.

Although my first impression of Frank wasn't favorable, all the years I rushed home from school to watch syndicated episodes of the show with my younger brother every weekday afternoon at 4 p.m. all through the early 1970s kept me open-minded. Maybe Frank wasn't such a loud-mouthed, complaining, self-centered guy—maybe he was a nice person and I had just seen him at his worst—after all, even though Lumpy was kind of a jerk, Frank is just an actor, and I hoped to speak with him about early days on the set and hanging out with the Beaver. Despite our trivia enmity, I made it a point to smile and nod at Frank.

Trivia is very serious on our 35-day cruise. Every sea day, about 75 passengers gather in a lounge and answer 20 questions. Ray, the cruise director, personally conducts trivia. He started his career on the maiden voyage of the QE2 in 1969 and has been on many round-the-world cruises and extended sailings. Early on, I recognized that trivia was both difficult and seriously played. It did not resemble my previous experiences on seven- or 10-day cruises, where trivia contests are merely one of many onboard ship diversions.

"On a cruise like this," Ray quipped in his inimitable British accent, "all the passengers will be very friendly the first week or so, shaking hands, saying hello, being good sports and so forth. After a week or so the little cliques will form and the civilities will start to disappear. Then about a week before the end of the cruise everyone will start hugging and greeting each other civilly again and make plans to meet again on next year's cruise."

If a trivia team answered, "What won best picture in 1959?" by replying *Bridge over the River Kwai* and the correct answer was *Bridge on the River Kwai*, Ray takes a democratic vote of all players present to decide if both answers are correct. On the first week of trivia, the majority of voting players would have accepted both answers. Now, at mid-cruise, every time we have a questionable answer decided by a vote, it loses. The niceties are gone, and precise facts are what matter. My team has won first place four times, and every day but one we have taken at least first, second or third. Several teams have placed only a few times. Trivia is the one game where there isn't much conviviality between opposing-team players. At this stage of the cruise, trivia is played to win.

It is fun to watch all the personalities emerge on the different teams. All teams have at least one or more of the following: A "queen bee" or a "king bee," a silent player who doubts his or her worth, a film and pop-culture expert, a history expert and an intelligent-looking but noncontributing player who has learned to nod agreement and lend support to whichever fellow team player he or she deems most likely to provide the correct answer.

Frank is a king bee, and he complains mercilessly anytime his team doesn't win. He sometimes challenges whether Ray's answers are correct, and for a while he was convinced other teams were sitting by his team to steal their answers. To combat the perceived cheating, his team created an outpost far removed from all other teams. It didn't help much, since so many of their answers are wrong, and his team continues to come in third or fourth with an occasional better showing.

There are prizes for trivia as well as for some other shipboard activities. "O" points are the prize currency, and entertainment staff award them for winning. In daily team trivia, each player receives three points for first, two points for second and one point for third. Points can be redeemed for Oceania logo merchandise. A basic baseball cap costs 15 points; an Oceania journal is 25 points and so forth. I noticed what I thought was an incredibly tacky kitchen towel for 15 points and thought it might be a joke, but I overhead a fellow passenger say, "I really hope I get enough points to buy the Oceania kitchen towel. I just love it." My mom has earned over a hundred points between her, my dad and me, so I guess we'll have our pick of the caps, thin T-shirts, kitchen towels, coasters and key chains.

I don't know which prize Frank has his eye on, but he comes to the daily team trivia as well as the frequent nightly music trivia. Despite his teams' lackluster performance he is earning some points. My mother, along with a few other players from our daily trivia team, has been winning first or second place on the evenings that musical trivia is played. Early in the cruise, my mom met two well-groomed older men, traveling together, while competing in a music-trivia contest featuring Broadway show tunes. She told me I should meet them since they might be a gay couple. I was amused by this, as the chances of their traveling together and meeting at, much less winning, the show-tune trivia and not being a couple, was extremely low. I met them; they have been together more than 30 years, and they recently married in their home city of Toronto, Canada.

The night after my mom went to trivia and met her new show-tune teammates, she, my dad and I were eating breakfast at the Terrace restaurant.

"We should have won first place," my mother said, referring to last night's music trivia. "The pianist from the ship joined the other team and I think he knows every song. They shouldn't let professional musicians play against us."

"Well, it sounds like you guys did pretty well. You came in second," I said.

"I still think we should have come in first, but that piano player knew every song. At least it was a lot of fun, and I can't wait to do it again," she said.

A few moments later, a loud indignant voice yelled from behind me, "He didn't know any of the songs. That piano guy doesn't know a thing. I knew all the answers." Frank belligerently interrupted as he accusingly stared at my mom.

Uh-oh. I might not get my photo with Lumpy now, I thought. Unbeknownst to us, Frank had been sitting by himself a few tables over intently listening to my mother describing last night's music-trivia game.

"Oh, uh, I am sorry," my mom stammered out. "I just assumed he knew lots of songs since he plays so many different ones on the ship."

"He didn't know a thing. If it wasn't for me, we couldn't have won," Frank said. "Besides, aren't you the one that couldn't identify 'June Is Busting Out All Over'?" Frank asked. "How embarrassing! That was the biggest hit of the musical!"

With that, Frank walked away, and my mom, dad and I were left speechless, gazing at the remains of our breakfast. I started to laugh and said, "Well, he is sort of like his character on *Leave It to Beaver*."

A few nights later, the music trivia featured classical music for teams of two. My parents love classical music. Their combined knowledge earned them second place. Frank's team went down in flames—they scored only six out of 20 points.

I continued to say hi to Frank at daily team trivia, and a few days ago brought my camera and asked if I could have a "picture with Lumpy." He happily obliged. I asked my mom to snap the photo, and when she finished I said, "Frank, do you mind if I get one with you and my mom too?"

"Sure, I'd be happy to," he said, so now I have my favorite photo from the trip—Mom with her nemesis, Lumpy.

Although it has been fun to try to beat Lumpy's team every day, I suspect when we are down to our last week, Ray's prediction will come true, and we'll love Lumpy again; I know life won't be nearly as interesting when I have to return home and instead of getting to face off against Lumpy's trivia team every afternoon at 4:45, I have to be at my office working. Since it is now 4:30, I have to go... Trivia is calling and I can't be late!

NOTE: I just returned from trivia. We tied for first. We would have won if I had remembered the computer from "2001, A Space Odyssey" was HAL 9000—I said HAL 2000 (no one else knew the number either). At least I knew the Beatles manager, Brian Epstein, died in the late 1960s—I guessed 1969, the answer was 1967, but the point went to the closest and that was my team. Who knows what salient facts I'll learn tomorrow.

*****

merryecho   *April 16th, 2007, 11:26 AM*
Jack, you just keep getting better! The Lumpy story is hilarious—it sounds like he has stayed in character all these years. I always thought his dad on the show was even more obnoxious than Lumpy, but can't for the life of me remember his name. If you need to make conversation with the Lump, you might bring up Whitey, another character, who died recently in Portland after living as a street person for several years. The obit talked about him regularly cashing his $15 royalty checks. I wonder if Lumpy got the same deal?

Aussie Gal   *April 16th, 2007, 06:01 PM*

Jack, I have enjoyed so much reading your latest post today. Your writing is wonderful, and I am so glad you are spending some your precious vacation time doing this for us. A big thank-you.
Jennie

tgg   **April 16th, 2007, 10:13 PM**
Jack, we howled when we read your description of team trivia—especially how the mood of the competition changes over time. Your descriptions of the team members was perfect. I still remember the guy on the other side of the room who argued about so many of the answers.

Thanks to team trivia, we brought home one O visor and two O caps from our last cruise. We passed on the towels and thin T-shirts, thank you very much.

Thank you for helping us relive the wonderful memories of our fantastic trivia team. We looked forward to seeing them every afternoon at 4:45. What a great time we had.

*****

JackfromWA   **April 17th, 2007, 06:11 AM**

A FEW RESPONSES:

Decebal: The cabana has been wonderful. I haven't used it as much as I hoped—some days are too darn hot—but between my mom, dad and me we are getting our money's worth from it. The Banyan Tree wasn't flooded in the 2004 tsunami, but they did have extensive wind and storm damage.

Update on Ty: My partner Ty has been referred to a specialist for his biopsy. He is scheduled to go in on May 3rd. Hopefully his appointment will be moved up, but if it isn't I'll be home about the time he gets his results. Thanks to everyone who sent positive thoughts/prayers/and wishes for his good health our way—I believe it helps.

Chapter 9

MID-CRUISE REVIEW

JackfromWA   *April 17th, 2007, 06:11 AM*

Today marks the middle of the cruise. For those looking forward to an Oceania cruise or contemplating a trip of this length, I wanted to share some of my thoughts and observations. Remember this review is an anecdotal nonscientific opinion about my first time on Nautica—some, or maybe all, of your experiences will be different

Earlier I said that Regent's Mariner is my favorite cruise ship. If price is not a factor, my opinion hasn't changed. The reason I prefer Mariner to Nautica can be summed up in three words: standard cabin size.

After 18 days I still haven't learned to enjoy the size of my cabin. I have adapted to it, I got what I paid for, but I find 165 square feet is too small for a 35-day trip for two. On the other hand, my parents seem to be doing just fine with sharing an identically sized cabin (with the exception of not enough closet space), so contentment with the cabin size depends entirely on what you are comfortable with. A friend and his wife onboard have a Vista Suite (approximately 800 square feet), and they prefer the layout of the 550-square-foot Royal Suite on Celebrity. They love their suite, they are perfectly content, but they miss having a walk-in shower. Another friend and his wife have a Penthouse Suite (approximately 325 square feet), and they couldn't be happier. I know I would be happiest in an Owner's or Vista Suite. I am a sybarite at heart, love lots of space and enjoy having my cabin resemble my living room at home. But since I don't want to pay the premium, I would try to purchase a Penthouse Suite when traveling Oceania with Ty.

In defense of the cabins, they are well laid out and the space is intelligently designed for maximum efficiency. Despite my criticism of the size, it has not interfered with enjoying my vacation—I just prefer the standard-cabin configuration on Mariner.

Food generally creates the most controversy when comparing cruise lines. After eating onboard Nautica for several weeks, I now have an informed opinion about the cuisine and how it compares to Regent, Silversea, Celebrity, Holland America and Royal Caribbean. In short, it is significantly superior to Celebrity, Holland America and Royal Caribbean and easily competes with Regent and Silversea.

Portions tend to be smaller than on some other cruise lines, but it is never a problem to ask for more and, like any longtime cruiser in good health, I have never gone to bed hungry. Some of the desserts are truly outstanding—a chocolate mousse with caramel and orange sauce served in the Grand Dining Room and a refreshing cassis sorbet spring to mind. Every night there is a vegetarian course, a spa or light-cuisine menu, a pasta course, a wok course, and a salmon, steak or chicken entrée on the Grand Dining Room menu. In short, there is something for everybody, and the quality, temperature, taste, incredible variety and portion sizes have been perfect for me.

One of my litmus tests for a cruise-ship dining room is a Caesar salad. On Nautica the lettuce is always crisp, so I know the salad is tossed when I order it, anchovy strips are available, and slices of aged Italian Parmesan cheese are plentiful and savory. On some cruise ships the Caesar consists of limp, wilted lettuce and grated Parmesan if you are lucky. Another test is orange juice. I love fresh-squeezed orange juice and purchase it by the half-gallon from Costco at home. Unfortunately, Nautica fails this test. The orange juice is good for reconstituted, but it lacks the flavor and zest of good, fresh-squeezed juice.

Another test is room service. While I don't order too much food to my cabin, after a shore excursion or a long day it is nice to just have something simple. Nautica has an excellent room-service menu. The French onion soup is particularly good, and steak, hamburgers, spaghetti and ice cream are always available. The room service is much better than most cruise lines and almost as good as Regent or Silversea. Since I am in a standard cabin, I can't order dinner from the dining room or the alternative restaurants—that privilege is reserved for suites—but if I could order from the dining room during meal hours I would rate the room service as high as any ship I've sailed.

While true gourmands might be happier on Silversea, the food on Nautica is superb, and I think 95% of the passengers will be just as delighted by the superb food on Oceania as I am.

My expectation for entertainment on this ship was very low. I assumed with only 600 passengers show entertainment would be an afterthought. I was wrong. The nightly shows have been good and well attended. While there are only four singers onboard, they manage to consistently produce outstanding (for a cruise ship) variety shows. Singers, guitarists, violinists and the cruise director, Ray Solaire, who puts on an incredibly entertaining variety show of his own, augment their performances. My only complaint about the shows is the lack of a proper venue. The Nautica lounge is not terraced or elevated, so unless you sit in the front few rows, part of your view is often obscured.

The highlights of the entertainment for me are bridge classes and trivia. I wrote extensively about trivia in my last post, and though I could write chapters about learning to play bridge, I'll just mention a few highlights. First and foremost is the instructor, Jean Joseph, a delightful, impish lady from Kansas City.

From what I can tell, Jean is the only person on the ship who can routinely and resoundingly put every passenger in his or her place. My father was an education professor for more than 30 years, and both of us left Jean's class exclaiming, "She is an excellent teacher."

Jean taught kindergarten and first grade for many years, and she brings her years of experience teaching children to the more challenging task of educating pampered adults. She tolerates no talking while her back is turned to write a bridge hand on the chalkboard.

"I hear talking, and I know you can't be listening if you are talking. You just can't do both at the same time, so you need to just be quiet and listen," she frequently says. When explaining a difficult-for-a-novice-bridge-player-to-grasp principle, Jean breaks it into simple steps such as counting, "You all know how to count to eight, don't you?" she asks. She usually ends her illustrations with, "Now that's not hard, is it?" And in the easy-to-understand way she conveys difficult principles, it isn't hard to understand.

A beginning-bridge class with Jean fills your head with new words like singleton and doubleton and old words like dummy, pass and void that take on new meaning in bridge lexicon.

Her greatest gift is her ability to motivate her students to "make her proud." She has that ineffable quality all great teachers possess— they make you want to please them—and they do it in a nurturing, wise, mentoring manner that makes their necessary criticism a relatively painless motivation to learn and do better next time. Watching a room full of successful, experienced, mature adults respond to the same techniques that motivate five-year-olds is one of the great joys of this cruise. I hope to find friends to play bridge with someday, but whether I do or not I'll fondly remember the 18 lessons at sea in Mrs. Joseph's class.

The second highlight of bridge is spending time with my mom and dad in a classroom. My dad has always enjoyed bridge, but since my mom has never had lessons, he doesn't play much. It is fun to sit in a classroom with my father, enjoy his greater knowledge of what I am learning and allow him to share his love of bridge with my mom and me. The hours in the classroom and hours spent practicing bridge is another opportunity to spend quality time with my mom and dad.

Nautica's onboard library is extensive and well maintained. There is a section for current *New York Times* bestsellers. The numerous bookshelves contain hundreds of biographies and novels, an extensive travel library and a very large guest-paperback exchange. In addition to several cozy leather chairs with ottomans, there are two computer workstations and a printer. Best of all, the library is on an honor system that allows guest to return and borrow books 24 hours a day.

I have taken only one of the ship's shore excursions, "Bangkok on Your Own," which was really more of a bus transfer. But I have listened to my fellow trivia-team players, bridge students and dining companions, and overall Oceania is earning high ratings. This may be due in part to an excellent shore-excursion manager, Cinthya, but I also think this is an area that Oceania recognized needed improvement and made substantive changes. I'll write more about this after taking the Luxor and Cairo shore excursions, but I haven't heard any complaints, and I have heard many compliments about the quality of the guides and the organization of the ship tours.

No review would be complete without a commentary on service. Service on a ship can be hard to define, but I suggest it is a genuine attitude of friendliness and consistently meeting and exceeding guests' expectations. By this standard, Oceania is the best I have sailed. I described the overall service last night to a well-traveled friend at dinner as, "Holland America's service on steroids."

Service is unfailingly consistent, feels absolutely genuine—they really want you to have the time of your life—and is usually accompanied by smiles and a friendly demeanor everywhere on the ship. For those critics reading this, I am not a travel agent, I am not trying to "sell" you on Oceania (remember I said if money wasn't a factor I would still pick Regent's Mariner over Oceania)—I have just had nothing but consistent positive service experiences everywhere onboard. The complaints I've overheard about service are things like, "Why do they change my towel every day. I don't do that at home!" or "These people are bugging me. They are always asking if I need something. I wish they'd just leave me alone." I wish my business had complaints like that!

A small example of the service: A pool bar waiter I didn't know approached me yesterday and asked, "Can I get you something from the bar, sir?"

"No," I replied. "I am doing just fine, thank you."

"How about a lemonade or a cold glass of water?" he asked.

"Actually, that sounds great. Thank you," I replied. Not many ships have pool-bar waiters who, although they get paid largely from tips for bar drinks, encourage you to enjoy a free drink they have to fetch on a hot, humid day. I think if I tried to order a free lemonade on Celebrity, the waiter would at best reluctantly disappear for five or 10 minutes and eventually fetch it. On Nautica, I had ice-cold lemonade in less than a minute, served with a genuine smile. Somehow Oceania has created a corporate culture that encourages all personnel to genuinely strive to make guests comfortable and happy.

The No. 1 complaint I have heard is the price of alcohol beverages (a beer starts at $3.75 + 18% service), water and sodas (a Diet Coke is $2 + 18% service). The No. 2 complaint is laundry. There is only one laundry room onboard, and to say the self-serve laundry is overtaxed is like saying Bombay is a little crowded.

Early in the cruise, some experienced, self-centered passengers attempted to buy all the laundry tokens from the purser's desk. Whether they were trying to replicate the Hunt brothers' silver exploits in the 1980s or simply trying to stop everyone else from doing laundry, I don't know. When the ship belatedly realized that they suffered a run on laundry tokens, they instituted a daily limit of two per cabin (it takes one token for one washer cycle and one token for one dryer cycle). Despite the new limit and frequently emptying the token receptacles in the laundry room, the desk shortly ran out of tokens. Two days ago, the purser took the unusual step of making the laundry room free, rendering all the tokens as valuable as Confederate dollars, in hopes that the laundry room would sort itself out—it didn't. Now that it is free, it is worse than ever.

Urban legends about the laundry room abound. I have heard tales of fistfights, shoving matches, stolen laundry, obscenities and lines forming at 6 a.m. (the laundry room is open from 7:30 a.m. to 10 p.m.). I don't know if any of these are true or not, I suspect some of it is hyperbole or an excuse not to do laundry, but I did hear from a reliable source there was talk of having a security guard posted outside the laundry room door on sea days and that ship's officers avoid walking by the laundry room. I can't help but be amused that on a trip that every passenger paid thousands of dollars to take, such a furor would erupt over laundry. I have sent most of my clothes out (my mom is aboard and has graciously offered to do some of my laundry along with hers and my dad's, plus she irons it for free. Thanks, Mom!). My total laundry bill is about $60, so I just don't get it. I must be missing something. I guess everyone has different priorities, but you won't catch me duking it out in the laundry room—I'll be lounging in my cabana, reading a book, writing, or studying bridge.

The greatest delight of a long cruise is the wealth of days. There isn't the sense of urgency I feel on a short cruise. There is enough time to eat, watch, listen and view everything. In my regular (not at sea) life, I live with deadlines, schedules and appointments. On Nautica, I have time to strike up a conversation with an 85-year-old woman from Nova Scotia, to assist a fellow passenger with adding titles to his pictures in Adobe Photoshop, to chat with Raquel at the Reception Desk, to attend bridge class, and to stop and "smell the roses." One of the most valuable things I have learned so far this journey is that my personality is much better suited to a less time-sensitive lifestyle. I feel physically, emotionally and spiritually better when I can interact with people without an impending sense of urgency. My self-imposed deadlines at home are not as congruent with my personality as the liberation from time I have on the ship. So when I get home I want to figure out how I can incorporate some of that wisdom in my everyday life.

If I could change 10 things about Oceania, it would be (in no particular order):

1. Fresh-squeezed orange juice
2. Faster Internet speeds
3. Free sodas in all dining venues and better prices on all bar drinks and water in staterooms
4. Larger standard cabins
5. More laundry rooms
6. More phones scattered around the ship to call staterooms
7. A terraced main showroom
8. A more sensible repeat-guest program (Regent counts the number of days you cruise for more benefits; Oceania counts the number of cruises, so for 35 days I have only one cruise with Oceania.)
9. Affordable single supplements (perhaps 50% instead of 100%)
10. A larger game and card room

All in all, I am more than satisfied. Oceania is in that rare strata that if you can't be happy and content here, you probably can't be happy and content anywhere. Although there is no perfection this side of heaven, Oceania comes closer than most vacations, and I plan to relish and savor the remaining days.

*****

CruisingSerenity   *April 17th, 2007, 10:32 AM*

This thread has been, by far, by miles and miles, my favorite thread on Cruise Critic ever.

And when you return home and find some of that "stop to smell the roses" time, I hope you decide to write a book. It is SUCH a joy to read your posts. Your writing ability is phenomenal. I get the feeling you could write about grass growing or paint drying and it would be interesting, informative and humorous. To think that people in this world have not discovered your writing is...sad to think about, actually.

I echo the gratitude from others: Thank you so much for taking the time to share your thoughts and observations with us. They are such a treat.

fjdelrio   *April 17th, 2007, 02:08 PM*
JackfromWA posts
Hi, Jack and Hi, everyone:

I just wanted Jack to know that I too, have joined his fan club.

Your posts IMHO are informative, funny, entertaining and accurate.

I agree with your opinions, both the positive ones and the negative ones. I wish I could enlarge the bathrooms (wait until you see the BR's on the new ships!!), add a second story to the show lounge etc. The OJ issue is a tough one. Although not fresh squeezed (only Owner's Suites and Vista Suites are served fresh squeezed), the OJ we serve is Tropicana, which I believe, is the best you can buy. Maybe we've had trouble sourcing Tropicana in the Far East, which could explain why the OJ onboard is not to your standards.

I understand your point of..."if money were no object"...But that is why Oceania is so popular; you just can't beat the COMBINATION of high quality (cuisine, service, ship decor, etc.) and reasonable prices.

I am so impressed with your posts that I hope you accept my humble offer to grant you FREE unlimited access to the Internet. I would not want money to in any way interfere with your posts; if anything, please add more juicy details!!!

I join the throngs of Jack fans wishing and praying for Ty's good health.

Again, I just wanted to thank you and to congratulate you for providing all Oceania fans such wonderful insights and for sharing your experiences with all of us. I hope you and your parents and friends continue to enjoy Nautica.

All the best,
FDR
[Frank Del Rio, CEO of Oceania Cruises]

tak2   **April 17th, 2007, 02:51 PM**
Good move, FDR.

Thanks for providing the free Internet time so Jack can keep entertaining those of us that are so looking forward to our turn on O.

Have you thought of publishing his journal, perhaps for those that wish to book long journeys with the broadening itineraries when the new ships come out?

meow!   **April 17th, 2007, 03:18 PM**
I agree with your analyses of things. The service on Oceania is very good, the people are jovial, and fellow passengers are folksy. As I have mentioned before, food is also very good, actually with more variety than on Silversea, for example, except that on Silversea you can have caviar and foie gras on demand. The entertainers on Oceania try hard, but that "hall" is more like a nightclub and not a multistoried, tiered theatre, and the sound equipment (at least in 2004) left much to be desired. I would prefer they turn off their loudspeakers! Again, as mentioned before, the standard cabin is no-frills, standard fare (with those on RSSC and Silversea being much larger at Oceania's PH size and much more elegant). As we have discussed on another thread, I have made some guesses (based on published data) on what the newbuilds' basic staterooms are likely to be. Your story has become a daily entertainment with interesting information, and thank you for the perseverance and effort!

Twiga   **April 17th, 2007, 04:32 PM**
I, too, have been enjoying your postings, Jack. I have been a "lurker," but now that you are at the halfway point I must come out in the open and say "Great writing!" I am eagerly awaiting the next

71

installment. I love Goa and all of India. It has been quite a while since I have been there, so I can't wait to read about your experiences in India.

I also want to say "Thanks!" to Mr. Del Rio for reading these message boards and responding to the comments made, both good and not so good, by Cruise Critics members. I am booked on the Nautica in September. It will be my first time on Oceania. I know I will become an Oceania convert. Until my cruise, I am enjoying my virtual cruise with you, Jack, and your parents. They sound like wonderful people and terrific cruise buddies. Thanks for sharing your cruise with all of us!

Wendy The Wanderer   April 17th, 2007, 05:27 PM
Jack, thanks so much, I'm really enjoying your postings. I'm a Regent fan who hopes to try Oceania some day, probably in a concierge-level balcony cabin. You've certainly painted a very positive picture.

china addict   April 17th, 2007, 05:30 PM
Laughs in the laundry room
Jack, you are a great raconteur, and I relish every word you write. The tale of the missing laundry tokens and drama over the washers and dryers made me laugh out loud. Actually, when I was on the Nautica last summer, the laundry room was one of the best places to hang out. We had chardonnay in there and great fun modeling weird garments discovered in the "lost and found" basket. DH wondered why I knew so many people onboard, and I told him we had bonded over our laundry. I am so glad you are enjoying these precious days with your parents and am praying for Ty's good health. Please please please start a new thread when you are back home and let us know how he is doing.

Aussie Gal   April 17th, 2007, 07:23 PM
Jack, another hilarious episode! We are thinking of you and Ty down here and are hoping for a good report. Having been there (am a six-year cancer survivor), I do know what you are both going through. It is not an easy time, and I am glad that you will be home when you will be most needed.

I have one question to ask and that is about the bridge lessons. We would love to learn but are complete novices. Do you think we would be eligible to sign up for the lessons? Secondly, when are they

72

held? Next April we hope to take the ship's excursion to Agra and the Taj Mahal so will be missing a couple of days. We also are thinking of doing the side trip to Angkor Wat. I would hate to miss out on lessons because we will be missing from the ship.

Keep up the good work. We were reading your post this morning at breakfast, and it certainly made our day, especially the laundry episode.

Jennie

ChatKat in Ca.   April 17th, 2007, 07:57 PM
Wow—Lumpy too!

Jack—I am thoroughly enjoying your posts. We are diehard RSSC cruisers and will be on Nautica in June.

Your Lumpy posts have me grinning from ear to ear. When we were kids, Frank lived in my neighborhood (on Guthrie Street) and was the idol of a bunch of us. We routinely would go and knock on his door to say hi. He later moved to Cadillac Avenue, and we still continued to knock on his door to say hi. He was always very kind to us little brats. Please tell him that we fondly remember him. His dad worked as a butcher, if I recall correctly.

lahore   April 17th, 2007, 09:40 PM
Hey, Jack, what a great post. Our last Nautica cruise was for two weeks, and the laundry room could get quite nasty then, so I will come prepared this time—with a different attitude, I expect, and a preparedness to spend more on getting it done for me. It's astounding that someone even thought of buying up all the laundry tokens—how gross can people get???

Good move, FDR—Jack deserves it if anyone does!

*****

JackfromWA   April 18th, 2007, 04:05 PM

A FEW RESPONSES:

CruisingSerenity: Like most of us, I doubt my writing ability, and your encouragement is overwhelming. I believe most of us have a story to tell—I love the expression "the greatest stories of a man's or woman's good nature are buried each day in the obituaries"— but few of us make, or ever even have the luxury of time to tell our stories. On a 35-day journey with 18 sea days, I unexpectedly discovered the luxury of time needed to share a little of my story with you. I am glad you like it—it warms my heart. Thanks for reading.

fjdelrio/FDR: I envy your initials! Thank you for your unabashed encouragement, well wishes and generous offer of free Internet access. I am sure other readers are as impressed as I am that you pay attention to such small details as our little cruise forum. Then again it is the attention Oceania gives small details that makes cruising on Nautica so pleasant. You and your partners have built a well-oiled machine, and the time you spent replying has cemented my already growing loyalty to your cruise line (not that I needed it, as any reader knows I am experiencing a fantastic once-in-a-lifetime trip with my parents). I have carefully budgeted my Internet package and as of mid-cruise yesterday I had used exactly half—590 minutes are remaining. While part of me wants to exploit this unexpected opportunity and download the last three episodes of *24* from iTunes, the mature and grateful aspect of my nature simply thanks you for your kind and generous gesture. I will continue my pattern of writing offline and going online to post. If I run out of my package before Athens, I'll take you up on your offer. Like most of us, I am totally excited to experience your new ships and new cruising innovations (after a few shakedown cruises, of course) when they come online. Can't wait to see what you have in store for us, and wish you all the best for your future well-deserved success.

Twiga: Thanks for posting. You will have a great time. Please feel free to contact me (or Jan—she seems to be a wealth of knowledge and posts regularly) if I can help answer any questions before your trip next September.

Wendy The Wanderer: Like you, I love Regent. Overall, considering the value, I like Oceania better. Can't wait to hear what you think when you try it.

Aussie Gal: No worries! Bridge lessons are held only on sea days, so you won't miss any classes if you take the trip to Agra or the side trip to Angkor Wat. Everyone I have spoken to that did the Taj Mahal last year enthusiastically recommends it. I would have loved to go but two things stopped me: finances and wanting to see it first with Ty. I hope you are lucky enough to have Jean Joseph as your instructor. I have overheard several classmates comment she is the highlight of their cruise. Make sure you try to attend every beginning class on sea days (on our cruise they last one hour and are always at 11 a.m.), as the instruction is sequential and it might be hard to catch up. I believe after 18 lessons I will at least know enough to sit at a table without completely embarrassing myself.

ChatKat in Ca.: I will pass your well wishes on to Frank a.k.a. Lumpy. I am going to wait till the last few days, as I would rather have him read my description of our time together after he gets home! Every story needs a villain, and Frank is an easy target. All in all, I am sure he is probably a kind man with a big heart—his wife is very nice—he is just a "loud" personality. Around Frank, I get the feeling it is Frank's world and I just live in it.

lahore: My suggestion for laundry is just send it out and do something other than the laundry on your holiday. These ships don't have the self-serve laundry facilities necessary for extended cruises. Hope you have a wonderful trip. Wish I were able to come with you, and I look forward to reading your impressions.

Chapter 10

GOA

JackfromWA   *April 18th, 2007, 04:05 PM*
Our first day in India...ever

We arrived at the port shortly after 8 a.m. My cabin is on the portside, and this was only the second time my window faced the dock when Nautica berthed. Goa is hot and humid. Since I carry a few extra pounds, I suffer from chafing between my thighs in hot, humid climates. I learned this the hard way a few years ago after a trip with my brother Jeff and his family to Disney World over spring break. In hot, humid climates, the chafing can become very painful—especially when walking from one end of Epcot Park to the other. Since then I have brought baby powder along to minimize my discomfort.

In Hong Kong I went to Watson's, a drugstore, to purchase more powder. The heat and humidity were incredible, and I didn't want to risk running out. While I quickly found my familiar Johnson & Johnson baby powder, near it on the same shelf was something new—St. Luke's Prickly Heat Powder. The label promised the powder to be "cooling, refreshing and soothing," as well as "effective in relieving itching and discomfort from prickly heat." It was packaged in a compact white tin adorned with ubiquitous-in-China red roses. It seemed to be exactly what I needed, and since it was recommended to "apply three to four times daily," it appeared to be perfectly benign. The only hint of trouble was a warning that St. Luke's Prickly Heat Powder is "not suitable for infants and children under 2 years." Since I was neither, and it was cheap, I purchased the tin.

This morning I noticed my supply of baby powder was low and the weather was quite humid, so I decided it was time to open the

Prickly Heat Powder. When I removed the lid, I immediately noticed it had an odd orangish-rust tint and a strong medicinal odor.

When applying baby powder to my inner thighs in the small bathroom of my cabin on the first few days of the cruise, I noticed I had left too much powder on the floor. In addition to wasting it, I was making quite a mess for my cabin attendant. So I figured a new way to apply it—immediately following my morning shower, I draped my semi-damp towel on the bed, sat down, leaned my head and torso back and lifted my legs high. Then I happily and successfully sprinkled away. If the image of a 270-pound, 44-year-old man assuming a position normally used for changing diapers is too much for you, I can only say that I wished I hadn't accidentally glimpsed myself in the eight-foot-by-five-foot mirror inconveniently located on the wall at the foot of my cabin's bed. (I learned to look away, and I would never allow Ty to see me like this—some things are best done in solitude). The position worked very well, I neatly captured the excess powder in my damp towel, and when I finished I rolled up my towel in a neat little ball and placed it on the bathroom floor. I have repeated this little ritual most mornings, and my inner thighs have been very comfortable in the "prickly heat."

Today I lay down, assumed my powder-application position and shook the new Prickly Heat Powder loose from the tin. The new powder didn't sprinkle the way my baby powder did, the size and spacing of the holes is different on the lid, so I kept shaking it to make sure I got enough applied. Like too much salt pouring from a shaker, far too much Prickly Heat Powder quickly escaped from the can. My cabin attendant is going to have a bit of a mess on her hands, I thought. Then something hit me. OUCH! THAT BURNS! From the very personal area located below (if your legs are up in the air) my inner thighs, I felt a painful, growing, burning sensation. As it grew more intense I yelped out in pain. I had powder all over me in a spot that Prickly Heat Powder was never meant to cover. Now I know why this stuff wasn't recommended for young kids—if it fell where it wasn't intended, they would scream and cry! It has a real kick to it and needs to be treated with caution. If medicated Gold Bond powder is a beer, this stuff was a fifth of single-malt scotch.

As my rear end continued to erupt in flames I happened to glance out my window and noticed the line of tour buses gradually drift in view of my open stateroom window. OH, NO!—There were Indians waiting to greet us standing on the pier outside, and I was dancing around naked in my cabin attempting to splash water around my lower posterior to relieve my burning bum. I quickly slammed the curtains shut; I don't think anyone saw me through the window. With my privacy restored, I carefully finished rinsing the intensely strong Prickly Heat Powder from my bottom, and I bravely, necessarily, gingerly applied more Prickly Heat Powder after the burning subsided; but I was as careful as a pastry chef sprinkling powdered sugar to decorate the captain's table desserts—I won't ever sprinkle it willy-nilly from the can again. When traveling, you never know what new things might happen, and this was an auspicious way to begin my first morning in India.

We walked down the low-rising gangplank stairs and were quickly met by 20 or 30 cab drivers for hire. All drove different makes and models of white-painted cars emblazoned with a red Tourist Vehicle logo. Dad and I made a plan to pay about 2,000 rupees ($80) to hire a driver from 9 a.m. to 3:30 p.m. We wanted to drive north of Goa to Anjuna's famous Wednesday flea market and then drive through Old Goa and visit some of the rustic old churches and see some of the Portuguese-influenced architecture. A driver agreed to take us for 2,000 rupees, and we drifted away in a sea of jabbering, sweaty cabbies, not too certain which one was our driver.

"Here, get in this car. This is your car," the man-who appeared-to-be-in-charge of all the other drivers said. Five or six other white-clad drivers pointed to the car, so we naively got in.

As we started to pull away I suddenly realized… "Is the car air conditioned?" I asked. It was very hot, getting hotter, and every window was open.

"Oh, no, that costs more," our driver replied.

"Well, we better stop. My mother suffers from heat exhaustion and we need a car with air conditioning," I said. My mother suffers from nothing of the sort, both she and my father are in excellent shape, jog regularly and can easily outrun me any day of the week, but she smiled and quickly acted as if she were unable to cope with the heat-drenched agony of a taxi without air conditioning. The driver reluctantly stopped, we got out and the man-who-appeared-to-be-in-charge came rushing over.

"We need a car with air conditioning," I told him.

"O.K., that will be a hundred U.S. dollars," he replied.

"No, that's too much. I can't pay more than $60." Obviously my on-the-spot computation of U.S. dollars to rupees was failing me as I was now offering to pay less than the 2,000 rupees or $80 my dad and I previously agreed to pay the other driver. There was some scowling and wringing of hands.

Suddenly a new face emerged and said, "You will pay $60?"

"Yes, I'll pay $60."

"OK, I will take you," he said.

"Do you have air conditioning?" I asked.

"Yes, I have. You will be very comfortable." And with that, off we went with David. Apparently David isn't one of the regulars working the pier. He had the proper documentation (everything in India seems to require documentation) to pick up tourists on the pier, but the man-who-appeared-to-be-in-charge came up to David's window and started reading him the riot act. I will never know what, if any, protocols of pier taxi driver rules David violated, but I was glad to have him; his English was excellent and his demeanor was pleasant. Like so many Christians in Hindu or Buddhist countries, David had a picture of Jesus inscribed with a prayer attached to his driver-side window, and a two-inch-high wooden dome-covered cross affixed to the center of his dashboard. J-E-S-U-S was spelled out in four-inch-tall vinyl white letters across the outside top of the front windshield. No one could doubt which team David was on.

I asked David to take us to an ATM, and I also informed him I needed to purchase a SIM card for my phone. Even though Nautica added coverage for cell phones last week, and the $2.50-per-minute charge is much better than the $9-per-minute stateroom phone charge, I still wanted to talk to Ty, my sister, my brothers, my office and some other friends without anxiously watching the clock.

David took us to a Bank of India ATM—my dad's card worked, mine didn't— and to a mobile-phone outlet. What in Vietnam was a 30-second SIM-card purchase, in India was a 30-minute lesson in patience, bureaucracy, and the inexplicable need for a passport photo. When I finally, politely, said I couldn't wait another half hour to go to a photo store, located somewhere over a hill and around the corner where they would gladly accompany me to pay for a photo from some relative or accomplice, they miraculously found a way to issue the SIM card with a photocopy of my passport photo. I once spent 30 long, hot minutes purchasing a chocolate bar at the automobile entrance in Paraguay to Iguaçu Falls; this experience was eerily familiar. What is it that makes a society think they are modern and globally competitive because they have an abundance of arcane, useless bureaucratic paperwork?

We headed north, functioning phone in tow, and started admiring the beautiful scenery along the roadside.

"I never knew there were so many palm trees in India," Mom said.

"It looks a lot like parts of Southern California, doesn't it?" I said.

The tropical scenery was broken up with ramshackle homes, foul-smelling piles of trash strewn along the road's edge, emaciated cows and King Fisher beer signs. It was wonderful. It felt like India—not the India I had imagined, prepared for or expected to see in Mumbai, but a unique, coastal pocket of the vast Indian subcontinent.

When we arrived at the market there were no restrooms, so my mom suffered and my dad and I found and frequented a semi-secluded patch of grass, then we walked into the flea market.

Goa has a reputation for laid-back hippie beach life, trance music and raves. The Anjuna flea market originally emerged from that culture. Today it is about a thousand booths, temporarily set up once a week in a hodgepodge layout atop a sandy coastal bluff. The prices were outrageously cheap—a beautiful wood stained-green Krishna mask for $6, a heavy, elaborate hand-sewn multicolored elephant wall hanging $26—but extensive bargaining was mandatory. My father rose to the occasion, and 90 minutes later our arms were filled with colorful India mementos, and we spent only about $150 between us.

"You know, Ray should have a white-elephant party on the last week of the cruise," my dad said. "Almost everyone ends up with a few things they realize back in their cabin they don't even want, but it was so cheap they just bought it anyway."

"That would be fun, but there'd probably be lots of complaining from people who thought they received worse things than they gave," I replied.

"You know, some things from markets like this look so much better and exotic back at home, but others make you wonder what you were thinking when you bought them," he said.

After two hours, the heat, dust and sales pressure grew overwhelming; I felt myself starting to get irritable. Not only were our hands full, but we are all expecting to be overweight for our luggage restrictions on the British Air flight from Athens to London, so we returned to David's air-conditioned car and headed back toward the ship.

Sensing my mom might need a restroom break, David said he would drop us off for 10 minutes at a mall with western-style toilets. When we pulled up, it looked more like an art gallery in San Diego's Seaport Village. David had mentioned the store was much more expensive than the flea market. He was right. The store was very expensive, but they had many fine, elegant, beautiful and unique items for sale.

Everyone has traditions. As a little kid I loved watching my mom and dad observe their tradition of kissing each other on the lips every time we crossed any state line, but especially on the bridge separating Portland, Oregon from Vancouver, Washington, while driving our station wagon. As I've grown older, traditions I used to make fun of such as Dad reading the story of Jesus Christ's birth out of Luke every Christmas Eve following dinner (I just wanted to move past all the religious stuff and get a few presents or eat more sugar), are now infrequently celebrated rituals I look forward to participating in. When my niece, Victoria, is frustrated by how slowly Grandpa reads the Bible on Christmas Eve, I smile inside, and remember when I felt that way, and wish for her the joy I now take in listening to her Grandpa's voice while our family celebrates being together for the holidays.

I have established a more secretive and personal tradition for myself. Whenever I visit a new region of the world, I try to buy a souvenir that has intrinsic value, personal attraction, and can accompany me some day to a nursing home. I don't particularly want to go to a nursing home, I know things get stolen there, they smell funny and aren't the nicest places to live, but I may end up there because I don't want to be a burden on my family. In a nursing home, since I am paying to be there, I'll feel entitled to be demanding. I want some things that can stay with me the entire journey of my life, that are well-crafted and solid, so that if I am lucky enough to live in good health long enough to someday get to a nursing home in bad health, I can say, "I remember when I was in the Peruvian Andes and bought that beautiful Incan wall hanging—it was $750 dollars—back then that was a lot of money…Can you find the six hidden Inca crosses in it? I'll bet you can't. Boy, was that a trip. We went to Mah-choo Pee-choo and hiked some Inca trail, it wasn't too polluted back in 2005 but I bet it is today, you should go there but if you do it sure is hard to breathe in Cuzco and don't drink tap water, you need to buy bottled water, did you know it is over 13,000 feet…" and other such nonsensical mispronounced comments sure to annoy the overly worked nursing-home staff but sure to bring favorite memories home to me. If I am a little forgetful and frequently repeat the same lines, stories and jokes, all the better— I've heard my share from old relatives and others I love, so someday it will be my turn to return the favor to my children, siblings, nieces, nephews, Ty and the poor nursing-home staff.

Today I found my lifetime souvenir for India—a pair of 40-ounce sterling silver intricately carved Indian elephants. I instantly fell in love with them. I also purchased the nicest carved sandalwood Krishna I've ever seen. My parents fell in love with an exquisite silk

Indian rug. After lots of negotiations, significant (but not significant enough) price reductions, we left with a large silk rug for my parents (shipped directly home via DHL included in the price), two silver elephants, a Krishna and an exquisite jeweled wall hanging for Ty.

"David, we just had the most expensive bathroom break of our lives," I laughed. I have never spent this much spontaneous money with my parents, rarely by myself or with Ty, but it just felt right to all of us. The treasures we found are all heirloom pieces we'll keep the rest of our lives, and decades from now I intend to gaze at my silver elephants and fondly recall the first wonderful day my mom, dad and I set foot in India.

Time escaped us. We couldn't get to all the sites we wanted to visit, but we didn't care. We had a great day. Fortunately we managed to stop at the Basilica of Bom Jesus where the sacred relics of Saint Francis Xavier lie. I snapped lots of pictures. A few miles from the ship we saw two cows scavenging like stray dogs in a trash Dumpster, right alongside the main highway from Goa to Mumbai. I asked David to stop and took a few pictures of that unusual sight, and far too quickly we arrived back.

We stopped at the security gate to enter the pier and the guard asked for our pink pier passes issued by the Goa police. My dad suddenly exclaimed, "I don't know where my pass is. I think I folded it in half in one of these pockets." He had two backpacks and too many pockets to search while restrained in the front passenger seat. My mom handed David her unwrinkled pass to show the guard. David returned it to her, and I handed my tattered, sweaty pass to David. The guard hardly glanced at it, and David returned it to me.

After my experience with the SIM-card purchase, I knew this was a nation enamored with forms and paperwork. I didn't want another bureaucratic boondoggle, and an idea quickly occurred to me. "Here's your pass, Dad. I have it right here," I said as I handed my mom's pass, pretending it was my dad's pass, over the front seat to David to show the disinterested pier guard. The guard gave my mom's pass a superficial cursory glance, accepted it as my dad's security pass and waved us through the gate.

"My pass had a fold in it," my dad muttered, still trying to take in what had just transpired at the security gate.

"Shh, Pete, keep quiet," my mom whispered.

It's hard to successfully practice deceit when your parental accomplices are inexperienced and honest, but I got away with it with no regrets, and derived a great feeling of accomplishment— nothing like fooling the cops on a meaningless bureaucratic matter for a pleasant endorphin rush.

David was such a pleasant man, considerate guide and safe, cautious driver that I gave him $100 (cash flowed like water today) and told him to keep the change. Even though the poverty in Goa was nothing like what I am afraid I'll find in Mumbai, being in India makes me so grateful for the material blessings I take for granted that I wanted to share what I have in some small way.

The ship is quiet tonight. One hundred twenty passengers have departed for two nights to the Taj Mahal. Wolfgang Maier, the executive chef, planned an Indian dinner in Tapas on the Terrace tonight. It was unbelievably delicious—maybe our favorite meal on the ship yet. After dinner I walked out on the softly lit Pool Deck, felt the warm Indian air brush my sunburned ears and neck as the ship sailed toward Mumbai and enjoyed the sight of mostly older, long-married couples curled up in Balinese daybeds together, watching a movie projected on a small outdoor screen under the humid, pitch-black sky. It was a good day. The kind of day it would be good to live over and over again. The kind of day you remember, and savor, long after it's passed.

Being with two of the people I love most in the world, setting foot for the first time in a new country together, each of us finding beautiful treasures to take home and enjoy for a lifetime, and indulging and tasting the exotic flavors of Indian food exquisitely prepared…We even had time to help our team take second place in trivia again as the ship left port. These are the best times—the times you remember long after they are gone. The times made possible by sharing 35 days at sea with someone you love.

Cruise ships are a palette replete with brushes, paints and canvas. We passengers are the artists, and whether I choose to paint an Old World masterpiece or fingerpaint is perfectly fine—as long as my brushstrokes, color and subject make me happy—as long as what I paint is true to me. Oceania is a wonderful starting point because they provide everything imaginable to create art—but you still have to paint your own world.

Thanks, everyone, for staying with me. Tomorrow, Bombay. Thanks for reading.

*****

zu zu's petals   April 18th, 2007, 07:56 PM
OK, it's time for me to come clean…I too have been a "lurker." Others have said it before but, Jack, your amazing prose profoundly touches me. You have that uncanny ability to transport your readers to whatever scenario you describe. I look so forward to your postings! Thank you for taking the time to share your experiences.
We will be embarking on our first cruise ever (Insignia Rome-Athens) in about five weeks' time. Whilst looking for sage advice from experienced cruisers, I luckily stumbled upon your posts. Can't wait to hear of your time in Cairo (we're going there as well). I'm certain once you've described the Pyramids/Sphinx, people of Egypt, etc., my anticipation of seeing them for myself will reach fever pitch.
Looking soooo forward to the next installment!

scdreamer   April 18th, 2007, 08:31 PM
Ah, Jack…you had me laughing so hard milk came out my nose at your desperate talcum-powder escapade, and then just a few minutes later I was sighing over your description of painting our world.
I have always taken mental "snapshots" of my own special times, just to be able to figuratively pull them out when life takes a turn or I just need a lift.
I am afraid we are becoming used to finding your wonderful journal on a regular schedule—maybe we will all have to take up a collection to send you on another exotic sojourn so we will be kept in reading material!
Thank you so much for your posts!
Leslie & Wayne

86

meow!   ***April 18th, 2007, 08:44 PM***

That is very altruistic of you. However, from what we know, nursing-home rooms are very small, and just one room with a small kitchenette and bathroom, and that is if you are lucky enough to get your own room—hardly enough to store the accumulated souvenirs of a lifetime. In many cases, there are many beds (people) in one common room!

A more practical question. Usually, when we are on a long trip, to lessen our load on our way home, we often mail back parcels from the various cities we visit on land. (Now often we just mail a local postcard to ourselves from each city, this is the best, cheapest, lightest and most memorable souvenir of all.) As you are on a long cruise and don't have the time to go to post offices, do you ask the ship concierge to mail back parcels of souvenirs for you, or do you intend to haul it on to Athens and mail it there? If you have to take all the goods back on the plane yourself, together with your other luggage, won't that be quite a burden?

Emdee   ***April 18th, 2007, 10:32 PM***

Jack, your posts are an absolute delight. I cannot wait for the next installment about Bombay—the city of my birth!

I have to wait until next March to take my Beijing to Hong Kong cruise on Oceania but I cannot wait.

Happy travels!

                                                        Miriam

*****

JackfromWA   ***April 18th, 2007, 11:27 PM***

QUICK UPDATE

I sort of overdid it after my Goa post. I was so stimulated by the day I couldn't sleep—Horizons lounge is strangely empty at 2:30 a.m., and Nautica is a wonderful place to have insomnia—I went to bed sometime about 3 a.m.

Unfortunately for my sleeping pattern last night, today is not a sea day. In fact today every passenger must appear in person for India Immigration between 8 a.m. and 9 a.m. in the Nautica lounge.

So after only four hours' sleep I had to get up—at least I am enjoying a cappuccino and orange juice in my stateroom. Not a great way to start Mumbai, but it will still be a great day.

I am taking the Elephanta Caves excursion from the ship this morning, and after that I splurged with Starwood Points and booked two rooms at the ITC Grand Sheraton Central. We will go to bed tonight and wake up tomorrow in the heart of Bombay. So if I don't post for a few days, I am touring, sleeping and vacationing. I am sure I'll have lots of time to catch up over the two sea days between here and Salalah.

china addict: I overlooked your post yesterday. Don't know how it happened... sorry about that. My mom has had similar experiences to yours and met several nice people in the laundry room, especially while ironing. I guess besides all the chaos, it is a good place to meet friends and bond. Thank you for your kind words for Ty and your compliments and encouragement to keep writing.

*****

Aussie Gal　　　***April 19th, 2007, 12:04 AM***
Jack, I just loved reading your post from Goa. It is always special to be able to take home something that you love from a country. We have done that many times, and most of the pieces are very small but do bring back wonderful memories.
Enjoy your night away from the ship, and we look forward to hearing about all your exploits in bustling Mumbai in a couple of days' time.
Jennie

lahore　　　***April 19th, 2007, 06:15 AM***
St. Luke's
Oh, very very funny Jack. As SOON as I read "St. Luke's" I swear it I knew what you were going to say. Suffering from the same problem as you, and having lived in Singapore and Malaysia for years I do exactly the same thing. I am a woman and can assure you that the pain is excruciating . Nevertheless, a tinnie of St. Luke's is the first thing I get out of my bag (or buy, depending on if I have any left over) whenever I return to my second homes. It works so well, it's utterly brilliant stuff. Don't worry, although it feels like

88

hydrochloric acid that first time, it won't do you any long-term harm. Actually I think it's the shock the first time, and the worry that it might cause permanent damage—after a while you just expect that tingling, cooling pain (sounds like I have actually come to enjoy it) and it doesn't worry you so much—although I am careful not to bucket it on. I am just so totally beside myself that you had the same experience and actually posted about it.

I adored your post and just can't wait to get to India myself. Although I have lived with Indian people and am most at home in the Indian sector of Singapore, I have never got to actual India. I must have read hundreds (literally) of books about the place, but the one time we were booked, visa'd-up and ready to go, I got as far as Hong Kong and got as sick as a dog and had to come home. Karma—I wasn't meant to get there that time. I just hope Lord Ganesh facilitates the return attempt. Keep enjoying. I am looking forward to hearing about Mumbai. Maybe we will see you in a Bollywood movie.

merryecho   **April 19th, 2007, 09:53 PM**
OK, a small-world story. While reading your Goa post I was sitting on the deck of my floating home looking at your parents' "kissing bridge" over the Columbia River.

Hope you have recovered from your prickly-heat treatment, although it did have the silver lining of adding another hilarious episode to the Jack Journal.

Toranut97   **April 20th, 2007, 12:36 AM**
Thanks so much, Jack!
Another lurker/Jackblog addict here! I am thoroughly enjoying your posts, and am traveling vicariously with you. What a dynamite trip!

Also am enjoying the sweet memories of our Nautica trip from Istanbul to Athens last year. We are utterly sold on O now! Hoping we can swing Athens to Rome in November of this year for our 20th anniversary.

I am praying for you and Ty. Hope all the tests come out benign, benign, benign!

Have fun and…um…keep on sprinkling!

                                        Donna

*****

JackfromWA　　　*April 21st, 2007, 04:00 PM*

A FEW RESPONSES:

zu zu's petals (what a delightful name!): I am sure you will have a great time—before you know it, five weeks will pass and you'll be on Insignia. Hope you have as good a trip as I've had on Nautica.

scdreamer: Thank you for the inspiring note to keep up this memoir of 35 days on Nautica in so many new places. I wish I could meet all you great people who post here! We would make an amazing group of friendly, well-traveled passengers if we could take a cruise together.

meow!: I can relate to sending postcards. I collect less and less as there is less and less space at home—I limit myself mostly to the "good stuff." On a trip this long I knew I was bound to find some memorable souvenirs to take home. American Airlines allows 70 pounds (you have to pay $25 extra per bag over 50 pounds) per bag, and I have two bags. Coming over, they weighed 90 pounds combined, but about 10 pounds were travel books that I will leave onboard. I should have about 60 pounds available, and if I need it I can purchase carriage for a third bag for $80. I think that is less expensive than using the concierge to ship items home, but I know Robert, Nautica's delightful concierge, is happy to arrange services like that for guests who need it. My brother Jeff and his family are moving to Athens for three years in August. Both my parents and I have lamented he isn't here when we disembark for the final time on May 5th so we could burden him with all our extra stuff! My parents did have their carpet shipped from Goa via DHL, and that is the only heavy piece (so far). Plenty of shopping days and new countries remain, so who knows how we'll ultimately cope.

90

Emdee: Have fun next year on your trip. I wish we could have done that this year. A few passengers aboard took the China cruise immediately prior to this one.

Toranut97: Thanks for the good wishes for a benign result. This morning I spoke to Ty through a computer video chat. He is doing well, and both of us appreciate all the positive thoughts and prayers coming in our direction. Thanks for the kind words and encouragement to devote a few hours each day to sharing my journey. It has become as much a part of my vacation as trivia, bridge and eating.

Chapter 11

MUMBAI

JackfromWA   *April 21st, 2007, 04:00 PM*

Our day in Mumbai started in the Nautica lounge, where every passenger had to participate in a face-to-face inspection with Indian Immigration. The timing was inconvenient (8 a.m.), but at least it was on the ship and took only a few minutes. After the inspection, our police certificates were endorsed, which we needed to exit the Indira Dock.

My parents and I purchased a ship shore excursion to Elephanta Caves. I wanted to use the security of Oceania's shore excursions to get the lay of the land. I knew Mumbai was fundamentally different than any city I've ever visited, and I was afraid to just walk out of the secure pier area into the sea of aging black and yellow taxis hovering at the gate.

We boarded our bus and drove out the gate. I don't recommend driving over tall, poorly spaced speed bumps on a 40-passenger tour bus! As we pulled away from the security gate at the end of the pier, I looked down at the cabbies, self-appointed city guides, beggars, postcard and peacock-feather-fan merchants. I caught a hawker's eye, and it was clear from his disappointed and slightly angry expression that in his opinion we should be forced to run his gauntlet to enter Mumbai. He seemed to think a tall, air-conditioned tour bus whisking affluent, well-fed passengers from the pier to tourist attractions qualifies as cheating. He may be right—part of the reason I paid the ship for a tour I thought I could do less expensively on my own was to circumvent being hassled.

Our guide started talking. Her microphone didn't work well, I found her thick Indian accent difficult to understand, and I was too enthralled by the view flashing outside my bus window, so I put on my iPod shuffle and hit PLAY. "Time keeps on slipping, slipping,

slipping into the future," Steve Miller sang, as I enjoyed listening to "Fly Like an Eagle" instead of to the guide (who still couldn't get her microphone to work). I love my iPod shuffle. It is the size of a matchbook and weighs practically nothing. I load several hundred eclectic, favorite songs, everything from The Who to *Peer Gynt*, and set it to randomly select. The iPod chooses the order of the soundtrack for my day. I can't wait to listen to it in Egypt and Petra. Besides providing a daily soundtrack, it cuts down on the number of vendors haranguing me, as most of my fellow travelers don't have earphones on.

Outside the window I saw multi-story stone buildings, poised women walking the streets wrapped in colorful sequined saris, pairs of men heaving and pulling long blue carts laden with everything from auto transmissions to reams of paper, western-clad businessmen crossing the road—appearing to me as brave as Moses crossing the Red Sea—and merchants, children, traffic police and hundreds of taxicabs. Mumbai hummed with activity as far as the eye could see. Our drive to the Taj Mahal Hotel and the Gateway of India lasted about 15 minutes. Our guide warned us not to stop for shopping and to stay with the group as we exited the bus. She held up our Oceania No. 11 sign high—the crew calls the signs lollypops— and we followed her past the arched Gateway of India, through hordes of merchants, beggars and tourist police toward our waiting ferry.

As I walked down the stone steps to the ferry, I was glad I booked this excursion through the ship. Most ferries to Elephanta Island were crowded with more than a hundred people. Crowded in India isn't like crowded in the United States. There are so many people here that no space for transport is wasted. A crowded ferry in India would be extremely uncomfortable by U.S. standards, and I would be hyper-vigilant for pickpockets and scams—I could never leave my camera bag unattended. On our reserved ferry we had fewer than 40 passengers, all of whom were fellow guests on Nautica; we were comfortable and our belongings were safe.

As the ferry left the terminal at the Gateway of India, I climbed a ladder to the upper deck. I was rewarded with fantastic pictures of the Taj Mahal Hotel and the Gateway of India. Several other brave passengers, including my mother, joined me, and we took photos of each other standing on the stern with a view of the Mumbai cityscape in the background. My mom has started practicing digital photography. I was proud of her as she snapped away like a seasoned pro. One of the great advantages of taking a few shore excursions with the ship, even if you are like me and enjoy more independent travel (I like to be able to roll down the window or stop and take photos at will), is the opportunity to befriend my fellow passengers. Since we are spending over a month together on Nautica, it is nice to strike up conversations and form casual friendships. For me there is a fine line—I am here to spend time with my parents, and I don't want to waste our precious time together on forming too many new, passing acquaintanceships—but I also enjoy becoming familiar and friendly with some of my exciting and diverse fellow guests. By the time our hour on the ferry together had passed, it seemed almost everyone knew someone else a little better than they did before our daytrip together began.

As Elephanta Island came into view, my mom asked, "Is that it, you think?"

"Yep, I can see King Kong's head," I replied. It appeared a little foreboding, like an island King Kong might live on. It seemed strangely uninhabited after our brief, shielded view of Mumbai. We departed the ferry, boarded a small amusement-park-style train and rode about half a mile to the entrance gate. The guide advised us there were over a hundred stone steps and long terraces to climb to reach the caves, and we could pay 500 rupees ($20) to be carried up the stairs on a sedan chair. Though this appealed to me—on a visit a few years ago to Bavaria, I hired a horse-drawn carriage to bring my nieces and nephew and me, warmly wrapped in wool blankets, up the steep hill to Neuschwanstein castle, as my friend Eric, my brother and his wife hiked up while watching me corrupt their happy-to-be-corrupted children—everyone else in our group chose to hike up the steps.

Part of me wanted to experience the thrill of going up the hill lifted like the Queen of Sheba by four strong attendants. But I let my visions of royalty evaporate and began my hike. Although it wasn't that far, being out of shape, overweight and prone to physical laziness, the farther I hiked, the better the sedan chair sounded. It didn't help that on both sides of the ascending staircases there were merchants loudly exhorting me to buy their wares. As a heavy, profusely sweating tourist, I must have appeared a likely sedan-chair prospect. Every time I saw a group of men carrying an empty chair down, their eyes lit up as they saw me approach them, sweating, huffing and puffing up the hill, and they excitedly asked, "Sir, would you like a ride?" Damn straight I would, I thought, as I verbally declined their offer.

Despite wanting a ride, pride, knowing my parents were right behind me practically prancing up the steps, and not wanting to look like Homer-Simpson-as-he-goes-to-India, I forced myself to continuously decline the ever more attractive offers to ride up the hill in style. When I finally reached the top, our guide reminded us to be careful of the monkeys, which are aggressive about stealing food, and invited us to follow her into the caves.

The caves instantly captivated me. Sadly, generations ago the carvings were severely vandalized—genitalia were destroyed, spiritual markings were mutilated—but despite the intentional destruction and age of the sculptures, the carvings remain powerful and relevant. Though little is accurately known about their history, the cave temples are dedicated to Shiva, who was conceived as the supreme deity, both the creator and destroyer of the universe. Inexpensive pamphlets containing theories and speculative history are readily available on the path between the ferry and the dock.

Our guide began lecturing in front of one of the many carved panels adorning the north entrance. I decided to wander about, let my eyes adjust to the darkness of the interior temple and explore the various carvings. After taking at least 50 photos, I asked my mother to let me know when we were leaving as I wanted to sit in a quiet, tranquil location and try to absorb some of the energy of this stone cathedral. There is a small shrine within the temple, where Shiva is still worshipped to this day. I settled into a corner of the shrine, mostly obscured from view, turned my iPod on and reflected on the age, spirituality and purpose of the shrine, the carvings and the temple.

A good friend, Carol Stewart, from Nelson, Canada had taken me and a small group of friends to numerous Inca ruins and holy places in Peru and taught me the value of being still while trying to take in the power of such places. "You can't just trek though them," Carol told me, referring to the majestic Inca ruins. "You have to sit, contemplate and make a connection with the beauty and spirit of the place." She traveled in India for three months last year, and she recommended visiting the Ellora Caves—they are similar to but larger than the Elephanta Caves and located several hundred miles from Mumbai—rather than visit the Taj Mahal. "I wouldn't make the effort to go back to the Taj, but I would go back to the Ellora Caves," she said. Everyone has different priorities when traveling, but I hold Carol's opinions in high regard, so I knew before I came to India that both the Ellora Caves and Elephanta Caves were special places likely to be of great interest to me.

After half an hour sitting cross-legged in the corner of the cold, stone shrine, a nasty looking red insect larger than a wasp kept hovering about me—I think it was attracted to the smell of my Coppertone coconut-scented sunscreen. It's time to leave, I thought.

Although we had been warned, both my dad and I wanted to feed the monkeys. Between us we had several apples and bananas. The monkeys react as excitedly as seagulls to food; when they see it, they congregate, hover and remain just out of reach. An enterprising monkey managed to grab most of an apple from my dad's hand, so Dad retaliated by trying to slice the remaining apple with his pocketknife and ration the portions. As he divided the apple a commotion erupted.

"LOOK OUT! SIR, SIR, LOOK OUT!" an Indian cave guard shouted as he shooed monkeys away with his feet, unintentionally kicking up the heavy, red dust. My dad had set his small backpack on the ground behind him and, while he was focused on their cohorts, two enterprising monkeys were bravely rummaging through his pack, tossing out his things as they looked for more fruit. Fortunately, the monkeys didn't steal anything but an empty plastic bag, but I did give my dad a good scare when I asked him where his camera was (I had it hidden in my pocket).

On the return ferry we captured some great pictures of Nautica docked against the Mumbai skyline, and before we knew it we were back on the ship. I had booked two rooms at the ITC Sheraton Grand Central. We packed overnight bags, retrieved our passports and left the ship for a night ashore in Bombay. There is nothing wrong with the ship—after three weeks we still weren't overly tired of sleeping aboard—I just wanted to wake up in the heart of Mumbai.

We hired one of the ubiquitous black and yellow, old Fiat taxis. Production of the most commonly used model of taxi in Mumbai ended 15 years ago, so every one you see (and there appear to be tens of thousands trolling Mumbai's streets) is at least that old or older. They are kept running with hundreds of mechanics who specialize in repairing old Fiat taxis. I observed at least six constants among all of them: They are not air-conditioned, they have no seat belts, only males drive them, the passing lights or flashers are never used, the horns are scrupulously maintained, and all have numerous small dents and scratches from driving in Mumbai.

The chaos of driving in Mumbai's choked streets exceeds anything I have ever seen. Imagine allowing two lanes on San Francisco's Golden Gate Bridge, to allow four cars wide instead of two, and then encourage hundreds of men, women, children, dogs, hand-pushed carts and motorcycles to dart between the moving cars, which are simultaneously practicing indiscriminate passing and constant jostling for position. Oh, and multiply the Golden Gate's traffic load by a factor of five and you have some idea of what driving in Mumbai is like. Traffic is incredible, incomprehensible and dangerous.

When our cab approached the port exit, I realized I'd left my police pass in my camera bag in the trunk. When I told the port guard my pass was in my camera bag, he replied, "Did you declare your camera to customs?"

Ten hot, humid minutes (without air conditioning or a hint of a breeze) later, we were finally allowed to leave the pier without registering my camera with India customs. I could write pages about the meaningless bureaucracy and paperwork I encountered at every level in India. Though it might make a good story, I'd rather share the positive things we did. Suffice it to say India is a bureaucratic nightmare: Forty minutes to change money, 20 minutes to check into a luxury hotel, 20 minutes to check out of a luxury hotel, 30 minutes to buy a SIM card, and 40 minutes to buy a stamp at the post office—all normal, everyday occurrences based on my short time in India.

For reasons I still don't understand, today was a fortuitous day to get married, and we encountered several loud, colorful weddings as we drove 30 minutes to the ITC Sheraton. Although the hotel was fine, the personalized service on Nautica had spoiled my parents and me. We found ourselves privately critiquing the service and saying that Emil (our excellent cabana waiter) would do this, or Raquel from reception would never do that. The Sheraton service had no chance of measuring up. After three weeks, Nautica felt like home and we'd be glad to be back.

Since we had intentionally eaten a late lunch on the ship—I didn't want to eat much onshore in India—we didn't make dinner plans, and my parents and I went our separate ways. My parents went to Phoenix Mills shopping center, a mostly fixed-price mall, and I went to meet with some fellow recovering drug addicts.

I have been abstinent from alcohol and all other substances (marijuana, cocaine, etc.) since 1990. I have the disease of addiction, so I choose to regularly meet with other recovering people to deal with my problem. Most cruise lines, including Oceania, place a meeting for Friends of Bill W. on their daily schedule. Bill W., along with Doctor Bob, founded Alcoholics Anonymous, and though I am not a member of that particular organization, I usually show up at the meetings when I am cruising and I am always made to feel welcome.

In the United States it is hard to be a recovering drug addict. It is harder in India. The best part of meeting with my new friends was listening to them tell of pressures at work, dealing with anger and resentment, having problems with a partner or spouse, learning to cope with wanting a glass of wine at a wedding—all the same issues I've had to deal with at one time or another myself. Our external circumstances are different; our feelings and struggles are the same. I quickly felt connected with this group of strangers, and I know some of them felt connected with me.

On the drive back, my chauffer—the only way I could get there was in a Sheraton limousine—asked how my appointment went.

"Did you arrive on time?" Panjac asked. Due to worse-than-usual traffic, we almost arrived late.

"Yes, I did. Thank you, Panjac," I replied.

"So your appointment went well?" he inquired.

"Oh, yes. It went fine." There was a moment of silence. Panjac considered whether he was crossing a line.

"So what kind of appointment was this?" Panjac finally blurted out. He had seen me leave the appointment with Indians hugging me and saying goodbye. He had probably never driven a Sheraton guest to this part of town before—we passed some of the slums that Mumbai is sadly famous for as we raced to my destination.

I thought a moment and told him the truth. "It was a place for recovering drug addicts to help each other stay clean," I replied.

He looked thoughtful. I think he already knew it had something to do with drug addicts, and he said, "My uncle's only son, my cousin, died from a heroin overdose last year. We tried everything to save him, but he just couldn't stop and we didn't have enough money to try to get him help. How much does this cost?"

"Well, actually, it is free," I replied. "Anyone can go, and you don't pay any money."

"It is free?" he asked incredulously.

"Yes, it really is free."

"How do I contact them? I know another person that needs this help," he said.

I gave him the information, and during the rest of our hour drive he told me about his family, how addiction had harmed people he knew, how difficult it is to survive economically in India, and how challenging, virtually impossible it is to rise out of Mumbai's slums and to its universities and thriving business community. In Mumbai, office space is as expensive as in downtown Manhattan, yet over

6 million of its 15 million residents live in filth, squalor and disease. Every day is a fight against sickness and starvation. It is impossible for me to move through parts of Mumbai, the places tourist buses try to shield us from seeing, without feeling a deep sense of sadness and loss for the plight of the poor. I returned to my hotel tired, grateful and a little more conscious.

The next morning I arranged for Panjac to take us on a whirlwind tour of Mumbai. The day started a little late, as the Sheraton had an excellent broadband connection and Ty and I had a video chat on our Mac computers. He showed me our dog Rusty and our cat Stewart. It was so good to see Ty. For the first time this trip I felt really homesick.

Our first stop was the dhobi ghats, where thousands of dhobi wallahs famously wring, beat, pummel and wash the city's laundry. As we stood above and snapped photo after photo, I couldn't believe how many clothes were hanging, drying in the sun.

"Panjac, how long does it take to get the dhobi wallahs to do your laundry?" I asked.

"This time of year about two days, but in the rainy season up to a week," he replied. "The clothes must dry outside."

After that we drove by the Jain temple as we made our way to Mani Bhavan, Gandhi's house in Bombay. As we approached the front steps, I knew we were someplace special. It reminded me of going to Anne Frank's house in Amsterdam. Neither home is ostentatious or grand, or particularly stands out from the surrounding homes (except for the flow of visitors and presence of street merchants), but I experienced the sense of approaching hallowed ground in both places.

We spent about an hour viewing Gandhi's sleeping and meditation room, visiting the library, gazing at irreplaceable photos, viewing a series of miniature dioramas displaying Gandhi's life and reading some of his quotes. My mom's favorite begins, "To call women the weaker sex is a libel...." Being in the home made me curious about Gandhi in a way I hadn't been before. As we left the house, I wanted to purchase a book, just as I had at Anne Frank's house. As we walked down the stairs to the exit where a small store is located I saw a familiar face—Frank a.k.a. Lumpy was sitting at the bottom of the stairs. He looked exhausted, and I was immediately a little concerned.

"Hey, Frank, are you doing OK? You look hot." He was sweating profusely and looked pale.

"Oh, I am fine," Frank replied. "Four of us shared one of those terrible taxis without air conditioning to come over here, and I am just burning up from the ride."

"Have you been upstairs yet? The dioramas are wonderful." I said.

"Oh, yes. We were here yesterday. I was so moved, I wanted to come back. I also wanted to get some more books as gifts. Did you see these?" Frank asked as he showed me a beautiful book of Gandhi's quotes printed on handmade paper and costing only 200 rupees ($5). "They are absolutely wonderful and make excellent presents."

"Gosh, Frank, those look great. Thanks for showing them to me," I replied. "I think I'll get a couple."

"I studied literature in college and always loved Gandhi's writing. These are really special books," Frank said as he passed his book toward me.

I wanted to sink in my shoes. My previous encounters with Frank hadn't been so warm, intimate or pleasant, and here I was standing in Mani Bhavan, Gandhi's wise visage gazing over us, as Frank knowingly recommended the best Gandhi books to buy. Life has many ironies. I considered the spirit of Satyagraha, Gandhi's beloved principle of practicing truth, relentless love and nonviolence, and I thought of my previous interactions with Frank. What a profound, unlikely encounter, I mused.

"Well, I'll see you later, Frank. Hope you have a great day," I said as I paid for my books and quickly headed out the door. I didn't want him to see us riding around in a comfortable, chauffeured, air-conditioned Sheraton sedan, while he suffered in a hot, cramped taxi. It is so easy to rush to judgment about others and make an ill-informed opinion. Sure, Frank was rude to my mom once, but clearly, as I suspected (and is so true for so many of us), there is much more to him than meets the eye. I never would have figured him for a Gandhi admirer.

We drove away, down Malabar Hill and past the Tower of Silence, the hidden place where the Zoroastrian Parsis lay out their dead for the vultures to eat. Apparently there aren't enough vultures left in Mumbai to eat the corpses, so priests add chemicals to accelerate the bodies' decaying process. We stopped at the Hanging Garden, took a picture with a monkey literally on my back, walked on Chowpatty Beach, drove past and photographed the imposing Victoria Terminal (we arrived too late to see any tiffin-wallahs carrying food), whiffed the pungent odor of the fish market, stopped for a quick photo opportunity at the High Court clock tower and finally arrived at the Chhatrapati Shivaji Maharaj, more commonly known as the Prince of Wales, Museum.

We had about 90 minutes before we wanted to return to the ship, and we browsed the stone sculptures, Nepalese and Tibetan religious relics and priceless Indian artifacts of painting, cloth, sandalwood and gold. The price of entry was 300 rupees for foreigners and 15 rupees for locals, but after seeing all the poverty, we didn't care. We were happy to pay a little more.

It was time to leave India. Even though we enjoyed our time here, I did not want to be stuck in Mumbai. Passengers who choose to sightsee independently have to be extra responsible about returning to the ship on time. A good reason to purchase ship shore excursions is that you never risk the boat's sailing away without you.

On the drive back, my dad purchased another 20 cans of Diet Coke for about 60¢ each. Oceania, unlike many cruise lines, does not prevent you from bringing your own alcohol, water and soda aboard, as long as you are willing to schlep it yourself. We arrived at the ship about an hour before our 4:30 p.m. deadline. The hotel charged about $10 per hour for the sedan and driver, so after a generous but well-deserved $20 tip to Panjac, our total cost was less than $100 for a chockfull day of sightseeing in one of the nicest cars I saw plying the streets of Mumbai.

The passengers who went to the Taj Mahal arrived back a little late, so it turns out we had a bit of extra time. If I ever take this trip again, I will take the Taj Mahal excursion. Despite the $1,600 price tag, all my friends who went said it was worth every penny. They particularly commended Oceania for flawlessly organizing the air and ground transportation, lodging, meals, and excellent, English-speaking guides. Someday I hope to stand with Ty in front of the Taj and have our pictures taken too.

As the ship pulled away, while playing trivia (our team took first), I reflected on the past three days. I still can't make sense of India; so much beauty, so much extreme poverty. I thought of the spiritual experiences at Elephanta Caves, meeting fellow recovering addicts and seeing Frank at Gandhi's house. I thought of the slums, teeming with disease and starvation and bereft of a glimmer of hope. I thought of the kindness of strangers I watched literally risking their lives to assist a cab driver they didn't know push his broken-down taxi through a dangerous traffic interchange. India is full of paradoxes. Today I am ambivalent about coming back (except to see the Taj, of course), but I said a prayer of gratitude last night for the life I have and of exhortation of help for the poor, the downtrodden and the hopeless who live in the streets and slums of Mumbai.

I don't know what I can do to improve life for the paupers in India. I don't know how to change the extreme poverty that still haunts the world, but I think Gandhi said it best in this quote from the book Frank shared with me:

> I will work for an India, in which the poorest shall
> feel that it is their country in whose making they
> have an effective voice; an India in which there shall
> be no high class and low class of people; an India in
> which all communities shall live in perfect harmony.
> There can be no room in such an India for the curse
> of untouchables or the curse of intoxicating drinks
> and drugs. Women will enjoy the same rights as
> men. Since we shall be at peace with all the rest of
> the world, neither exploiting nor being exploited, we

should have the smallest army imaginable. This is
the India of my dreams.   —M.K. Gandhi

*****

Druke I   **April 21st, 2007, 04:25 PM**
*Jack, like many others, I have read your reports and enjoyed
them very much.*

*We were in Mumbai (Bombay) on Nautica 12/14/06 (Istanbul to
Singapore). I was told a different tale about the taxis—the old Fiats.
Our tour guide told us that they were made in India, the dies, etc.,
having been bought from Fiat when that model was discontinued,
and that they were still in production—unmodified. I found it
interesting how the cab's meter was mounted outside on the fender.*

*In Cochin two days later, the cabs were of a completely different
design, which I took to be Toyopet (predecessor of Toyota), but I
could be wrong. Those were also being manufactured in India.
I can't recall the Indian name. They were very similar to the
"kamikaze" cabs we had on Okinawa during my Army service there
in the mid-'50s!*

Michael

Emdee   **April 21st, 2007, 05:11 PM**
*Jack, really enjoyed your Mumbai adventures. It's five years
since I have been, and I could smell the smells and hear the sounds
of the city. Made me a bit homesick…though I have lived here in
Canada for the last 27 years.*

*I have never been to the museum and studied at Bombay
University directly near the Clock Tower. I will be going back for
a week this year en route to a Kenyan safari and shall make a
point of going to the museum and maybe take my 22-year-old to
Elephanta Caves.*

*You may want to publish this journal. It would be a pity to limit
it to Cruise Critic—it is a sheer pleasure to read.*

I eagerly look forward to the next installment.

Miriam

meow!   **April 22nd, 2007, 12:48 AM**
*After your vivid experience on this voyage, what is your opinion on
the United Nations' helping Third World countries practice birth
control? Might that be helpful? Just curious.*

Aussie Gal   ***April 22nd, 2007, 05:04 AM***

Jack, again thank you for giving us a look at Mumbai through your eyes. I could picture the chaos, the traffic and the people in my mind even though I have never been there. I know that is an assault on all your senses and am looking forward to visiting India next year.

I am so glad that the people who did the excursion to Agra enjoyed it and felt it was worthwhile. If you do happen to speak to someone who did it, please ask them if they felt they saw enough in the time allowed and was the accommodation up to scratch. Thanks again.

Jennie

esther e   ***April 22nd, 2007, 10:48 AM***

Jack, I just have to jump in and tell you how much I'm enjoying your journal. You're in a part of the world I'll never get to, and yet I feel I'm there with every sentence. Please continue. This is a pleasure to read, and I'm enjoying each experience.

My best wishes to Ty. I pray it's not serious.

Esther

Toranut97   ***April 22nd, 2007, 11:16 AM***
Keep up the great work!

Jack, your writing is so eloquent! You are wonderful with your portrayal of images. When I read the account of your conversation with Frank at the home of Gandhi, I felt like I had reached a fascinating plot twist in a novel—isn't life amazing!!? A fiction author could hardly dream some of the stuff that happens in everyday life!

Your contribution to the cruise devotees here—and your fine account of the joys and oys of Oceania travel (mostly joys!)—are marvelous. I look forward to your installments. I think FDR should purchase the reprint rights and have a copy placed in the Nautica library!

Happy cruising,

Donna

KIWP   ***April 22nd, 2007, 11:50 AM***
Hi, Jack—

Just got back from a quick trip to London, Milan and Dubai (all personal to see friends and family) and could not wait to catch up on your most wonderful writing. I totally agree with your list of the "areas for improvement" at Oceania and hope that some attention is paid to your suggestions. Over our numerous cruises with "O" (and it is still our favorite of all), we have also mentioned the same categories.

I see that you did not go to Agra, and I'm sorry that you missed an amazing sight. Sunrise and sunset there are as special as seeing the Pyramids, looking down from Mt. Kilimanjaro, and seeing the world in the same lights. Frankly, I could go on and on (actually we are to Tibet). Hopefully you will take other opportunities to go back. Please don't miss Petra, or the trip to Luxor. The only challenge is trying to get to Cairo in one day. We've spent 10 days there and explored every corner of the city and still think we missed a few things. But a quick glimpse of the Pyramids is better than not seeing them at all.

I hope that Ty is well and will keep our fingers crossed that all turns out well.

Robert is a terrific concierge. Not only is he knowledgeable but also a great guy.

Who is playing piano in the Martini Lounge?

Please keep writing, and perhaps consider a compilation of your diary for publication. You have a great style of presenting your views. As long as people travel and take opportunities to expose themselves to other cultures, then they will definitely broaden their perspective of the world and all that it offers.

Twiga   **April 22nd, 2007, 06:02 PM**

Jack, I loved reading about your visit to Mumbai. I spent a month in India, including almost a week in Bombay (Mumbai), many years ago. Your descriptions of the city, the traffic and the people were marvelous. I could hear the car horns honking and smell the scent of India as I read your words. Thanks so much for sharing with us!

merryecho   **April 23rd, 2007, 12:08 PM**

[QUOTE I think FDR should purchase the reprint rights and have a copy placed in the Nautica library! END QUOTE]

I have a better idea. Jack's journal has inspired me to sign up for the Oceania cruise Jack has been describing. I think it would be *great advertising to give Jack and Ty free trips on Oceania in exchange for Jack's writing a journal on each journey!*

raffeer   **April 23rd, 2007, 02:48 PM**
Jack, thank you so much for making it possible for me to travel this route with you. Many memories and much longing for the day when I can dispense with vicarious travel and dust off my passport.

Good thoughts for Ty. The waiting is not fun.

merryecho, what a brilliant idea! Ty and Jack can taste all the routes and report back.

What better sales force could Oceania have?

On second thought, maybe not such a good idea. Booking would end up being 18 to 24 months out.

Beatrice

Chapter 12

A NOTE FROM ANN

JackfromWA   *April 23rd, 2007, 02:50 PM*

I asked my mom to share some of her thoughts about Oceania, Oman and cruising together. I'll write my entry on Oman sometime in the next few days (we have four sea days ahead, just left Salalah, Oman en route to Safaga/Luxor). I hope you all enjoy a different voice for a day and my mom's impressions.

A POST FROM ANN (JACK'S MOM)

Today you will hear another voice. This is Jack's mom. Like all of you who are reading his thread, I am a big fan of Jack's writing. He has done a beautiful job capturing the spirit of the many places we have been. As you can imagine, he is funny, talented, and a blast to travel with. He suggested that I give some input to his narrative, and I agreed.

This cruise has been a wonderful experience for us. The best thing has been the amount of time we have been able to spend with Jack. Not every parent is fortunate enough to be able to take a long vacation with a grown child. The memories and the fun we have had together will stay with us all of our lives. This is truly a great cruise line. The food is delicious, the crew is extremely friendly and personable, and the activities are fun and educational. We have had wonderful interaction with various crewmembers as well as other passengers. That being said, there is always a wish list of changes for any cruise line, but in this case I think they are minimal. I would like to have more laundry facilities, and I would like to see a few changes in the gym. We use the treadmill almost daily and it is first-come, first-served, with a 20-minute limit if people are waiting. We have learned to go a little later in the day so we can spend longer on the machines. I personally prefer ships that have signup sheets for the treadmill and allow you 30 minutes on the machines. It eliminates waiting around for someone to finish up. But the positives on this ship so far outweigh the negatives that I hesitate to even mention them. We are experienced cruisers, and this is probably the nicest cruise we have ever taken. I would not hesitate to recommend this line to my friends.

Today we arrived in Salalah, Oman. It is not as exciting as most of the ports we have visited, but we were curious about the country and the culture. We got off the ship and, unlike all our other ports, there were no taxis and only one small stand with a couple of vendors. We were told that due to local regulations, guests were not permitted to walk in the port area, so a shuttle-bus service was provided to transport us from the gangway to the port gate. At the port gate, there were numerous taxis. After a bit of haggling, we found a taxi to take us into the town for $30. Jack offered him $55 if he would take us round trip. At first he said no, and then he realized we did not expect him to wait but to return at an appointed time. The fare quickly moved from acceptable to desirable, and he was eager to come back for us. Pete suggested 4 p.m. (it was 10:30 a.m.), and Jack and I looked at each other and wondered what we would be doing all day. We suggested we wait and see the town and then decide on a time. The Omani official who had boarded the ship had written down an address where we could shop and where the men could get haircuts. When we arrived, we saw sand, a few buildings and a barbershop. We asked about the market and the driver said, "Oh, sure, there are fruits and vegetables here." With all we have to eat on the ship, that is the last type of market we wanted to see. We finally got to the market street where there were many small shops with a variety of souvenirs. Jack had already decided to have a haircutting experience in Oman, so our first quest was to find a barbershop. He found one he liked and asked for the works. The barber was friendly and did a pretty good job with the scissors. Next came a shave with lots of lather and a straight razor. The final touch was a head massage for about 20 minutes. I took several pictures of the process. The bill for this elaborate treatment was $2.50. Pete had a haircut and massage but no shave, and his bill was $1.25. Needless to say, they were happy campers.

While the men were getting their beauty treatments, I walked to the market area. On the way, I saw more tailor shops than I have ever seen in my life. On one street alone there were 20. Most of them were for men, but I saw three for women. I went to the windows to investigate and felt like I was peeking into a dressing room for a harem. The dresses were in bright colors, often sheer and with lots of sparkles and spangles. This was in total contrast to the women I saw in the shops in plain black dresses and often with veiled faces. I did see two or three women wearing colorful silk scarves, which covered every speck of hair. I'm sure the fancy dresses were for husband's eyes only. Although I looked at clothing, I bought only one top and a few scarves for gifts. When the shopkeepers showed me the long dresses that the women wear on the street, I politely said "No, thank you," but in my heart I knew I could never wear one of those dresses. We saw very few women. I think they must stay home most of the time. When a friend of mine asked a woman if she could take her picture, the woman first got permission from her husband. That is so foreign to my thinking that I can barely comprehend it. My heart goes out to women all over the world who live in societies that dictate how they dress and what they can and can't do. I know that it is embraced by some and that is their choice. Throughout this trip, I have had so many occasions to ponder the wonderful circumstances in which we live at home. I hope I never take our freedom for granted.

*****

tak2   ***April 23rd, 2007, 03:09 PM***
   [QUOTE I have a better idea. Jack's journal has inspired me to sign up for the Oceania cruise Jack has been describing. I think it would be great advertising to give Jack and Ty free trips on Oceania in exchange for Jack's writing a journal on each journey! END QUOTE]

   If O is reading this, will you consider a new ship for this route? With the 35 days it'll be nice to have the 50%-larger staterooms, and the demand generated by Jack and Ann's journal, we also need extra cabins to fill the need.

scdreamer   ***April 23rd, 2007, 03:27 PM***
   Now we all know where Jack's wonderful writing skills and his observant and compassionate manners come from. Thank you, Ann, for your post—and also for doing a superb job in raising your son Jack! Wonderful read...
                                             Leslie & Wayne

111

KIWP   *April 23rd, 2007, 06:18 PM*

Well, now we know from whom Jack gets his creativity. Thank you for your addition.

I agree Salalah is not much. Should you have a chance, to see Muscat and parts of the north you would see more, but Oman is truly subdued compared to the various emirates of the UAE (especially Dubai and Abu Dhabi), Egypt, or Jordan.

I am a transplanted European who has lived in the U.S. for many years and other parts of the world and have often been to the Middle East. I agree that the western mind (especially for us women) it is most difficult to observe the very definitive separation between the sexes. But the cultures are so amazing and rich that there are other aspects to be gained from being there.

I hope you go to Petra, and would love to hear your further impressions as you explore. We did this cruise in '06 and loved it so much we will repeat it in '09, even though we've been to all the destinations numerous times.

I wish you a most enjoyable rest of the trip, and please keep writing.

PennyAgain   *April 23rd, 2007, 08:12 PM*

Absolutely fantastic thread. Truly my favorite on CC as well! A pleasure and treasure!

Wadadli1   *April 24th, 2007, 05:17 PM*

Do you reckon Jack also got his Prickly Heat Powder application technique from Ann?

*****

JackfromWA   *April 25th, 2007, 08:28 AM*

A FEW RESPONSES:

Druke I: Thanks for your encouragement and information about the cabs. I forgot to mention the meters attached outside the cab; I had never seen that before.

Emdee: I love Kenya. To this day I don't think I've enjoyed any day more than one spent watching lion cubs play while seated in a

112

Governors' Camp Land Rover in the heart of the Masai Mara. Have a great time when you take your safari.

meow!: I'm not informed enough to even offer an opinion of what is best to control population in India. I do think Dr. Jeffery Sach's book, *The End of Poverty: Economic Possibilities for Our Time*, is chockfull of the best ideas I have heard on solving the problem of 20% of the world's population living in extreme poverty. Dr. Sach's work formed the basis for the successful global ONE campaign (Bono is the lead spokesperson) and is truly compelling. I highly recommend reading it.

Aussie Gal: I spoke to several friends, and the accommodations (this year Oceania used the Taj View hotel which—not surprisingly—has a view of the Taj Mahal) were definitely up to snuff. I asked Cinthya, the destinations manager, for you, and they will use the Taj View hotel again next year. Everyone I spoke to who went to Agra felt that the time given for the Taj was sufficient—they didn't feel rushed. You should probably book from home as the Taj excursion quickly sold out and several people on the waiting list couldn't go. Also, watch what you eat in Agra; there have been some passengers with diarrhea and upset tummies (my cabin is on Deck 4, directly across from the ship's medical center, so between that and being socially active, I see and hear quite a bit about medical problems). You can't be too careful, and no one wants to suffer from digestive problems while taking a 35-day cruise. Please don't be afraid to go, just brush your teeth with bottled water, don't eat salad, etc.

esther e: Thanks for the well wishes for Ty's good health and for your encouragement to keep writing.

KIWP: As you know I will go to Agra next time and won't miss Petra, Luxor or the brief visit to the Giza Pyramids. As always, thanks for sharing your experience and offering excellent suggestions.

raffeer, Twiga and PennyAgain: Thank you for the kind words and encouragement to write.

merryecho: Glad you can take this trip next year. You will have a great time; it is a fabulous, exciting itinerary.

<u>tak2, scdreamer, KIWP:</u> I made sure my mom read your replies and compliments. She and my dad are great parents and did a wonderful job raising my two brothers, my sister and me.

Chapter 13

SALALAH, OMAN

JackfromWA   *April 25th, 2007, 08:28 AM*

My research on Oman revealed little of interest in the port of Salalah. The possible exceptions were the Sultan's Salalah residence and the historical and biblical significance of Job's footprint and tomb, but I was skeptical that the footprint even belonged to Job. If all the fragments of Jesus Christ's cross displayed in cathedrals and monasteries across Europe were genuine, his cross would have been larger than the tallest redwood tree in California

Maybe I'm missing something, I thought, but after talking to Cinthya, the destinations manager, and Robert, the concierge, I decided that Salalah didn't have too much outside of beautiful beaches and a taste of everyday life in Oman that piqued my curiosity. Since sightseeing choices were limited, I decided to get a shave and haircut from an Omani barber.

"That's an excellent idea," Robert said. "After they cut your hair, the barber will take little strings and roll them across your cheekbone and ears to pluck any stray hairs. Then you will get a wonderful little scalp massage. I am going to do the same thing in Port Safaga. I have never gotten a haircut in Salalah, but I am sure it is very similar."

With a plan in place, I began to look forward to going ashore. The excursion desk had a handout on visiting Oman that covered tourist points of interest (not many), appropriate attire (strongly advised for men and women), etiquette, heritage and shopping. The headline of our daily program is usually either historical information about the current port of call or information about the sea being navigated (today is "Cruising the Gulf of Aden"). In addition, the excursion desk distributes free handouts tailored to the local port. I have found them quite useful in planning my day and gaining a bit more insight into our destinations. Between my Frommer's guides, Lonely Planet guides, Rough guides and the ship handouts, I have covered my reading bases for our ports of call.

The Salalah handout had half a page on male Omani fashion. The section described traditional Middle Eastern garb. The photo of a man in a dish-dash-ah (the robe) and ogal (the headdress) looked exactly like stereotypical Arabs in U.S. television news broadcasts. I decided I'd like to purchase a dish-dash-ah and ogal to take home. It might be comfortable to wear, and if I needed a costume for a holiday or special occasion, I'd have a unique one—I have never seen any of my friends dressed as an Arab at a party or for Halloween.

The Salalah representative on board—in every port a local representative has come aboard for three or four hours and sat at a table on Deck 4 near the excursion desk to answer guests' questions—advised that I could easily find a barber and a dish-dash-ah at the local market. We took a short, free shuttle ride from the ship's dock to the pier gate and negotiated a taxi for 11 rial (about $30) to take us on the 20-minute drive to town. Our Omani driver spoke a little English, so on our way into Salalah I explained that I wanted him to stop at an ATM. I withdrew 75 rial—I always prefer to shop in local money, but in Salalah it wasn't necessary; U.S. dollars were accepted everywhere—and arranged to meet our taxi a few hours later.

Salalah is desert country. All the buildings reflect the deep tan color of desert sand, and during our visit I didn't see any trees, shrubs or greenery except where man had irrigated to create artificial lush oases. I live in the far Northwest of the Pacific Northwest (Ty and I live eight miles from Bellingham, Washington on five secluded forested acres with a large lawn and a salmon creek cutting across the back corner of our property—it's like living in a park), and I take lakes and ponds, babbling creeks, rivers with strong currents (and inevitable annual flood alerts), tall evergreen trees, needles and pinecones, snowcapped mountains and rugged coastlines for granted. If my home has a geographic and religious opposite, it could be Salalah.

We left the central market area and started searching for a barber. After wandering several blocks from the market hub, and passing at least 50 or 60 small tailor shops—it seemed every tailor shop was about 15 feet wide, 20 feet deep and was filled with mostly white bolts of fabric to make dish-dash-ah robes—I spotted a sign that said HAIRDRESSER in English and Arabic. The business signs are easy to see as the vivid red, green and blue colors used to advertise stand in stark contrast to the sand color of the buildings.

"That one looks good to me, Dad. Let's go in and check it out," I said.

"All right, but I want to come in and see how long it is going to take," my mom said.

"That's fine. I probably want to have a few pictures, and it'd be great if you could take them."

We entered the barbershop, and the familiar interior reminded me of a traditional small-town barbershop in America. Two dark-skinned men were quietly chatting as a television blared Arabic music and videos in the background. They looked up, surprised to see us.

"Can I get a haircut and a shave?" I asked, as I made pantomime scissor motions with my fingers and a cutting motion on my chin.

Despite their initial shock, they seemed happy to have customers, and I was quickly motioned to the chair. Uh-oh, I thought. I better set a price before this starts.

"How much will this cost?" I asked, pointing to my money.

"One rial," the barber replied. He pointed his index finger skyward to make certain I understood he meant "one." Seemed like a great deal to me—one rial is $2.50.

"O.K.," I said, and my haircut began. With two more weeks before I fly home, any misgiving I had about a bad haircut were nullified by the knowledge that any damage done was likely to be gone by the time I reached Athens.

To my delight, the haircut was great. I have very straight hair, and the barber seemed quite adept at dealing with it. My mom snapped a few photos, and my dad stepped outside to look around. It was at least 90 degrees outside, so my dad quickly returned to the air-conditioned shop, and my mom decided to return to the main market and meet us at noon.

My barber, in an apparent effort to make me comfortable, kept changing the TV to find an English-speaking station. Unfortunately, he found a Christian fund-raising channel based in Florida, so out of politeness I was forced to listen to a plea to send money to help missionary efforts and hungry children. Whatever their problem is, it can't be any worse than the poverty in Mumbai, I thought. Since I paid no attention whatsoever to the television, the barber eventually changed the channel back to the much more interesting Arabic music station.

Since we had a language barrier, I wasn't sure if I was actually going to get a shave. I have never been shaved in a barber chair in my life, but when the haircut was done, my scalp cleaned, and all errant hair removed, he applied the first of many layers of lotion to my face and my first barbershop shave began. After all the lather was applied, the barber asked, "Where are you from?"

"The U.S.A., near Seattle," I replied.

"Oh," was all he said. I liked him, he seemed nice enough, but I wondered what he thought about Americans. He had a well-coiffed American in his barber chair, with my head leaned back and my neck fully exposed, while he held a long, sharp razor just under my chin. Though I was never frightened—if I had been I would have abruptly left—this was my first time in an Arabic, Muslim country, and I couldn't imagine that the United States is currently held in high regard in Oman. I received a good, close shave, a long, invigorating and relaxing head, scalp and shoulder massage—the massage alone was worth $5 to me—and then got up so my dad could get his haircut.

My father is mostly bald, but I think the reason his haircut cost half a rial is that he didn't have a shave. While my dad's haircut was going on, the barber's two young sons arrived. I think a phone call was made, and the children were invited to come view the unusual sight of Americans in the barber chair. The boys appeared to be about six and 10 years old. I overheard the dad say "U.S.A." to them, but of course I couldn't understand the rest of what he told them. The children watched me intently. I wish I had brought the kids some of the Oceania chocolates they place on my pillow every night; I have a drawer full of them and I'm not going to eat them all before the end of the cruise. My dad's small backpack was sitting next to me; he loves candy and usually has some. Sure enough, there was a yellow bag of peanut M&M's. I ate a few, offered some to the two boys and they happily accepted and started munching them.

"You are from the U.S.A.?" the 10-year old asked me in halting English.

"Yes, I am," I replied. He thought about that for a minute.

"I like 'Pirates of the Caribbean,' " he finally decided to say.

"Me too. Jack Sparrow!" I said while swishing my hand like a pirate wielding a sword.

He laughed, and his younger brother shyly smiled. Their father seemed pleased by our small conversation and his son's proficient English. Soon he and his brother left, sure to tell about meeting the Pirates-of-the-Caribbean-loving Americans. I took a few more photos of my dad getting a haircut, tipped the barber (I gave him double the price of the haircuts; our net cost with tip for two haircuts, two massages, one shave and a great tip was $7.50) and left the comfort of the barbershop for the heat of the Salalah streets.

As we went back to the central market to meet my mom, a deep, male Arabic voice was broadcast across the downtown over speakers as loud as the ones used at Yankee Stadium.

"Is that…?" I asked my dad.

"Yep, that's the call for Muslims to pray. The announcement is coming from the mosque. You haven't ever heard that before?" he asked.

"No, I never have." I said. It was my first time. My parents have traveled to Istanbul and other places where they have heard the loud, public exhortations to pray, but I never had. At first it made me feel uncomfortable. Why was a religious action broadcast so loudly to the entire town? As I thought more about it, I recalled the bells of the Assumption Catholic Church loudly ringing every Sunday morning through my bedroom window as I tried to sleep after finishing my early-morning paper route. Growing up, the bells announcing mass seemed normal to me—and I am sure the call to pray broadcast five times a day in Salalah didn't bother most residents any more than the bells from the Catholic church bothered me as a child.

As we approached the market, merchants warmly, genuinely greeted us. Unlike many of our previous ports, and though the greetings were subtle invitations to enter their stores, they did not pressure us. Almost every man was clad in traditional garb: dish-dash-ah robe and hat. The few women I saw were covered in black and their faces and bodies were concealed from view. The only two children I saw were the boys in the barbershop, dressed in T-shirts, long pants and sandals.

Salalah appears to be a traditional, conservative Arab country. Because of the war in Iraq, I expected to encounter hostility as visitor from the United States. My experience was the opposite. When a merchant overheard my asking my dad about a toilet, he interrupted and offered me his bathroom and expected nothing in return. Whenever I was asked where I was from and I answered "U.S.A.," eyes lit up in pleasant surprise and I was warmly welcomed.

I am starting to think that extremist Muslim terrorists bear no more relationship to the traditional Muslims I encountered in Salalah than the extremist use-the-Bible-to-justify-their-behavior Ku Klux Klan terrorists bore to traditional American Christians a hundred years ago in the United States. My expectations of how I would be greeted in an Arabic country were largely formed from watching the *NBC Nightly News* and reading the *Bellingham Herald*. My reality was very different; I found the residents of Salalah friendly, interesting and polite. After the poverty, begging and hassles of

120

Mumbai, the calm roads and friendly residents of Salalah were a pleasant respite.

As a tourist port, Salalah was fairly boring. According to a handout Nautica gave us the first week of the cruise, we use 22,000 gallons of fuel daily if traveling our maximum speed of 20 knots. According to my calculations, we use roughly 45 gallons of fuel to travel a mile (we get 45 gallons to the mile), so a significant portion of our ticket cost is used to pay for fuel. (45 gallons times approximately 9,500 miles from Hong Kong to Athens is 427,500 gallons for this entire trip. At an average cost of $2 per gallon, total fuel is about $850,000. There are close to 700 passengers aboard so each ticket contributes a little more than $1,200—$850,000 for total fuel divided by 700 passengers—toward fuel costs).

I think the primary reason so many ships repositioning from Asia to Europe stop here is that Salalah has cheap fuel and cheap berthing. Oceania is a for-profit company, and in the economics of cruising, berthing at a port like Hong Kong or Venice probably costs considerably more than berthing in a port like Salalah. It increases profitability for a cruise line to include some inexpensive ports like Salalah along with more expensive ports like Singapore or Athens. I'm not sorry we came to Salalah. I personally found it very interesting, but unlike Ho Chi Minh City, Bangkok or even Mumbai, I don't have a desire to return with Ty.

With our haircuts under our belts, it was time to buy my dish-dash-ah and hat. There were so many shops that the problem wasn't finding one; it was choosing which one to shop. I selected a store at random, proceeded inside, and with words and pantomime explained to the shopkeeper what I wanted. Although I am a large American, dish-dash-ah robes are very forgiving. For the first time since Hong Kong I purchased clothing that I knew would fit me. The young shopkeeper showed me how to tie my shumagg (the scarf-like headdress). It looked great when he tied it, but I didn't devote the time to learn how to properly fasten it. In Oman they also wear a headpiece that is a cross between a fez and the style hat you expect to see a 1950s-era movie usher wearing. I purchased one of those along with my shumagg. I knew if I couldn't tie the shumagg I could always wear the hat.

After a few more souvenir purchases from the souk, my parents were ready to leave as well. Our driver had been loitering in the market to get our fare back to the ship, so we returned to his cool cab and left for Nautica. As we approached the cargo container port about fifteen miles from town, I caught a view of Nautica rising over the top of containers and sand dunes. The pure white paint of her smokestack appeared out of place against the muted sun-bleached containers, cranes and sand-colored port buildings. To me, Nautica appeared an oasis in the desert of Oman, and I couldn't wait to get aboard and loll around in the lush, comfortable confines of my traveling home.

After 24 days aboard, Nautica feels like home and the passengers and crew feel like my neighbors and friends. It is a good home, and with the exception of the absence of Ty, Rusty (our beloved wheaten terrier) and Stewart (our mostly beloved cat), it is a home I would be content and happy to live in for a long time.

Ray Solaire (his last name is Hook, but his stage name and thus his last name on Nautica is Solaire), the ship's cruise director, invited my mom, dad, Sukey and me for dinner. I decided to wear my new dish-dash-ah and hat. It was great fun. I took photos with Robert the concierge, Raquel and Rosie from reception and garnered many amused looks in the dining room. Someone warned me not to wear my dish-dash-ah home on American Airlines; they might be correct that wearing this would cause some concern on a U.S.-bound flight. But if more overweight American men tried wearing a dish-dash-ah, the garment could become very popular very quickly. You don't have to wear a belt and, after I discovered it contained a pocket for my room key, I wore nothing but a T-shirt, undergarments and sandals underneath. The whole outfit looks quite imposing while feeling light and comfortable. I told my mom the next time I am on a cruise line with a formal night, I am taking my dish-dash-ah.

At dinner Ray regaled us with interesting stories of his 39 years at sea. He is actually retired, makes his home in the Lake District of England, and is working part time for Oceania to balance his retirement with his love and talent for being a cruise director. Ray embodies everything a cruise director should be: imminently approachable, friendly, extremely talented (he sings, dances, hosts, writes, acts and is a world-class marionette puppeteer) and has decades of experience creating happy passengers. Like so many of the top staff on Nautica, including general manager Michael Coghlan, executive chef Wolfgang Maier, concierge Robert Kinkhorst and destinations manager Cinthya Pavan, Ray previously worked for Silversea and brings a Four Seasons level of service and proficiency to Oceania. I love getting Silversea service for Oceania prices.

We are in the middle of four days at sea. Yesterday was the dreaded day the disembarkation questionnaires were distributed, and I had to tell the ship when and how I was leaving. In bold letters I was informed I had to be off Nautica by 9 a.m. on disembarkation day. Unfortunately, none of the options on the questionnaire included the choice of staying aboard! Along with the questionnaire, each stateroom received a preliminary summary of charges—they were smart enough to hit us with all the bad news at once—mine wasn't too bad as I purchased the Cairo and Luxor excursions and cabana rental over the Internet from home. While it is a necessary evil, seeing the first telltale sign that soon this trip will end wasn't enjoyable, and though I long to get home to see Ty, I don't look forward to taking my last walk down Nautica's gangplank. Fortunately, the sightseeing highlights for my parents and me remain ahead of us, and there are still 11 nights and 12 days in front of us.

Ray has canceled trivia today, and the staff are converting the Pool Deck into an Olde English Country Faire—the Pool Deck is closed from 3 p.m. to 4:30 to accommodate the transition—and this ship is abuzz about what will happen at the fair. Ray promised some unusual, exciting activities for the remainder of our trip. "On a cruise this long you have to hold back some of the most exciting things until close to the end," he said at dinner, and I am looking forward to seeing what he and the rest of the crew have in store for us.

This has been a wonderful journey—it feels too long to call it a vacation—and as we begin to enter the last laps I look forward to watching the remainder of our trip unfold.

Next stop: Luxor—our first time in Egypt—but in between there are still a few more wonderful, relaxing sea days to enjoy.

*****

lahore   **April 25th, 2007, 09:14 AM**

Hi, Jack,

Thanks for yet another fabulous report. I am quite looking forward to Salalah; we have booked a taxi driver (through a backpacker e-friend who recommended him) and were thinking of going down the sea road a little to the next little town, which is apparently a picturesque fishing village. Do you know if anyone did that? Or did anyone go driving anywhere out of Salalah—and if so what were there impressions? Thanks, the cheek thing with the string is called threading, by the way, and is commonly used by Asian women. It is remarkably efficient and the skill required is unique; they hold one end of the thread in their mouth and deftly ensnare the errant hair with the other end and rip it out by the roots. My Indian girlfriends said, "Oh, good, you haven't tried threading. Let's go, our shout" —they just wanted to see me suffer—it hurts. Did they do that to you? Maybe I'll get them back with a Brazilian when they come to visit next year. Keep on enjoying...we all are, vicariously.

Magicnelly   **April 25th, 2007, 11:29 AM**

Cabana review?

I am so enjoying reading your wonderful journal! Thank you so much for sharing it.

We are booked on a back-to-back in May and have booked a cabana for the entire time. I am anxiously awaiting your review of these controversial spaces!

In my imagination, they shall be little havens to escape to after a long day in port...after changing into something cool and relaxing, slipping off the "functional" shoes and settling down to sip a much-needed adult beverage with my DH while sharing our thoughts on the day!

An in-depth, honest review of these written in your wonderful style would be a treat!

meow!   **April 25th, 2007, 12:05 PM**

JackfromWA: Thank you kindly for continuing to post. This has become my "daily reading." I especially appreciate your effort in replying to all questions posted to you from everyone. You are truly thorough and responsive!

124

Mom, Dad and Jack on the first day of the cruise

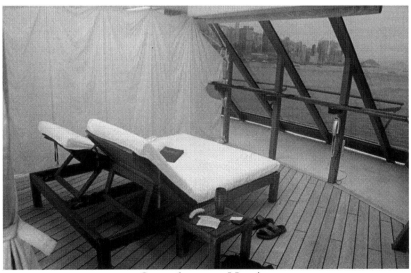

Our cabana on Nautica

Dad having his pants hemmed in Vietnam

Mom and Dad buying counterfeit purses in Saigon

Dad and Jack at the Vietnam War Museum

Mom with Frank Bank, who played Lumpy in *Leave It to Beaver*

Jack and Mom at the Grand Palace, Bangkok

Dad buying his Travelpro luggage in Bangkok

Raffles Hotel, Singapore

Mom and Dad at the Kranji War Memorial, Singapore

Mom and Jack at the Banyan Tree, Phuket

Dad buying a shirt at the Anjuna Market in Goa

Mom, rug salesman and Dad in Goa

Jack and Mom going to Elephanta Caves near Mumbai
(Taj Mahal Hotel and the Gateway of India in background)

Dad on the tram to Elephanta Caves

Dad rationing fruit to monkeys in India

Nautica in Mumbai

Jack at Mani Bhavan, Gandhi's house in Mumbai

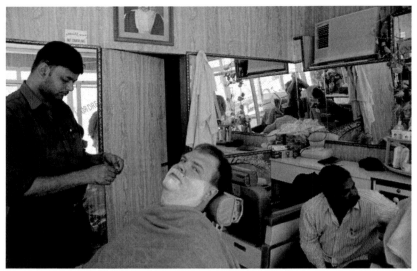

Jack and his barber in Salalah, Oman

Dad buying a new hat in Salalah

Saga Ruby　　　*April 25th, 2007, 04:16 PM*
Travels with Jack

　　Jack, many thanks for writing this most marvelous travel diary. The elements of your writing are as layered as a croissant— delectable, fresh, insightful, amusing and touching.

　　I would like to take this opportunity to echo your sentiments about Arab hospitality, especially the barbershop in Salalah. As a single white woman traveling alone, I didn't know what to expect on our Nautica repo from Istanbul to Singapore last year. I am always a solo traveler, never took a group tour off the ship, so I was on my own with admittedly a bit of trepidation for Islamic countries.

　　But the Turks in Istanbul, at all levels, were so very accommodating and truly happy to welcome me, give me directions, and assist me. I had a young driver for five days in Istanbul who was leaving shortly to enter military service. Although Mehmet spoke very little English, he understood what I was saying, just couldn't reply very well. We were able to make a connection, and his openness to driving a single woman all over both sides of the Bosporus encouraged me about the other Arab countries on our Nautica itinerary. With the wonderful Turkish people in mind, I sailed off on Nautica and looked forward to the adventures ahead.

　　When I walked down the gangway in Muscat, Oman, I didn't know what to expect from the Arab men. I was dressed properly for a Muslim country in a long, cotton broomstick skirt and long-sleeved blouse, but my head was not covered. I felt silent approval from the Arabic men—mostly taxi drivers and hotel staff—and had a marvelous day in Muscat, which I have discussed in another Oceania thread.

　　I would like to take this occasion to relate that I left the States with a mental chip on my shoulder toward Muslims because I am tired of being regarded as "The Great Satan." However, as a single woman, 100% of the time I was welcomed in Arabic countries with true hospitality and a "hands across the borders" attitude. I was wrong about the believers of Islam. As an Egyptian businessman told me at dinner in Luxor, 95% of Muslims are good people, 3% are not believers, and the remainder are fanatics.

　　I encourage everyone reading Jack's thread to discover Arabic lands with an open heart, to enjoy their fine hospitality, and to learn the joys of travel in Muslim countries.

　　An editorial comment—for my 25-day cruise, I carried two mystery novels, copies of Smithsonian, *and bought English-language* newspapers along the way in Muscat and Phuket. The Nautica concierge, Bruno, and I had a deal that I would put the books and newspapers in his chair and he would pass them along to crewmembers. The superb library onboard supplemented any reading needs I had, but the reading materials I left with Bruno seemed to be warmly welcomed by the crew. I would encourage other passengers to consider doing the same.

One day I hope to find a bound copy of Travels with Jack in the library of all Oceania's ships.

Ruby

meow!   ***April 25th, 2007, 06:00 PM***

While I remember, I have a little suggestion: Perhaps on such a long cruise, Oceania can provide those interested on board a "bridge tour." Silversea has bridge tours for most voyages. I understand that the current Oceania ships have twice the number of passengers as Silversea. However, for a 35-day voyage, at no cost to the cruise line and just a little extra work, organizing a bridge tour should not be too much to ask for. After spending so many days together on the ship, "security risks" for letting passengers see the bridge should be minimal, especially on those long sea days. Perhaps Jack and his parents can have a picture taken with the captain, the hotel director, the chef and whoever is important to him on the bridge and post it here later. (That can be a nice addition if Jack is going to compile this thread into a booklet some day.)

I remember in April 2001, on our return flight from Sydney, the purser was so kind as to invite the male and female cats (the two of us) into the cockpit and took our picture with the captain and co-pilot. That was the first and probably last time we were in an airplane cockpit. Five months later, there was the 9/11 tragedy, and such opportunities became a thing of the past! That picture has been a well-treasured souvenir for us.

Aussie Gal   ***April 25th, 2007, 06:27 PM***

Jack, thanks so much for finding out for me all the info re Agra. We will certainly book on line as soon as the excursion is released.

We have traveled extensively through Asia going back to the '70s and know not to eat anything that has been washed, e.g., salads, or anything that you cannot peel or cook, and to drink only water that comes out of bottles with a special top so that they have not been refilled.

We took our children away at an early age and were particularly careful with them, so the consequence is that we have never been ill in any third world country.

I have now printed out Episode 13 of your travels and have enjoyed each and every one. Please pass my compliments on to your Ann for a woman's perspective of Oman.

Jennie

*****

JackfromWA   **April 27th, 2007, 02:58 PM**

A FEW RESPONSES:

lahore: I didn't hear of anyone leaving Salalah, but assuming you have plenty to time to return to the ship I would do it. I am sure you would enjoy something unique by leaving Salalah for the fishing village your friend recommended.

Magicnelly: A short cabana review is part of the entry below. Something I forgot to mention in the review is the closest bathroom to the cabanas is two decks below on Deck 9.

Saga Ruby: I loved reading your post, and I was pleased to learn my impressions in Oman weren't unique to me. I do envy that you were able to visit Muscat; uniformly I have been told it is a better tourist port than Salalah.

meow!: I remember the Silversea bridge tours. In years past I understand some small lines maintained an open bridge policy. I also toured the Silver Winds engine room. It was immaculate. The bridge of a ship is special, especially at night when the glow of the instruments panels and radar dimly light the helm and navigation stations, and the sea appears dark and mysterious through the bridge window.

Aussie Gal: I passed your comments on to my mom, and she was delighted someone appreciated her perspective as a woman in Salalah.

Chapter 14

FOUR SEA DAYS

JackfromWA   *April 27th, 2007, 02:58 PM*

Today marks the end of four wonderful days at sea. Other than one night the first week, the seas have been calm and pleasant every day since leaving Hong Kong. Though the weather has been hot (usually over 90) and humid at times, we have had only one rainy sea day. Every port day except Singapore has been sunny, warm and dry—today is a balmy 80 degrees, the light breeze makes it feel cooler—and shortly I'll head to my cabana, put on my iPod and gaze across the sea and cloudless sky.

Tomorrow 400 passengers disembark for an overnight shore excursion to Luxor. My parents and I are part of the group, and we are excited to finally see the cradle of human civilization firsthand. The day after we return from Luxor we arrive in Aqaba, Jordan, the gateway to Petra and Wadi Rum. My parents and I are taking the ship tour, which includes Petra, Wadi Rum and a Bedouin dinner with belly dancing in the desert. After the laziness of four sea days filled with bridge, reading, shows, meals, naps, sun bathing, team trivia and conversation, the next three days almost sound like work—but seeing the sights of Egypt and Jordan for the first time are something I'll remember long after the memories of these sea days have faded.

Nautica has several fine guest-enrichment lecturers, including Richard Tallboys, the former U.K. ambassador to Vietnam. Today at bridge class I was fortunate enough to play with his wife Margaret and two of her friends. If I were casting a film with a role for a British ambassador's wife, Margaret would be the perfect choice. Her upper-class accent, impeccable manners and slight eccentricities make her delightful to converse with and play bridge with. All three women are skilled players, and they generously encouraged me to play every hand to further my bridge education, whether it was my

139

turn or not. So, I exchanged seats after each bridge auction to play out the winning hand. After we finished, they urged me to keep playing at home and enthusiastically assured me I have a future in bridge. Between Jean's excellent tutelage, and a natural affinity for counting, structure, rules (I like knowing what the rules are since I can't bend them until I understand them) and competition, I hope to find a way to continue playing at home. I never anticipated learning a new skill onboard Nautica, but attending every beginners' class is paying off, and I am having fun with an exciting new card game. Bridge makes my friendly poker games look easy—it reminds me of the difference between snorkeling and scuba diving.

The mood on the ship is enthusiastic for our three exciting ports of call, but interspersed with the excitement are conversations about airline routing home, baggage allowances and shipboard-account balances. Earlier today I saw one woman with a calculator borrowed from the purser's desk sitting at a desk in the reception lobby adding up, and then disputing, the total of her 15- or 20-page stateroom bill. I saw another man angrily and rudely refuse to sign something at the reception desk. I don't know what the circumstances were or if his refusal to sign was valid; regardless, his rude, angry behavior was inexcusable, and his traveling companion was clearly mortified. Some nerves are a little frayed as the reality and anxiety of going home sets in—pretty soon it will be midnight for Cinderella; the chariots turn to pumpkins, the ball gown turns to rags, and my piping-hot, savory French onion soup in the cabin turns to Lipton Cup-a-Soup in the microwave at home, and the closest I get to eating crème brûlée is a refrigerated Jell-O pudding. My desire to see Ty pulls me toward home, but I will sorely miss the artificial luxurious world I am happily ensconced in on Nautica.

A reader asked me to comment about the cabanas. To be brutally honest I have mixed feelings. Initially, I thought the cabana was the wisest choice I made, especially since neither my mom, dad nor I have a veranda. I envisioned using the cabana daily, enjoying attentive service, receiving chair massages, and watching the world sail by from my bird's-eye view. On this itinerary, it has been so hot and humid that I have used the cabana only a fraction of the time I hoped to. The short chair massages included are offered only on port days, and of course on port days I am off the ship. It doesn't help that it is hard to type in the cabana due to the glare of the sun reflecting off my laptop screen, so despite the fact I am typing this from my cabana, in general I don't write here. Yesterday was very hot, about 95 degrees, and after 10 minutes I left the cabana for the air-conditioned comfort of my cabin. Later in the afternoon, my parents came to the cabana, and as the sun set and the temperature fell, they lay on their Balinese daybed for two and loved watching the ocean and sky at sundown and nightfall. "It was the best time we had in the cabana the entire cruise," my mom said.

I would probably take the cabana again since between my parents and me we have two cabins without verandahs, and we all use the cabana as a private spot to enjoy being outside. If I were here with Ty, I would probably rather have a veranda. I think I would use it more often than the cabana, as the balcony is connected to the stateroom—and I could easily sit on it at night or in the morning when I drink my strong cappuccino. On an itinerary with more moderate climates, or if you really enjoy heat, the cabana has its benefits—in fact, just as I typed this sentence the attentive, young, attractive Indonesian deck steward brought me a plate of fruit skewers. I told him I didn't need anything, but he has been watching me for almost a month and knew if he brought fresh pineapple, watermelon, cantaloupe and strawberries accompanied by a tart berry sauce for dipping, that I would eat at least some of it. The service here is like that across the board—desires are anticipated—and after four weeks the crew has learned my tastes.

Last night's entertainment was a fantastically funny variety show. In a sense it was a "leftovers" show since each act was comprised of previously seen performers. But the acts and arrangements were so enjoyable that in many cases last night's "leftovers" were tastier than the original meal. Tonight, for one night only, we are being treated to an original play written by Ray Solaire entitled *Last Tango in Little Grimly: A Sex Comedy in Four Short Acts*. The Nautica lounge has been closed much of the day for rehearsals, and if Ray's original play is as good as the Olde English Country Faire held a few days ago, we are in for a treat.

The fair was held for a little over an hour in the late afternoon and hundreds of passengers turned out. Scattered about the Pool

Deck were 12 or 15 stands, everything from fishing (held in the Jacuzzi) to darts. Several of the events involved getting coated with whipped cream or flour, and I saw lots of crew and guests laughing, pointing, taking photos and having a rollicking good time despite the heat and overcrowded pool deck—to a small degree the fair was a victim of its own success. Each passenger received 10 Nautica dollars to play the games—each game had a small, usually one-dollar entry fee—and prizes were awarded to the guest who won the most money. The winner earned $124, second place earned $110, third place earned $104, and my mother earned $99. She did extremely well!

A hallmark of a trip this length on Nautica is the innovative entertainment. It seems the longer I am aboard the more interesting the entertainment gets—whether it is actually improving or I am more easily amused is an open question—but rather than being bored by the sea days I am enjoying them more than ever. The past four sea days flew by, and I am sad that the long stream of days at sea is behind us now.

We have had six or seven time changes on this itinerary. There would have been fewer, but when we left Saigon we had to move an hour forward for Singapore time. All the other time changes we have turned our watches and clocks back, so we have had at least seven 25-hour days, which is very pleasant for sleeping in. For some bizarre reason the time change for India was 30 minutes rather than an hour, so the day we left India we set the time back one hour, and the next day we set the time back an additional 30 minutes. Last year the ship attempted to set the clock back half an hour at midday, but the change was so confusing to passengers that this year we had two time changes on consecutive nights. I don't know why we couldn't just go back 90 minutes, but I heard that was too confusing as well. In any case, for one day we were on a unique "Nautica time zone" as, according to my Apple MacBook Pro, no known time zone in the world matched ours.

Last night was my final meal at Toscana. Over the course of this trip, I managed to sample every pasta on their extensive menu. My favorite is the fettuccini carbonara; it's as good as any I've ever had. All the pastas, entrees and appetizers are excellent there. My only complaint is their portions are often too large, unlike the Grand Dining Room, and it is challenging to make even a half-hearted effort to eat lightly.

All in all, as my mother said, this is probably the best cruise we have ever taken. In fact, I know it is the best cruise I have ever taken—the itinerary alone assured that—but more than the destinations, the level of genuine, friendly, competent service tailored to my likes and dislikes, the superb cuisine, the surprisingly enjoyable entertainment and the educational opportunities in the form of bridge classes, enrichment lectures and most important spending 35 relaxed, placid, unhurried days with my parents has made this my best cruise. I would happily take a self-serve car ferry to see Luxor, Petra and Cairo, but having the luxury of one of the best cruise ships in the world escorting me to the three upcoming exotic locations is incredibly exciting and I am filled with gratitude for having this unique opportunity.

I overheard someone on the ship talking about reading some of these posts. Word is getting around that a passenger is posting on Cruise Critic about this journey. It is strange to hear people talk about what they read when they don't know I am the author. It has been an honor and privilege to share my thoughts, observations and feelings with each of you, and the encouragement so many of you have generously given me to pursue writing is one of the memories that will always stay with me. A part of me has always wanted to write, but like so many things I have never done, I doubted my ability to do it. Knowing that I have successfully shared some of this cruise-of-a-lifetime experience with so many of you, with just the help of my keyboard and the power of the Internet, has far exceeded anything I expected when I began this simple thread. Although I look forward to finishing—every story needs an ending—it won't be just Nautica I miss when I get back home; it will be the time I have spent in all your living rooms, kitchens, bedrooms and computer screens, as we shared the opportunity of virtually traveling together in this unique 21st-century style. Just as you imagine me on the ship and in the ports of call, I imagine your reading this at home, and somewhere in between I like to believe we make a connection.

Thanks everyone for reading—nothing motivates my writing more than your desire to read it.

Next stop: Luxor.

*****

Marebear   *April 27th, 2007, 04:28 PM*
Another lurker here—I have thoroughly enjoyed all of your posts of your cruise—a real treat for me —you have made me feel as if I were along for the ride! Thank you!

Magicnelly   *April 27th, 2007, 04:48 PM*
I will gladly buy 10 copies of the first book you write! The subject doesn't even matter.
The ability to bring words to life on paper is rare…you definitely have it. Cherish it, use it, enjoy it!

Toranut97   *April 27th, 2007, 06:04 PM*
I will be sad also…
…when the cruise ends! I have felt like I am traveling vicariously with you all on this trip! Jack, you are indeed gifted, and I can understand why many on ship are enjoying your account also. Reading about your feelings—knowing that the cruise will end soon…the bittersweet feeling that it will be sad to leave but good to go home…(someone needs to coin a new phrase for it! "Pre-disembarkation tristesse"?) made me remember the exact sentiment on my previous vacation journeys.
You and Ty remain in my prayers, and when the cruise ends I sure hope you will let the gang here know how you both are doing. And when you are traveling again!

Donna

scdreamer   *April 27th, 2007, 08:11 PM*
Thank you once again, Jack, for another entertaining and informative post. You have more than whetted our appetites for our first Oceania cruise this coming fall. I'm looking forward to your next impressions, and like many others, wish to send on best wishes for Ty's test outcome.

Leslie & Wayne

Decebal   **April 27th, 2007, 08:31 PM**
Egypt

　　Hi, Jack...Egypt...sigh...oh, how I love reading about your travels. Egypt...sigh...the Pyramids, Luxor...sigh...

　　Thanks for keeping us updated on the cabanas...Petra...sigh...Aqaba...all right! end of another workweek...vacation on Nautica...siiiiiiiighhhhhhhhhh...

lahore   **April 27th, 2007, 09:37 PM**
Hi, Jack,

　　I think it goes without saying that we are all continuing to enjoy your superb postings. A thousand thanks.

　　Don't get stressed about not finding time to write about the upcoming ports—we don't want you to get stressed about anything. Maybe later, when you have got home and to a hopefully fit and well Ty, you can tell us about the Egyptian ports.

　　When and if you do get time, I will be absolutely fascinated to learn about the convoy and how effective...noxious (that's a continuum I can imagine) it is. When we do the same cruise we don't get Jordan, which is a bummer as it sounds more interesting than some of our ports—from the sounds of things they could drop Salalah and even Muscat in favor of Jordan for Petra. But then you never know, on our Panama cruise the stop that everyone seemed to like least—where there were no major "sights"—was our favorite place. We just went to the market square and played with some kids and dagged around. So I shouldn't write off Salalah; it may be like that too.

　　Can't wait to hear about Egypt—but in your own time. Enjoy.

potterhill   **April 28th, 2007, 07:06 AM**
　　Jack, I have enjoyed reading about your cruise, as has everyone else. Before reading your account, I wanted to do this cruise. Now, I have to do this cruise! I can hardly wait until the last child is out of school in three years so we can be away for an extended length of time. We did a TA last November because we really enjoy the sea days, and it was great. The first thing I do when I look at a cruise is count the sea days!

　　Sending you positive thoughts for Ty.

　　　　　　　　　　　　　　　　　Mo

145

meow!   ***April 28th, 2007, 11:16 AM***

Looks like we have to find alternative reading material soon! Jack, wish you the best of luck when you return home. Please keep us posted for the rest of your story when you are free, and thank you for sharing with all of us the experience of your voyage.

merryecho   ***April 28th, 2007, 01:07 PM***

O.K., this is to Mr. FDR. We take quite a few cruises, and I think I am not alone in saying that a large part of the enjoyment is planning and expectation. One thing I find lacking on EVERY cruise line is an acknowledgment of this. I would love to know more about the places we are going to visit, from someone who has been there. It seems to me that an inexpensive and tremendously effective marketing tool would be to add a feature to the O website with stories like Jack's (not that there are that many people who can write like Jack).

In other words, click on "visit the ports" and be able to read Jack's story about Vietnam, Mumbai, etc. Instead of the usual dry brochure blah blah, it would be along the lines of the old Peterman catalogue, which I think was hugely effective. You could even make it a contest—best port story wins an onboard credit.

Just my two cents.

PennyAgain   ***April 28th, 2007, 06:08 PM***
Jack, my most sincere thanks!

The magic continues. I read your posts in my office, which is isolated from the world. You have given me the most remarkable adventure.

Blessings and safe travels to you and to Ty. You are an absolutely wonderful travel writer.

I do wish to keep reading your new writings in future.

Emdee   ***April 29th, 2007, 09:51 AM***
Oh, to be in Luxor again!

Jack, thanks again for another wonderful posting...like everyone on this board I second the thought of a Jack's journey on an Oceania website but I am sure you could serialize it for a travel magazine as well....

When we were in Luxor we flew in from Alexandria for the day,

146

and it was a spectacular day in 46 degrees Celsius. I have a vivid memory of dropping ice cubes down my blouse in an attempt to cool off and the cubes just evaporated without a trace! Enjoy Luxor and the Valley of the Kings.

Eagerly await your next post.

Miriam

Chapter 15

SAFAGA AND LUXOR

JackfromWA   *April 29th, 2007, 06:16 PM*

As I tied my New Balance hiking shoes, I smiled. I knew it would be a good day. I bought the shoes a little over two years ago for an intensive 15-day trip to Inca ruins throughout the Sacred Valley in Peru. I wore them every day, and they safely carried me through Machu Picchu, Cuzco, Ollantaytambo and Pisaq. They worked so well and every day was so good that a year later I took them on safari to Kenya. While wearing them I finally saw close-up leopards and witnessed my first cheetah kill. I reserve wearing them for special occasions (basically when I need a guaranteed good day and hiking is involved).

I briefly debated whether to bring them on this trip, as there aren't too many ports with hiking, and I already had four pairs of shoes: a pair of dress shoes for dinner, Birkenstocks for relaxing, tennis shoes for the gym, and a pair of comfortable Mephisto loafers for airports and walking. Even though I wouldn't wear them often, I decided to put the shoes in my suitcase as I didn't want to set foot in Egypt or Jordan without them. As crazy as it sounds, I have assigned them magical properties. I believe wearing them guarantees a good day. I wore them to the orphanages in Vietnam, to the Grand Palace in Bangkok, through Goa and Mumbai and, like Cal Ripken, my shoes consistently brought me good days. I know that attributing good experiences to my choice of shoes is extremely superstitious, unreasonable and silly, but my grandmother's influence runs strong in me. She was raised in the coal counties of West Virginia where kids are sent to bed with a ghost story—and both the storyteller and listener believe every word is true.

The stories my grandma told my brothers, sister and me were wonderful, believable and, often as not, scary. She had a favorite recurring character, the Button Witch, who among other magical

149

traits revealed her presence by stealing your buttons. Whenever I put on a white shirt to go to church on Sunday and discovered a missing button, I knew the trickster Button Witch had slipped into my room and stolen my button as another trophy for her collection. Somewhere around 10 or 12 years old I forgot about the Button Witch—when my buttons went missing it was just another case of bad sewing or bad luck. But in 1996—after my 91-year-old grandma's stroke, which left half of her body permanently paralyzed, her once razor-sharp wit on a permanent holiday, and her exterior world reduced to an unpleasant-smelling room in a friendly nursing home in Chehalis, Washington, and just before she died in 1998— my mother discovered thousands of buttons stored in Mason canning jars in an alcove off Grandma's small, cold study. When we heard about it, both my brother and I immediately recalled the Button Witch. "It was Grandma all along," Jeff said. "She was the Button Witch!" I loved my grandma so much. Throughout this trip I can't help but think I wish my grandparents could have seen this, or I wish my long-gone uncles could have seen that. The greatest gift I could give my mother, father or Ty would be one more day with each of their deceased mothers, but of course that is a gift I can't give.

Egypt is old. It raises feelings of mortality and the meaning of life in me. It feels as if civilization as we know it started here, yet to me the monuments and remnants of Egypt's past feel completely disconnected from our modern world. I look at the work of men and women performed thousands of years ago, and I wonder: Does it matter? Like the pharaohs, I used to want to leave my footprints in the sands of time, but now I don't care. Even the greatest pharaohs have all been upstaged in popularity by a relatively minor pharaoh named King Tut. I realized a few years ago that I have to go back only a few centuries and I can't even name a single person who lived. The only person I can name from the 1400s is Columbus, and for the 1300s my best guess is King Arthur, Guinevere, Lancelot and Galahad. Instead of leaving a mark on the world, I want to leave a mark on the people I live with—my family, my friends and the strangers whose lives briefly intersect mine. I don't know if all you need is love, but I think it is true that the greatest gift you can give is love. The monuments of Egypt are a stark witness to you can't take it with you, so it seems wise to give love away. It has a chance of lasting in one form or another, and love is like rabbits, tribbles or fleas—it multiplies quickly when its passion is inflamed.

So despite knowing I fell prey to ignorant superstition, I happily pulled on my shoes, comfortable in the knowledge I would have a good day. Thinking warmly of my grandma, I got ready for my first day in Egypt. As I gazed out my stateroom window, at least an hour before my "alarm clock" of room-service breakfast was scheduled to wake me, my first view of Egypt was tall, brown, dusty hills, a few cinderblock construction buildings, and docks rolling past my cabin window as Nautica made her way to the Port of Safaga.

With over 400 passengers going overnight to Luxor, the excursion staff had their work cut out for them. A few days earlier we were divided into 11 different buses going to two different hotels. Everyone chose between the Nile Palace and the Sonesta—both are among the nicest hotels in Luxor. About 12 of us (most of my trivia team and a few other friends) requested the same bus and the same hotel, so when all 11 bus groups met simultaneously in an overcrowded Nautica lounge at 8 a.m., the group my mom, dad and I were assigned was filled with many familiar, friendly faces.

We were escorted off the ship by group number, and since every bus traveled in the same police convoy, it didn't matter which group left first; we were all arriving in Luxor together. By the time our convoy pulled out from the dock, our tour guide had lectured us on how to say "No, thank you" in Arabic, given her credentials (she had a letter from the U.S. ambassador to Egypt attesting to her skills, and she passed around pictures of her and Bill Clinton at the Pyramids) and given a brief outline of our day's schedule.

As we pulled away from Safaga and passed through police checkpoints, young and old Egyptians smiled and waved. Almost everyone we passed made a friendly overture.

"I don't think they see this many Americans too often," my friend Carol said. It did seem like we attracted an inordinate amount of attention from the locals.

As the scenery passed by the bus window, I noticed my first pyramid. Look dad, there's a pyramid ruin, I almost said. But when I looked again, it was just a triangular hill nestled between two mountains. As I kept looking, I noticed more pyramid shapes—even the triangular traffic warning signs looked like a pyramid. Since I was clearly obsessed with Egypt and pyramids, I decided to keep quiet about any future sightings until I was certain it was a relic from Egypt's past.

"This looks like the area outside Las Vegas," Carol's husband Bob said.

"Yeah, except in Vegas there are some red tones and color in the rock. Here it's all one color. I sure see why no one wants to live out in this desert," I replied. I also realized why researchers believe Egypt contains many more treasures to uncover—there could be tombs, statues, even a whole temple right in front of our very eyes and no one could tell. The landscape was hot, dry, desolate and barren.

Our guide announced that water was for sale—$1 for two bottles of Aquafina—and that our bus was equipped with a "temple of relief," which she claimed was a literal translation of the Egyptian word for bathroom.

"That's one temple I hope I don't have to worship in," I whispered to Bob and Carol. They both laughed, and Carol assured me she had brought her own tissue paper in case she felt the call to worship. Later on, when toilet paper ran out on the bus, I started referring to the bathroom as the Temple of Doom.

As we drove on, the stark, bleak monotonous scenery repeated itself. "Anybody want some chocolates?" I asked. I had hoarded about 30 Oceania chocolates left on my pillow every night and intended to give them to some Egyptian kids. However, the chocolates proved popular, it was a little piece of Nautica, and my fellow passengers smiled when the Zip-Loc baggie made its way up and down the bus. When it finally returned to me, most of the chocolates were gone.

Three hours later we cleared the last police checkpoint and arrived in the suburbs of Luxor. Many of the homes had primitive barns attached, filled with emaciated cows, old donkeys and horses trying to find relief from the heat. Despite their rundown appearance—indoor plumbing looked questionable in many cases—

satellite dishes sprouted from many of the roofs. As we drew closer to Luxor, the Egyptians on the side of the highway grew even friendlier.

Since time was extremely limited, we were driving directly to the Temple of Karnak, and after touring for two hours we were going to our hotel for a buffet lunch. After we ate we were scheduled to go to the Temple of Luxor and then return to the hotel about 4:30 p.m. to receive our room keys. After two hours' free time, we had dinner at 6:30 p.m. and left for the light show back at the Temple of Karnak at 8:45 p.m. As the bus pulled into the parking lot I grew excited. The Temple of Karnak was now merely walking distance.

"The temperature outside is 69 degrees," our guide told us.

"That isn't too hot," my mom said.

"It's got to be a mistake," I replied. "Just feel how hot the bus windows are."

"She said it is 39 degrees Celsius," the woman behind my mom corrected us. That made more sense, and sure enough when we walked off the bus it felt about 100 degrees. Off in the distance I got my first view of the Temple of Karnak grounds. There was a long row of rams (or lions or sphinxes) guarding either side of the entrance to the complex. Cameras were clicking left and right at our first Egyptian photo opportunity.

"Keep walking. Follow me," Eman, our Egyptologist guide, said as she briskly led us past the stone animal sentinels and toward the tall obelisk at the temple entrance. As we entered the first set of walls the age, majesty and intensity of Karnak began to reveal itself. Although I hate to admit it, the first I ever heard of Luxor was in 1993, the night my friend Eric and I watched the Dunes casino demolished in Las Vegas and the new Treasure Island and Luxor casino open. That evening we took a "boat ride around the Nile" and saw the "tombs of the pharaoh" all within the air-conditioned comfort of a Nevada casino. The only dangers were the slot machines, secondhand cigarette smoke and too much booze.

Ever since I was a child, I always wanted to see the Giza Pyramids and the Sphinx, but I didn't have any interest in Luxor—I had never heard of it until the casino opened. Ten years ago, my brother and his wife took a Nile River cruise. When I expressed my interest in the Pyramids to him he said, "The Pyramids are interesting, but to me the most exciting attractions in Egypt are around Luxor. You can see the Temple of Karnak, the Temple of Luxor and the tombs in the Valley of the Kings. There is a lot more to do and see in Luxor than what you see visiting the Pyramids in Cairo." His informed opinion notwithstanding, I had secretly believed he exaggerated Luxor at the expense of Cairo. He didn't.

Everywhere I turned, the obelisks, statues, hieroglyphic wall carvings and pillars staggered me. I couldn't believe all this survived so many thousands of years. How did anyone move this much stone, create this much art and design these, much less build these temples in this climate?

"I can't believe people worked this hard in all this heat," I told Carol.

"Well, I doubt they were lining up to volunteer to get on that team," Carol replied with her slight southern accent. She had a point. Much of the work was probably done with forced labor.

As we entered the Great Hypostyle Hall, my jaw dropped. I was speechless. Trying to capture this with a camera is as futile as attempting to capture the majesty of the Grand Canyon or the sound and motion of Niagara Falls with a camera. Every direction I looked, carved stone columns, at least 50 feet tall and 10 feet in diameter, were arranged in neat rows like perfectly placed 50-foot-tall cribbage pieces. There must be over a hundred columns, each weighing incalculable tons. Every angle offered a different artistic perspective as the columns are evenly spaced and of uniform height and diameter. The labor necessary to create this was unimaginable. I can think of only one reason to create a space like the Great Hypostyle Hall: to force a reaction of awe and wonder. The pharaohs succeeded. It is impossible not to be affected by the sight of standing here, looking at the columns, hieroglyphics, statues and walls. Anyone who enters the hall will never forget the sight of the stone columns, silently standing as a reminder of the temple's antiquity and acting as mute witness to our ephemeral existence.

Past the hall there were more obelisks, more statues and, unfortunately, more heat. Later that day I learned the high in Luxor was 110 degrees. Though I wanted to see more and stay longer, the excursion staff wisely sent us back to the hotel to hydrate and eat. The lunch buffet was good, I didn't eat much as I was limiting my food choices to bread, rice and potatoes on shore—I didn't want to be sick this week, as tomorrow is Petra and Thursday is Cairo—and after lunch we drove to the Luxor Temple.

Having just left Karnak, the Luxor Temple wasn't quite as impressive as it would have been if I had seen it first. The site is right in the heart of town. From the interior boundary I could see a McDonald's sign reading LUXOR: I'M LOVING IT, and the temple was overwhelmed by all 400 ship tourists descending simultaneously. Despite a great effort by the ship, and Cosmos, their ground-tour operator, our group is such a behemoth that everywhere we go we crowd our surroundings.

After dinner, my parents had to pick up our cartouches—little custom-made gold or silver amulets with a name of your choice spelled out in hieroglyphics. Our guide told us we had to meet in the hotel lobby at 7:30 p.m. to pick up the cartouches we ordered on the bus. Since I was tired, my mom agreed to pick up the gold cartouche I ordered for Ty. When she and my dad arrived in the lobby, Eman, our tour guide, informed my parents they had to pick them up at a jewelry store. She offered to take them, so they went on the bus with about 20 other members of our group. When they arrived at the store, Eman explained the cartouches weren't ready yet, they could get them later, but since they were here they should look around the shop.

My dad doesn't get angry easily, but he detests being taken for a fool. He refused to buy anything, left the store, and waited on the bus. After he and my mom left, several other disgruntled passengers left too. Despite the unhappy passengers, Eman kept the bus outside the store for an hour.

"She lied to us," my dad said. "I am not giving her a dime for a tip." It was the most upset he has been the entire cruise. It is too bad that the economics of touring in Egypt force guides to betray the trust they earn through friendliness and excellent historical knowledge by preying on their tourists. To make a few bucks in commission, our guide upset at least a third of the group that went to the store to pick up their cartouches. If they weren't ready, she should have arranged for the customers who wanted to leave to go back to the hotel. It was a scam and cost my mom and dad over an hour of their precious time in Egypt. The worst part of all this is we knowingly overpaid for the cartouches so we wouldn't have to deal with any hassles. My parents weren't alone though. I overheard one passenger exclaim, "We were in some store until 2:30 a.m., we didn't get any sleep, and they wouldn't let us leave unless we bought a carpet." The wonders of Egypt are the world's oldest manmade continuous tourist attraction, so the locals have hundreds of generations of experience of separating the marks from their money. They do a good job of it, and while I admire their technical expertise, I dislike our guides' wasting our limited time to make a quick buck.

We left for the night show at the Temple of Karnak. The moon was half full and, between the light of the moon and the lights of the show, Karnak was awe-inspiring and magical in its ancient mysterious glory. During the first half of the show we walked through the complex. The second half of the show we sat on stone overlooking the sacred lake while recorded narrators gave a history of Egypt. Lots of people fell asleep—it had been a long, hot day and the sonorous amplified voices and lackluster staging didn't create much excitement after their initial appearance.

At eight the next morning, we went to the Valley of the Kings. Our first stop was the tomb of Ramses VI. It was eerie walking through the long stone tunnel toward the sarcophagus thinking about the Egyptian priests who walked this path thousands of years ago. On both sides of the 12-foot-wide passage, the walls are carved with hieroglyphics.

"I can't read them, but I bet they say he was a great king, he took good care of his people, his family loved him and he deserves rich rewards in the afterlife," I whispered to Bob.

"Don't forget he was beloved by all his people," Bob said as we both laughed.

The next tomb was Ramses III, and it was longer and even more ornate. The colors painted on the tomb walls thousands of years ago are still visible, and despite the fading and deterioration it is easy to imagine the pristine opulence of his tomb. From my perspective it seems wasteful to expend so many human resources to make one man's tomb, but I am sure from a different, ancient Egyptian theological perspective it all made perfect sense. In all the tombs the walls were adorned with thousands of original hieroglyphic carvings. I would love to walk through them alone, with a candle at night.

On our way back to the hotel, we stopped at the Memnon statues for a 10-minute photo shoot, and we stopped at Hatshepsut Temple but didn't have time to go in. Inexplicably, our guide offered us our paid tickets as souvenirs; it didn't seem much of a souvenir to have a ticket for something I wanted to see but didn't have time to tour, so I politely declined and told her she should sell them. We arrived at our last stop, Medinet Habu. Although I had never heard of the Habu temple before, I enjoyed this stop as much as Karnak.

The grounds are almost as large as Karnak, and the statues, carvings and immense stone exterior walls instantly took my breath away. Of all our stops, this was the one where I wanted to find a quiet spot to reflect on the mystery of the ancient Egyptians. There wasn't time, and quiet reflection isn't part of the tour, so I reluctantly left with the group after making a mental note to come back here when I can and devote at least a day to experiencing the mystery of Medinet Habu.

"Does anyone know how many children Ramses II had?" Eman asked over the bus P.A. system. She liked to give us quizzes and reward correct answers with cheap ink pens shaped like King Tut.

"Seventy?" someone shouted. "Fifty?" another woman guessed.

"No, Ramses had over 200 children and uncounted wives. He even married three of his own daughters," Eman said. The announcement of Ramses marrying his own children was met with groans of disgust.

"You know what, Jack?" Bob said.

"No, what?"

"That must be the reason they named those condoms Ramses," Bob said. Once again we both started laughing. Bob's wife Carol told us to quit cutting up, and a passenger sitting across the aisle overheard his comment and gave both of us the same withering glare I've earned for swearing in front of children.

Soon enough we were back at the hotel. We checked out, ate lunch, formed our convoy and started the drive back to Port Safaga. Our guide let us sleep for a few hours and then started lecturing on the religions of Egypt. I put in my iPod, and James Taylor sang, "The secret of life is enjoying the passage of time." Another successful random selection by my iPod, I thought. As we approached Safaga, the bus slowed down. There was a wreck ahead. As we drew closer I could tell it was serious. "It's a tourist bus," someone gasped. As we looked in horror, a bus just like ours lay on its side, windows broken, blocking a lane of the highway. As we drove past I saw the stunned driver sitting in the hot sand staring forlornly across the desert. Fortunately, the crashed bus was empty. With a new sense of gratitude, we quietly drove on. Soon the most bountiful oasis in Egypt, Nautica, appeared on the horizon, and we made our way through the town and to the dock. The Silver Cloud was berthed next to Nautica, and I was happy to see the familiar Silversea logo. I hoped her passengers were having as good a time as we were.

We got off the bus, the Nautica band was playing, and waiters passed out cool towels along with glasses of apple juice and water. A red carpet was rolled from the dock to the gangplank and a banner proclaiming WELCOME HOME was strung over the first stair. Twenty or 30 ship's officers, headwaiters, chefs and butlers enthusiastically welcomed us home. Even though today was bittersweet since it was the last Sunday of our cruise, it was good to be back.

Tonight was rushed. I ate dinner with my parents and some friends at Polo and then stayed up too late to finish this, before today's memories begin to fade and blend into tomorrow's adventures. Before crawling in bed I laid out tomorrow's clothes: my shirt, pants, underwear, socks and of course my hiking shoes. Tomorrow I am going to Petra and, after all, I want another great day.

*****

Aussie Gal   *April 29th, 2007, 07:20 PM*
Jack, what a wonderful episode. I think it is the best so far. I loved the story of your grandmother and the buttons. She must have been a wonderful lady.

Your description of Luxor and the temples has whetted my appetite, and I cannot wait until this time next year when it will be our turn.

Thanks for spending half the night writing this. It was well worth it.

Jennie

Emdee   *April 30th, 2007, 05:40 AM*
Jack, after reading your last episode, I just had to get out my own pictures and relive my time in Egypt. I am also resolved to do this itinerary—it will have to wait as neither of us will be able to take off for 35-plus days for a few years, but I have put it "on my list."

I am equally sad that your cruise is coming to an end. Shall miss the wonderful long reads of your travels. Today I am reading this at 5 a.m.

Take care,

Miriam

lahore   *April 30th, 2007, 08:54 AM*
Hi, Jack,
Your fan club is still out here. Was so interested to read about the convoy, the rip-off, the little things that happened along the way—they are what makes your writing more entertaining than the average travelogue to me—it's why it's real. Hope Petra is fun too, without any big hassles.

wildduck   *May 1st, 2007, 08:22 AM*
Thank you, Jack, for sharing all your wonderful adventures of Asia on Nautica. I began reading them only one week ago as I

159

*searched for information about the Hong Kong to Athens cruise as
we have booked to do the same cruise next April 2008. Now I can
hardly wait. Last May we sailed on Nautica (Deck 4) from Istanbul
to Athens through the Greek islands; it is certainly a special ship. I
remember seeing her for the first time from the terrace of our hotel
in Istanbul sailing up the Bosporus River gleaming white in the gray
of the overcast morning.*

*Thank you for your information regarding the trips to Agra to
the Taj Mahal and also to Luxor; this will be very helpful in our
planning.*

*We are keeping your journal of your trip to read many times
while we wait until it is our turn. We know it will be an amazing
journey as you have experienced. Once again thank you, and I wish
you safe return home.*

aneka   **May 1st, 2007, 08:49 AM**
Hi, Jack,

*Thanks for a wonderful installment on your fabulous adventure.
I would love to do this trip in the future and plan to print out your
postings and save them. I would love to see some pictures from your
trip. Have you thought about posting your pictures and a link so that
we might enjoy them also? Thanks again for spending your time on
your cruise to enlighten us all on this great itinerary.*

Annette

PennyAgain   **May 1st, 2007, 10:28 AM**
Jack, thanks so much. Just wonderful!

*I am looking forward to reading about Petra, as it is one of those
places I doubt I will see on my own.*

CruisingSerenity   **May 1st, 2007, 01:35 PM**
*Jack, in the beginning, you made me laugh. Boy, did you make
me laugh! Your last three entries have also been entertaining and
I've laughed, but you also made my eyes well up.*

*Don't ever doubt your ability to write. Wow. Someone else said
you are gifted. You truly are.*

*You hoped you have made a connection with all of us, your
faithful readers…you have. You make us feel many things and that,
Jack, is a fantastic talent.*

*I'd also like to thank you for your words of wisdom on this last
post…I won't get in to it here, but you have said some things that*

160

have put in to words something I've been trying to figure out for a few years. Without your even knowing it, you just made a big difference in someone else's life.

Hey, maybe you can start a blog when you're done with the trip!

*****

JackfromWA   May 1st, 2007, 02:30 PM

A FEW RESPONSES

<u>Marebear:</u> Thank you for coming out of the shadows and posting. I love hearing from fellow cruisers.

<u>Magicnelly:</u> If I am ever fortunate enough and talented enough to write something worth selling, I will e-mail you and get you a free copy! Thanks for the encouraging words and sage advice.

<u>Toranut97:</u> Thanks for the prayers and positive thoughts for Ty—his biopsy is Wednesday, and so keep the good energy flowing. Thanks for your compliments.

<u>scdreamer:</u> Thanks for the well wishes for Ty and me, and enjoy your first Oceania cruise. Cruise Critic is a great, maybe the best, place to get "real" information before your vacation.

<u>Decebal:</u> Wish you were here… sigh.

<u>lahore:</u> I surprised myself and find time to write while not losing joy in my vacation. But I appreciate your encouragement to postpone if necessary and enjoy this unique and wonderful experience. I am sure you've read about the convoy in the Luxor post by now.

<u>potterhill:</u> Thanks for the kind words and optimism for Ty. Put this trip on your list. Since you like sea days, as I do, you will love the balance on this itinerary.

<u>PennyAgain:</u> Thanks for calling my writing magic—what a humbling compliment!

<u>Emdee:</u> I know what you mean about the heat! Luxor was awe-

161

inspiring but soooo hot! Glad I motivated you to look at your photos, and if a writer ever received a greater compliment than being read at 5 a.m., I don't know what it could be!

wildduck: Don't you love Deck 4? After an excursion, I am in the cabin in less than a minute. I would gladly trade it for a veranda, but the location is ideal.

aneka: I might do some photos when I get home. Even though FDR graciously gave me free Internet, I am still using the 1,200-minute package I purchased and uploading photos is expensive. Besides that, between my parents and me we have over 1,500 pictures (most of which aren't of interest to anyone but us—some we don't even want to look at) and they haven't been sorted yet. I'll hope to post something with a photo link within a few weeks of getting home.

Aussie Gal, meow!, merryecho, lahore: I think you are among my biggest supporters. Thank you so much for everything you have written to bridge the distance between us. Your encouragement, contributions, well wishes for Ty and compliments mean the world to me.

Chapter 16

AQABA, PETRA AND WADI RUM

JackfromWA   *May 1st, 2007, 02:30 PM*

Desert sky, dream beneath the desert sky
Rivers run but soon run dry, we need new dreams tonight.
                —"In God's Country," U2

After two days in the lifeless desert and brutal heat in Egypt, the living desert and mild heat surrounding Aqaba were as welcome as Popsicles in Luxor. When we disembarked Nautica, the temperature was at least 20 degrees cooler than yesterday in Luxor. I overheard several passengers say, "This is like touring in air conditioning!"

Aqaba occupies a unique geographic location. From the city, I could look across the water and see Egypt and look north and see Israel. Despite the proximity to Israel, guests were requested not to spend the day there due to the thorny issue of passport stamps from Israel when entering Arabic countries. It didn't bother me, as my day was full with visiting the city of Petra and the desert of Wadi Rum. About 300 guests were taking the Petra and Wadi Rum tour, and I guess at least another 300 guests—basically most of the rest of the ship—were seeing either Petra or Wadi Rum on a ship tour, or made private touring arrangements to visit one or both. Going to Jordan without seeing Petra is like going to Paris without seeing the Eiffel Tower, London without seeing Big Ben, or going to Kenya without seeing a pride of lions in the savannah.

I had initially made private touring arrangements at a substantial savings (cost for Petra and Wadi Rum from the private operator was about $250 per person, and cost from Oceania was $399), but five things changed my mind. 1) I didn't have any information on the reliability of the company I found on the Internet offering my private tour. 2) Nautica's Wadi Rum tour included a private dinner with Bedouins under tents in the desert night sky. 3) Oceania's tour lasted from 8 a.m. to 10:30 p.m., and the ship docked at 8 a.m. and left at 11:00 p.m., so by going with the ship I could spend every minute possible on tour. 4) My parents and I have grown comfortable with some of our fellow passengers, and by taking the ship tour we enjoyed the pleasant company of 10 of the 14 people we had traveled to Luxor with. And 5) I learned that Oceania's ground operations were conducted by the venerable and reliable luxury-tour operator Abercrombie & Kent. I have never taken a land tour with A&K, but I didn't want to lose the opportunity to see how they performed, even though I knew a group of our size wasn't the best indicator of their talents.

Cinthya, Nautica's destinations manager, has earned my trust. She freely shared advice and recommendations on ports where I didn't purchase excursions from her—in fact in one case, Salalah, she validated my decision to go on my own, but she encouraged my parents and me to take the Petra and Wadi Rum tour. "It is our most popular tour, Jack," she said in her slight Brazilian accent. "You simply must try it." I knew she had my best interests at heart and her persuasion was meant to enhance our experience, not to simply sell more Oceania tickets. So once again we find ourselves at 8 a.m. in the overcrowded Nautica lounge—the heat, stimulation and exertion from the past two days in Luxor still fresh in my body and mind. It didn't matter. I had two days at sea to recover from Petra. I might never get here again.

I had gathered 12 tickets so our little group of team-trivia players and fellow Egypt travelers could be assigned the same bus again. My friends Kirk and Tony showed up at the last minute, and I grabbed their tickets as well.

"Jack, can you also get Frank and Becka's tickets?" Kirk asked. I realized Frank a.k.a. Lumpy was standing right behind him. Frank is a smoker and so is Kirk. Since smoking areas are extremely limited on Nautica—I think there are only two, one under cover outside on the Pool Deck and one in a small section of Horizons lounge—every smoker on board has spent time smoking with every other smoker on board. There are too many days together and too many cigarettes to smoke to be able to avoid each other. Consequently, a natural smokers' fraternity developed. I envied the smokers their esprit de corps. On the first week of this trip, I noticed the smokers had formed a bond, and even though I quit smoking almost 20 years ago, I still relate to smokers. I would smoke if I could—I just don't need the health problems. So when Kirk asked me to get Frank's tickets, I replied, "Sure, Kirk, I'll get them."

My perceptions about Frank were mixed. He was rude to my mom; he is loud, boisterous and competitive. But he also loves Gandhi, I have watched him physically help fellow passengers, and he is married to a very friendly, kind, attractive woman. Although it was ironic I would spend the tour day on the bus with Frank, it was how the day unfolded. After spending a full day around him, my impressions are: His wife Becky is beautiful, warm and friendly, and Frank has a cantankerous, sometimes rude, persona, but inside I think he has a heart of gold. The real villain of my story isn't Lumpy—it is the few "too good for the rest of the ship" passengers who isolate and complain about the nerve of someone wearing dress sandals to lunch in the dining room, or the passengers who berate, bully and ridicule the defenseless waiters, maids, front-desk staff and other workers who risk losing their jobs if they fight back. I haven't seen Frank do any of those things. Fortunately, I haven't seen much of that behavior from anyone this cruise, but I have witnessed just enough, and overheard just enough, to know it goes on.

When we walked off the gangplank, the A&K representatives greeted each woman with a single rose. The buses were much nicer than the buses in Egypt. Our bus was only a little over half full, and the mood aboard was jubilant—like kids Christmas morning, wondering what gifts would be in their hands by the end of the day. Just like in school, the smokers, along with those of us who have problems with authority figures and wish to escape the eye of the bus driver, sat toward the back of the bus. Instead of boxed lunches we carry expensive digital cameras, and instead of candy we carry our prescriptions, Aleve and Imodium. With a few other exceptions (as a group, we are more conditioned to having our own way and being treated subserviently than any bus of high school students), the social atmosphere on our bus wasn't much different than a long-ago high school field trip. My mom turned around from her seat in front of me (she and my dad had come toward the back of the bus to stay near me but remained one row in front) and said, "You can tell this is a much more upscale operation than the tour company in Luxor."

Our guide, who spoke impeccable English, described the history, economy, religions and social structure of Jordan as part of a well-organized lecture throughout most of the 2½-hour drive. Outside the window, I saw someone had painted RAED + KOELED on a cinder-brick wall; graffiti professing love is universal. As we left Aqaba, he pointed out the blatant flagpole—it is the second largest in the world. The tallest is three feet higher and is at the Jordanian palace several hundred miles north. It towers over the entire city, measuring about 450 feet tall. The flag, which flapped loudly in the cool, sea breeze, measures about 260 feet by 150 feet and is visible for miles. The residents of nearby Israel and Egypt are forced to view Jordan's gargantuan, imposing flag waving daily over their homeland skyline.

The desert between Aqaba and Petra is full of life. Petra is located 5,000 feet above sea level, so as we traveled we climbed a windy road and saw small tufts of grass and purple desert flowers. Camels and sheep dotted the desert landscape. "Petra is the petrol of Jordan," our guide said. "Tourism is the most important and growing sector of the Jordanian economy, and we are very glad to have this brief opportunity to show you our beautiful country." He carefully outlined where to use restrooms before entering Petra, where we would have lunch, what to expect when we reached the Treasury, and what to do if we got separated or chose to leave the group.

We got off our bus, used the bathrooms at the Petra visitors' center (the next bathroom is near the bottom of the two-mile hike down) and made our way toward the ancient stone facades, dwellings and carvings of this mythical city. As we walked, our guide talked about Moses' brother Aaron, and told us that much of this region's history was contained in early chapters of the Old Testament. I had never thought of the Bible as a history book; the Bible was a somewhat boring, not very engaging to read, guide of how to behave properly to get to heaven. But for the first time I saw how in this culture the Bible was a historical record. Moses and Aaron were Jordan's George Washington and Abraham Lincoln. If kids at home could visit Petra for Sunday school field trips, church would be a lot more popular, I thought, as our guide's words brought the Old Testament alive to me.

We walked along a stone path that followed a gentle downward slope through colorful ravines carved by countless years of wind and water. The gorge was stunning as the sun draped across the rocks, boulders and canyon walls. Hundreds of shades of tans, reds, yellows and oranges graced the sun-suffused stone surrounding us from either side of the narrow canyon and reached as high as the wondrous fractured rock formations, some towering several hundred feet above our heads.

"I want you to close your eyes, form a single line, and grab the back of the shirt of the person in front of you," our guide said. We stumbled blindly on, shuffling across the uneven stone knowing our destination was almost in front of us. "Now open your eyes!" he excitedly ordered.

Gasps of wonder echoed in the stone ravine, as the Treasury facade revealed itself through the tall, narrow, stone crevasse directly in front of us. As the light reflected across the hundred-foot pillars, arches and columns of the magnificent edifice carved in the face of the stone, I walked out of the Siq ravine inexorably drawn toward this ancient wonder. Despite the crowds, camel jockeys and vendors, the attraction was undeniable. I had never seen anything like the Treasury—it looked almost as if part of the Unites States Supreme Court had been gracefully carved in stone, and then a romantic Greco-Roman temple was stacked on top of it. According to our guide, the Treasury was carved over 2,000 years ago, and its original purpose has been lost in the annals of time. It is called the Treasury because some intrepid explorers expected to find treasure in it. The treasure is intrinsic in its beauty, design and architecture—no gold or silver was ever reported found there.

Having never ridden a camel, I transformed into a caricature of a tourist, hired a camel, rode through the swarming crowd and seized my photo opportunity of Jack-on-a-camel-at-Petra. I forced my parents to do the same. My mom happily obliged. My dad wouldn't do it until I had already paid the camel jockey for him, and he either had to ride the camel or I lost my $3—his Dutch background and natural aversion to wasting money got the best of him and, swept up in the moment, he joined my mother and me in riding a camel in Petra.

Our guide walked us farther down, to an amphitheater and many more but not as well-preserved facades, and then stopped at a shop for refreshment and the ubiquitous selling of trinkets, mementos and souvenirs. Somehow my mom got separated from us, and my dad grew worried. When you have been with each other as long as they have—they were married in 1958 and are best friends—it is stressful to be accidentally separated in a large, crowded site like Petra. Even though I am sure he knew she was probably fine, the thought of her lying on the ground with a sprained ankle or worse propelled my dad to anxiously search until he found her. After half an hour, my dad and Carla from the excursion staff found my mom, along with Sandy from our group, about 500 yards past the shopping stop.

Once again an excellent guide didn't communicate well with his tourists when the lure of a sales commission reared its ugly head. After reuniting with his wife, my dad was about ready to go. We were supposed to leave Petra to go to lunch, but since it was only 1 p.m., and the hike back up required one hour, and we didn't leave for Wadi Rum until 4 p.m., I told the guide I would stay in Petra another hour and catch up with the group around 3 p.m. at the hotel.

I hiked a small hill with a small Greek-temple-looking facade on top, situated directly across from the amphitheatre. Despite the hundreds of people wandering Petra, the site is large enough that with 10 minutes' effort I found a cool, quiet, peaceful retreat. The first cave entrance I tried smelled of old urine, so I found another cave, made a small pillow from my fleece jacket, put on my iPod, and leaned back to take in the surreal view. From this height, the tourists in the distance looked like large ants marching in an identical line from one spot to the next. Off in the distance, more stone-carved fairytale buildings beckoned, but with too little time I chose to simply watch and experience the magic of Petra's legacy from my cave's view.

As I lay on my stone dais, I wondered what other men and women watched from this same exact spot, hundreds or thousands of years ago. The property taxes, Visa bills, episodes of *Lost*, and the weeds in the yard back home were relegated to the trivial place they deserve, as the hand-carved stone walls of Petra, like their counterparts in Egypt and Greece, bore stark witness to the short time humans live, and the fleeting nature of so many temporal tasks I deem important. If there is a lesson for me in the stone monuments of Jordan and Egypt, it is that I need to look at the world with new eyes. I need to do the things that are truly important, the things that matter, such as raising a child, having a good relationship, honoring my parents, grandparents, siblings and friends, helping others recover from their own addictions as I am recovering from mine— and donate less time to my TV show addictions (*24* really is crack TV, and I am hooked), earning one more dollar beyond what I need, and the countless meaningless but urgent tasks that I allow, invite and encourage to rule my mental, emotional and spiritual energy on a daily basis. The potential for profound thoughts and spiritual shifts in ancient environments is great.

Far too quickly my extra hour in splendid solitude passed, I hiked down the hill, hired a camel for a short ride to the Treasury, and walked the mile-and-a-half, gradually ascending path to the trailhead. Close to the top, a man asked where I was from.

"Bellingham, Washington, about a hundred miles north of Seattle," I replied.

"I'm from Philly," he said. "So where are you coming from?"

"Egypt. We were at Luxor the past two days, and unfortunately have to leave Petra tomorrow."

"Did you fly up here?" he asked.

"No, I am on a ship."

"Where did you get on? In Luxor?" he asked, his curiosity growing.

"Um, well, actually I got on the ship in Hong Kong. It is a 30,000-ton cruise ship with 700 passengers and 400 crew. The trip ends in Athens on Saturday," I said.

His eyes grew large, and in a slightly envious tone he said, "Wow, you guys went around the world."

I thought about what he said. I had never considered our 35 days from Hong Kong to Athens as a true round-the-world cruise—those last three months, cost $50,000, and we only cruised a little less than half the globe—but I realized in the eyes of the stranger from Philadelphia, and in the eyes of my friends and family at home, I did go on a round-the-world cruise. In that moment I realized I took the world cruise I always dreamed of taking with my mom and dad.

"Yeah, I guess we did," I proudly replied. "It has been absolutely fantastic."

With a new spring in my step, I smiled, bade him good-bye and walked the remaining few hundred yards to the hotel. I informed my parents and our guide I was back, and I ate a quick, light lunch.

At four o'clock I reluctantly left Petra—with a large mental note to return with Ty—but the excitement of the jeep safari, desert sunset and Bedouin dinner made the departure easier. It was a 90-minute drive to Wadi Rum; I half-slept for an hour, and then started looking at the amazing landscape. Interspersed between vast expanses of air-rippled sand were tall oases of deep-red-hued rock. The huge, craggy rock formations, rising out of the desert sand, like tall, stone atolls standing proudly against the ocean sky, oblivious to wind, water, rain or sun, dominated the desert landscape. I put on my iPod, and Bono started singing about the beauty of desert sky. The song "In God's Country" is one of the lesser-known titles from my favorite pop album of all time, U2's *The Joshua Tree*. My iPod has never randomly picked a more appropriate song. A warm, tingling sensation ran through my head and up and down my spine while I basked in the beauty of the red sand and rocks of Wadi Rum listening to Bono's musical homage to God's glorious juxtaposition of red desert against clear blue sky. The song ended, the moment passed, and I quietly engaged my father in a brief conversation about his day.

At the visitors' center we were placed in small groups of six per jeep, the "jeeps" were old Toyota and Nissan pickup trucks with opposite-facing benches welded in the truck bed. We sat three per side as we entered the desert. Sandy, Bill and Nancy joined us in our jeep. They were also on our bus in Luxor, and Sandy and Nancy are on our trivia team. Nancy just retired at a young age and Bill is her uncle, so she and I have the shared experience of traveling with two members of an earlier generation of our family. Bill was born in the same small town in eastern West Virginia where my mom was born and my grandma is from (after they mutually discovered this, he "adopted" my mom, and she received the same chivalrous care from Bill that he reserved for his wife and niece). I liked him immediately—I like anyone who reminds me of my grandma, and no one reminds me of her more than Ty—and it was special to have that evening in the desert with Bill, Nancy and Sandy. Even though we have all lived long enough to realize the zenith of our friendship is likely to be this cruise, Bill, Nancy and Sandy are the kind of people worth staying in touch with.

After several photo stops (here is where *Lawrence of Arabia* was filmed, etc.), and about a half-hour ride, we arrived at the perfect outcrop of rock to watch the setting sun. As we pulled in, I realized the moon was almost full and rising above an L-shaped rock formation directly behind us. I pointed this out to Bill, and he and I dashed a few hundred yards back. Our cameras captured the blue sky, red rock and almost-full moon aligned in perfect symmetry. After the desert sunset, we headed to our Bedouin dinner.

Our first glimpse of our dining place was hundreds of lights twinkling in the deepening black of the desert night. As we drove closer, the lights revealed themselves as Japanese paper lanterns creating a path leading to the U-shaped arrangement of dining tents. Bedouin musicians played indigenous music, and we were welcomed as we made our way down the candlelit path. The only fly in the ointment was our fellow travelers. Our jeep was one of the last to arrive, and each tent contained several tables for six. We were encouraged to eat Bedouin style, without chairs, and for our comfort foam cushions were set up as benches to seat three guests on either side of each table. Although hardly anyone was sitting at a table, every available place setting was reserved by a camera, purse, hat or jacket belonging to our fellow passengers. It was like trying to find an open deckchair at noon on a sunny sea day on Carnival. I found an A&K representative, who finally found us a place to sit.

Dinner was tender lamb cooked in the sand, chicken skewers, rice, potatoes, salads, desserts, pita bread and fruits, accompanied by unlimited beer, wine and soda, all served beneath a clear, moonlit desert sky. A large concert-worthy speaker system had been set around the tents, and as we ate, live music was broadcast over the speakers. A line of watch fires blazed along the perimeter of a large dance area surrounded on three sides by our dinner tables. After dinner, a belly dancer appeared, and she selected men at random to perform her routine with. Her first choice was our friend Kirk, but so many other passengers tried to get a photo I couldn't really provide him with a great picture.

"That belly dancer is like a fox at a traditional English fox hunt," I said to my dad. "There are a hundred people trying to take a photo, and only one of her." He laughed, and as the dance went on, photos became easier to take. After the dancing, the Bedouin DJ played a few more songs, but by the time he put on the "Macarena" we decided it was time to return to the buses. We were told to just get in any jeep for the dark ride to the bus, as it was too difficult to find our original vehicle. Shortly, we met our new driver.

My friend Bob commented that his driver looked about 12 years old. I thought he meant he had a 20-year old-driver who looked young, but when I saw his driver, wearing a red Nike hat in a useless attempt to appear older, he looked about 10 or 12 years old. He told Bob he was 14.

"Bob and Carol's driver doesn't look 14 to me," my mom said, "I don't think he has reached puberty yet. Maybe Bedouins look younger than some other people, but he still doesn't look 14."

"If that kid is 14, I'll eat this hat," Sandy said as she pointed to her white Arabic headdress.

Our new driver was about 19, wore a navy blue T-shirt asking, GOT GOD? and spoke no English. He took off with a jolt and soon we were recklessly passing other jeeps in the nighttime shifting desert sand.

"He may have God, but I haven't even got a seat belt," I announced. Even though they laughed, it was obvious everyone was nervous from his reckless driving. My dad banged on the window and made a slow-down motion with his hand. The temporary reprieve from Mr. Toad's Wild Ride lasted less than a minute. Like a dog chasing a Big Mac, with a glance at a jeep pulling toward us, our driver forgot his momentary commitment to our safety, comfort and peace of mind. He resumed his sport of racing other jeeps in the

172

sand. "Maybe his favorite movie is *Smokey and the Bandit*," I offered, in an effort to distract everyone from their concern for our safety. It didn't work; no one laughed. Fortunately, the buses were just ahead of us, and we arrived safely.

We drove back to Aqaba. As we drew near the ship, I saw the world's second-largest flagpole, so tall it has a red blinking aircraft-warning light fastened to the tip. It will be good to be back home and see the Stars and Stripes again, I thought. With everything going on politically in the world, there have been times I have felt ashamed of our flag. But after seeing all these different countries, seeing all the different flags, I look forward to seeing the familiar red, white and blue. Despite our many problems, I remain grateful to be a citizen of the United States from birth.

Once again a red carpet was rolled from the gangplank to greet us, the Nautica band played "Bye, Bye, Blackbird," ship staff flanked either side of the red carpet and greeted us as we made our way along the carpet and up the stairs home. The Oceania tradition of greeting returning guests in this manner is a fine one; it reinforces the feeling of coming home and making those who missed you happy simply by setting your foot in the door. There is an eight-year-old wheaten terrier I love at home with Ty who will be beside himself when I set my foot in our door next Sunday. Whether it is a spouse, a housekeeper, a friend, a babysitter, a child or a dog, it feels good to be greeted warmly when you come home.

When I woke up this morning I could still smell the smoke from last night's campfire in my hair—it was an unforgettable evening in the desert. Today is the first of three remaining sea days, and we are at the tip of the Red Sea. Land is close on both sides—Egypt is off both the port and starboard bow. If the ocean weren't so warm and blue, and the landscape so arid and barren, we could be traversing the Inside Passage from Vancouver to Ketchikan. Tomorrow we transit the Suez Canal, and the day after that we get up at 4:30 a.m. for the trip from Port Said to Cairo. The Pyramids are singing their siren song—I can't believe I finally get to see them.

Dinner tonight in the Grand Dining Room was the best of the cruise. For gourmets, there were caviar and foie gras for appetizers, and for the rest of us beef Wellington, lobster, monkfish and savory handmade pasta. I tried the caviar, and it didn't taste any better now than it did the last time on Silversea. At least this time I didn't have to wear my tuxedo. I told my mom I was going to try caviar again since it was on the menu and my tastes might have changed.

"When you're my age you'll know when you don't like something," she wisely said as she enjoyed her fruit appetizer.

I ordered the Manjari chocolate passion-fruit volcano for dessert. It is a perfect dark-chocolate pyramid with a white-chocolate center served with an eye-opening, tart passion-fruit reduction sauce on the side. I chose how sweet or how tart each mouthful is by harmoniously mixing the dark and white sweet chocolate with the tangy fruit sauce. If Ty and I ever get married, it is what I want to serve our guests.

Not even Oceania can control everything, and tonight the gods smiled on us. During dinner, the sun set in a vivid orange ball of fire just off the forward port dining-room window. As the last glimmer of the sun sank in the blue ocean, and the dining room reverted from the bright orange glow of the sun to the traditional glow of incandescent lights, the full moon was rising on the aft starboard side. As the daylight faded, the moonbeams grew brighter, cutting a wide swath as they danced across the rippled waves of Nautica's smooth wake. From my dining-room table located center stern on the window, I enjoyed the ageless, beautiful tango of the sun and full moon on the Red Sea, while relishing the fine company of just my mother and father.

Back in the cabin, at the foot of my bed lay a personalized certificate stating I had successfully completed the Hong Kong to Athens cruise and traveled 9,162.5 nautical miles, along with an announcement that I'm the newest member of the Oceania Club.

Thanks for traveling with me this far. It has been a perfect trip filled with calm seas, sunny skies, exotic ports, and stimulating company both here onboard Nautica and with all of you.

scdreamer   *May 1st, 2007, 03:30 PM*

What perfect timing for your latest post to arrive, Jack. I was just getting ready to take a lunch break and thought I'd check CC to see if there were any interesting posts. When I saw that you had just posted, I knew right away I was going to have an enjoyable lunch today!

As corny as it may sound, I almost feel as if I know you personally now…I so appreciate your philosophical musings—they complement the descriptions of your travels perfectly.

(A small suggestion—if you have never read much of the Old Testament in the Bible, as I haven't—you may enjoy reading the book The Red Tent *by Anita Diamante. Much of the historical story takes place in ancient Egypt—and after I read it, I found a Bible and looked up the obscure verse upon which the story is based. Quite intriguing.)*

Thank you once again for your taking the time to share your experiences…looking forward to "seeing" the Pyramids with you!

Leslie & Wayne

zutalors   *May 1st, 2007, 04:54 PM*
Another fan

Hi, Jack,

First let me say how much I too am enjoying your posts! Funny and warm! I love your "Lumpy" stories, having watched Leave it to Beaver *in my childhood! It is funny how people can start out annoying you and then a glint of something really good shines through just when you feel like you have them pegged.*

There is something magical about travel that makes you see things more clearly and pull away from the little day-to-day worries and get the bigger picture somehow. Having said that—I have realized I am not traveling enough!!!

My husband and I are booked on Insignia Athens to Rome next September for our 25th anniversary, so there's a start! We are going to be in Egypt for two days, so I have been anxiously awaiting your Egypt posts, especially Cairo and the Pyramids!

Thanks again for putting yourself out there…It's all those little anecdotes about how you feel and relate to the passengers, the bus rides, your parents, that make it so good. Keep on writing!

meow!   *May 1st, 2007, 07:22 PM*

While your voyage is 35 days and most world cruises (we have not been on one) are supposed to be 100-plus days, I am sure you have had the most exotic portion of any world cruise! What is left compared to other world-cruise itineraries may be crossing the oceans, the Mediterranean, the Panama Canal, and perhaps the northern edge of Australasia or Japan and China. I believe you must have been to those places before. So in "segments" you have been around the world. I don't think we have the means (in several aspects) to do what you have accomplished! It is nice to read your account; if it were in film, it would be like a National Geographic program.

Aussie Gal   *May 1st, 2007, 07:39 PM*

Jack, I am so sorry your wonderful journey is coming to an end. I have enjoyed reading every word and, as you know, I have printed each episode out, am now up to number 15 to reread many times over the next few months.

I will always think of you on our wedding anniversary and send a silent "Happy Birthday" to you across the thousands of miles separating us.

I hope everything positive works out for both you and Ty and look forward to reading another wonderful saga when you next cruise.

Thanks for taking us with you this time.

                 Jennie

ChatKat in Ca.   *May 2nd, 2007, 12:59 AM*

I wish you and yours a safe journey home to the Stars and Stripes and to Ty and your beloved wheaten.

We experience Nautica next month. I am sure your many comments will replay in our head during our Istanbul to Athens cruise.

Thank you for sharing your cruise and wonderful writings with us.

Lagunaman   *May 2nd, 2007, 02:09 AM*
Thank you, Jack!

I have also been an ardent fan of your superbly composed travelogue, EXTRA especially interesting for me due to my brother and his wife sailing with you.

In fact I had an e-mail this morning, from my sister-in-law, telling me that her writing prowess is incomparable compared to Jack's and to read about their magical visit to Petra, click on to Cruise Critic. I actually do so daily!!!

So thank you for enabling me to follow their journey since seeing them here (unfortunately I nearly caused them to be stranded in Phuket, as Songkran causes horrendous traffic chaos), and I take this opportunity to wish you and your family a very safe journey home and trust that you will continue to post your future travel stories on this site.

Sawadee from the Land of Smiles

P.S. Looking forward to your Cairo report, a long time since I was there.

esther e   **May 2nd, 2007, 02:47 AM**

Jack, rather than getting some much-needed sleep, I sit here at 2:47AM reading your wonderful postings. I have printed out everything and will re-read them often.

I wish you and your family safe travels and pray Ty is well.

I look forward to photos when you post them, also.

Esther

monina01   **May 2nd, 2007, 05:19 AM**

Again what a wonderful post. I cannot believe this journey is soon coming to an end...as I read this last post, I really felt I could see through your eyes and almost smell and hear the surroundings...

Thank you once again...

lahore   **May 2nd, 2007, 06:52 AM**
Sail on, Jack.
The other day I was reading a book called Culture Shock Australia, *thinking of using it with some of our overseas students. One of the first comments for people doing business in Australia was "Don't try to impress an Australian...they are cynical and have well-tuned bull$#!+ meters, and are very hard to impress." As a generalization, I think this is a fair enough comment. But you've impressed this Australian, Jack; you have entertained us, given us a wonderful vicarious travel experience and remained humble throughout both your travels and the well-deserved accolades you have received. Thanks, may the peace and blessings of all the gods of the world be upon you and your loved ones.*

aneka   ***May 2nd, 2007, 09:02 AM***

Hi, Jack,

I have just copied and pasted your wonderful travel notes into a Word document (74 pages so far!), so that I could save it for future reference. What a great diary of a very special trip. Thank you for your personal and warm reflections during this trip. I will look forward to reading the final installments and seeing any pictures you post after you return home.

                                   Annette

PennyAgain   ***May 2nd, 2007, 09:35 AM***

Jack, your writing is magic. Certainly a great pleasure to read and to savor. Today is Wednesday. I have good thoughts going to Ty and wish you a happy homecoming.

I have long wished to visit Petra. You have given me a wonderful tour. My thanks!

Please keep writing when you get home.

Wendy The Wanderer   ***May 2nd, 2007, 10:58 AM***

Really, Jack, you should compile your journal and get it published somewhere. You're a really gifted storyteller.

molomare   ***May 2nd, 2007, 09:28 PM***

Jack, I recently found your postings, while messaging to Lahore. We will be joining them Nov. 24th on our 27-day Nautica cruise Rome to Singapore. I could never put into words the joy I have experienced following your journey. There is so much talent in you, Jack—pathos, humor and a strong sense of the true appreciation of life's privilege bestowed upon you and your family. I, too, feel as if I know you. Thanks for the "head's up" on some of the same ports we will be traveling to. My best regards to your wonderful mom and dad (we are a just a little older than your mom and dad), and prayers for you and Ty.

                           Sincerely, Marcia Neiman

merryecho   ***May 3rd, 2007, 01:41 PM***

Jack, it has been wonderful getting to know you, if only electronically. Isn't it funny how life brings you wonderful things when you are least expecting them? Who knew that on this trip, along with treasured moments with your parents, you would find abundant confirmation that you have a gift for writing? Thank you for sharing some of your most personal thoughts with us, as well as a few details most of us might have left out (O.K., I am talking about the heat-rash powder). This would be the point where you say, "Go, Trojans!" if you went to USC, but as Fairhaven alumnae I don't think we have an equivalent. The only thing close to a motto I remember is "Pass that ____ over here."

Jack's mom—it sounds like Jack gave you his share of gray hairs in his younger days. What a joy it must be to see him grown into a talented, caring person and loving son.

Please keep us posted on Ty's progress; he has the good wishes of many people on his side.

cathi   ***May 3rd, 2007, 04:43 PM***

Jack, I have just spent over two hours reading the last half of this thread!!! It is incredible!!!!! A link was posted on our Roll Call for next year's cruise, and I started to read it a week ago and got tied up with the real world (you know the stuff—work, family, living!). You have an amazing ability to cut to the heart of things. We will surely do some of the things you have talked about in the different ports. Not sure I want to do the Luxor trip after your description but am waiting for the Cairo report. Keep up the incredible work!

Cathi

Chapter 17

PORT SAID AND CAIRO

JackfromWA   *May 4th, 2007, 06:41 AM*
The Pyramids and the Sphinx

> My name is Ozymandias, king of kings:
> "Look on my works, ye mighty, and despair!"
> Nothing beside remains: round the decay
> Of that colossal wreck, boundless and bare,
> The lone and level sands stretch far away.
> —Percy Shelley, "Ozymandias"

Three thirty a.m.: My cabin phone rang from across the dark stateroom. Fumbling in the dark, I finally found it.

"Are you up yet?" my dad asked in a far-too-alert-for-the-hour voice.

"Yep, I am already awake," I lied.

The night before I had ordered a glass of milk from room service to complement the box of cereal and bowl I had stashed from yesterday's breakfast. The milk, cereal and a croissant purloined from the Nautica lounge were my meal. My Prickly Heat Powder and New Balance hiking shoes were on the couch. I had everything prepared before I went to bed, so following my morning ablutions I could sprinkle on the Prickly Heat Powder, put on my shoes and clothes, and get to the bus on time.

The burning of the Prickly Heat Powder was comforting—the multiple sprinkling applications and aftermath have reached the "hurts so good" stage—as I intended to walk around the Pyramids and Sphinx in the intense Cairo heat. The forecast was 100 degrees Fahrenheit: one more blazing-hot shore excursion.

A group of us have commandeered the last bus on the past few shore excursions. By going last we make sure we get to ride together, and it is much easier to make a plan to be last than it is to try to be first. Frank a.k.a. Lumpy and his wife Becka are now part of the group on the last bus. On the trip to Petra and Wadi Rum, they left their camera on the bus with more than 700 pictures (most of their trip), so yesterday I made Frank a DVD-ROM of 1,200 of our pictures.

About 5 a.m., Becka came up and sat behind me for a few minutes to thank me for the photos. I decided to tell her about writing about Frank. The unforeseen popularity of this thread (some passengers have passed parts of it around on the ship, and some fellow guests have come up to me and asked that I write about how expensive the medical doctor is, or that I mention their favorite staff member favorably; I politely explain that I don't have any influence and that they should write it on their comment card) makes it inevitable that some day Frank and Becka will hear about and probably read my portrayal and description of my initial encounters with Frank. So I wanted to address it head on and explain that, though I stand by my writing, if she keeps reading she'll see I slowly realized there is more to Frank than first meets the eye. As the darkness faded and the early light gently lit the desert sky, we discussed my writing, moved on to more interesting topics, and eventually both took naps.

Around seven I needed to use the bathroom. The layout was identical to the bus in Luxor, but when I opened the door I was assaulted by the nauseous smell of warm urine and feces. Most fruit- or vegetable-field outhouses smelled better than the bus latrine. Despite a natural aversion to locking the door and containing the odor, my need for privacy prevailed, and I pulled the door toward me. Just as the latch clicked shut, I was sprayed full on in the face. DAMN IT! I shouted. My glasses were covered with liquid, and my first thought was the sewer pipe was leaking. Instead, I realized I had been hit directly in the face with an automatic battery-operated, totally useless, air-freshener sprayer—this bathroom needed much more olfactory help than any artificial scent could supply. I did my best to remain upright as the bus swayed left to right; the slick floor made traction difficult. Fortunately, my trusted hiking shoes have sure footing, even in urine-drenched floors. I got out of there as quickly as possible—I was trying to hold my breath while peeing—and slammed the door shut behind me.

My mother was holding a small bottle of antibacterial gel that I gratefully rubbed over my hands. Frank was waiting for my reaction as he watched me leap out of the bathroom—he had already been in there—and as my mom squeezed the gel into my hands he enthusiastically nodded his head in approval.

"That is one of the five worst bathrooms I've ever been in. It is nasty!" Frank said as he shuddered in disgust.

If I had rented the bus, I would have demanded a new bus or a refund. The bathroom was unacceptable before we boarded for the trip to Cairo—we were living in the sewage and stench of the previous riders. Word got around quickly, and it was the least-used bathroom I have ever seen on a 3½-hour bus ride.

"Are you starting to wake up?" our perky guide asked over the P.A. system. "So who knows how many pharaohs built pyramids?"

"Why doesn't she just tell us'" Judy, a sleepy fellow passenger, muttered. "I am getting tired of all these guides asking questions. If I knew the answers already I wouldn't need to listen to these fools. I could run the tour myself."

The guide went on with her inane questions and simplistic Cairo & Pyramids 101 lecture. Finally she told us that today each of us were her "special pharaohs" and she was thrilled to serve us. "How do you like that? You are all my pharaohs today," she gushed. I rolled my eyes and gave my mom an I-can't-believe-she-thinks-we-are-this-dumb look. She then proceeded to work the bus aisle with her pitch for cartouche sales—both tour guides I encountered in Egypt wore the most expensive gold cartouche in their catalog and pressured everyone to buy from them—I successfully countered my status as a captive sales audience by shutting my eyes and pretending to sleep.

Around 9 a.m. we reached Sakkara. I knew the pyramids at Sakkara were no match for the Giza Pyramids—going to the Sakkara pyramids after seeing the Giza Pyramids would be as pointless as spending an afternoon at the San Diego Zoo after returning home from a two-week African wildlife safari—but they were even more disappointing than I expected. In hindsight I would rather have gone to the Egyptian Museum and seen King Tut's treasures again, especially since the last time I saw them was on a high school field trip to the old Seattle world's fairgrounds in 1978. In their decrepit state, a few of the pyramids looked like they could have been the remains of a long weekend of heavy backhoe and crane work.

The Temple at Sakkara was more interesting than the small pyramids. It was the first large stone surface I saw in Egypt that is still polished and gleaming. The stone facade of the temple entrance is similar to the smooth, gleaming, rich gold-tinted surface of the cobblestones in Dubrovnik.

Since Frank and Becka didn't have a camera, I volunteered to share today's photos and take their pictures at the Sphinx and the Giza Pyramids. "I want to make one of those crazy David Letterman pictures," Frank said. "You know, a 'HI, MOM!' photo," as he made a funny face while frantically waving his hand. I burst out laughing. Frank is a gifted professional at making entertaining funny faces. I snapped his "Letterman photo" with the small pyramid behind him.

"Hey, Mom," I asked. "Will you take a picture of Frank and me in front of this tomb? Frank and I want to make a funny picture." She obliged, and I knelt down, forced my face into an unnatural smile, and waved like a madman. Frank did the same as my mom snapped away. I showed Frank the results.

"That's great!" he said. "You just wait till we get to the Sphinx. We're going to make a really great picture together there!" It was fun—it felt good to enjoy Frank's company and to be his friend. Since we were getting along so well, I decided I could ask him something personal about his *Leave It to Beaver* days.

"Frank, can I ask you a *Leave It to Beaver* question?"

"Two-eleven Pine," he quickly answered, mistakenly thinking I was testing his trivia recall from the show.

"No," I laughed. "I wanted to know about Mr. Cleaver. When I watched the show, Hugh Beaumont seemed like such a nice man. Was he anything like that in real life?"

Standing in the gloomy, half-lit pharaoh's tomb, Frank's eyes momentarily looked far away, and for a moment he almost seemed misty-eyed.

"Those were wonderful days," he reflected. "Everyone was pretty much like they were on the show. Hugh was a wonderful, wonderful man. He was so good to all of us. It was a special time." As Frank shared a few other memories with me, I thought about what life must have been like for him. He was famous at puberty, and for the rest of his life he was linked to Lumpy's character. His show-business fame was prior to actors' receiving significant residuals for reruns, so unlike the financially-set-for-life cast of *Everybody Loves Raymond* or other successful syndicated shows from the late '80s to the present, Frank and the rest of the actors from *Leave It to Beaver* never earned significant royalties. When the show ended, they were dependent on their own ability to get work. Frank served in the military, became a successful bond trader, married well, and made himself a good life. Unlike so many young actors, Frank avoided the pitfalls of childhood celebrity. A few weeks ago he celebrated his 65th birthday in the Polo Grill, surrounded by some friends and his loving wife. Frank did pretty well for himself, I thought. I respected him, and I appreciated that the 35-day cruise gave me enough time to get past his cantankerous exterior and see some of his warm inner personality.

"Thanks, Frank," I said. "We are going to make an amazing picture at the Sphinx." I joined my parents for a few more photos, and we got on the bus to go to Cairo for lunch.

As we left Sakkara, we passed the Nile Carpet School. It might be interesting to see a school for young people learning to make carpets, I thought. A few hundred yards later I saw the Oriental Carpet School, followed by the Ramses Carpet School, Valley of the Kings Carpet School, Pyramid Carpet School and El Sultan Carpet School—apparently I was in the educational epicenter of carpet schools. I quickly reached the obvious conclusion that the "schools" were contrived tourist attractions. My first clue should have been all the signs written in English instead of Arabic. I changed my mind about wanting to visit them, and I was glad we didn't have to stop.

Riding through the streets, I watched the everyday life of local Egyptians. Litter was rampant, and since air conditioning appeared nonexistent, most doors and windows were open. The building exteriors were mostly concrete adorned with paint faded from the sun. Old wrought-iron grates covered most windows and doors. The street level was mostly businesses with small stores selling vegetables, rice, fruit or Coca-Cola. The upstairs were living quarters. I saw a man pulling an engine from an old car. He had positioned a child's swing set over the hood of the vehicle and attached a heavy chain from around the long bar at the top of the triangular-shaped swing to the dangling engine. It didn't look very safe; engines are heavy. I doubt they have workers compensation insurance or OSHA safety requirements here, I thought.

As our convoy of 11 air-conditioned tourist buses whisked by, jeeps with rifle-toting soldiers positioned at either end, small children waved and locals watched with mild curiosity as the parade of Americans drove past their homes, businesses and mosques.

We arrived at Memphis and saw a 100-ton reclining statue of Ramses II. The detail was beautiful—his chest was rippled with muscles, and his sinewy legs were strong and handsome. Time had taken its toll though. His right side was mostly unscathed, but his left side was pockmarked and mottled—as if stone-eating termites had voraciously attacked his arms and leg. Even a stone statue of Ramses II doesn't last forever—Shelley got it right with "Ozymandias," I mused.

Outside was a statue garden. There was a small stone sphinx, and Frank and I did a rehearsal shot for our big photo in front of the large, famous Sphinx at Giza later that afternoon.

"Come on, my pharaohs, shake a leg," our guide instructed as she attempted to herd us back to the bus. If I hadn't found her silly commentary so funny, she would have annoyed me. "Now we are going to the hotel for lunch, then we will go to the Giza Pyramids and Sphinx."

186

I climbed aboard the bus for the half-hour ride to lunch. I was listening to my iPod when I overheard someone say, "Look! There are the Pyramids." I immediately turned, but our bus moved too fast and I didn't see them. I stared out the window, like a hunter peering from his blind, carefully scanning the horizon for any sign of my Pyramid prey. Trees, buildings and power lines clipped by my window at a rapid pace, but there was no sign of any Pyramids. Momentarily, there was an opening in the line of buildings and trees and, like seeing a fleeting mirage, I caught my first glimpse of the Great Pyramid of Cheops. An electric charge ran down my spine as I exulted in my first glimpse. Scanning even more intently I waited, and then there it was again! No, wait…I see two of them! As quickly as they appeared they were gone. For about a minute, my eyes danced with the Pyramids—they appeared for a moment, and then vanished as the buildings obstructed them from view. My intent focus paid off as we passed a clearing and for a few seconds I could see all three Giza Pyramids in their solitary, ancient glory. There they were! I couldn't believe I was actually seeing them. As we drove to the hotel, we drew closer to the Pyramids. My view improved and soon I was within a quarter mile. I could see that the Pyramids were made of large blocks, and their surface wasn't smooth. We pulled into the Le Meridien Pyramid View Hotel for lunch. I didn't want to eat; I wanted to go to the Pyramids!

"We are going to be here for one hour, then we are going to the Pyramids and Sphinx," our guide told us. I decided to join my parents and friends for lunch. After eating a little rice and potatoes, I announced I was going to go outside and try to find a good view of the Pyramids, and I would meet everyone at the bus.

"Mind if I go with you?" Bill asked.

"Of course not. Let's go check it out," I replied.

A hotel employee took us outside to a balcony, and Bill and I caught our first good look at the Pyramids. We snapped some photos, and Bill went back to join his wife. I grabbed a chair, put on my iPod and just sat there for 20 or 30 minutes. Looking. Thinking. Being at the Pyramids was so surreal that I needed to keep staring at them to convince myself I was really there and not just dreaming. The heat, flies and my dry throat convinced me I was awake and lucid. As the reality of sitting in the shadow of the Pyramids set in, I became overwhelmed with feelings; tears welled up in my eyes. I looked around to make sure no one could see me. After everything I have been through, how did I finally get here? I wondered. The reality of standing in the shadow of the Giza Pyramids humbled me in a way nothing else ever has. Soon, the feeling passed, and a calm wave of gratitude, joy and a desire to go out and play washed over me.

The most significant feature about the Pyramids other than their appearance is their age. If someone could build them today, they would be impressive, but knowing they are thousands and thousands of years old made my mind swim. When I go back home and pick up my life where I left off, the Pyramids will still be here. When Moses left Egypt, when Socrates and Plato lectured in Greece, when Jesus and Mohammed preached, when Richard the Lionhearted was King, when the Mayflower came to America, when Lincoln gave the Gettysburg Address, when Neil Armstrong stepped on the moon, when everyone I have ever loved was born or died, the Pyramids stood here just as they stand here on May 3rd, 2007, just as they will stand here the day I die. They are the silent witness to everything. I recalled something my brother Jeff once said, "When you go on a field trip in third grade to the Pickett House in Bellingham, it seems pretty old. Then, when you go to the East Coast, up to Boston or Philadelphia and see buildings from the 1700s, they seem really old. Then you go to Holland, Germany, France, Italy or England and see things from the 12 and 13 hundreds and that seems pretty old. Finally you go to Greece and see the Acropolis and realize it is thousands of years old. Then you go to Egypt and see the Pyramids, and realize this is it—this is the most ancient manmade monument on Earth." Standing in their shadow, I understood what he meant. I have made the trek and it was worth the effort.

I was enthralled with the Pyramids. I couldn't take my eyes off them. Soon the buses left the hotel, and we made several stops. The first was near the base of the Great Pyramid of Cheops. Despite the haranguing, annoying camel jockeys, postcard sellers and conmen, I was in a childlike state of unbridled bliss—I wanted to do and see everything. My parents and I snapped lots of photos, and we walked completely around the perimeter of the largest, the Cheops Pyramid.

Like most people, I have been socially conditioned to politely reply when asked, "Where are you from?" The conmen around the Pyramids know this, and that is almost always their opening line. One man tried to hand me a "free gift," a rock from the Pyramids, and became upset when I allowed it to drop from his camel and hit the ground. "You pick that up! I gave you a free gift!" he yelled.

"I don't want it. I didn't ask for it. Pick up your free gift yourself," I said.

Another one asked where I was from, and I kept ignoring him. He continued to ask me, and finally I blurted out, "Just go away. I don't want to talk to you. It is against my religion."

He looked at me strangely then grabbed my forearm, dug his uncut fingernails in my flesh and said, "My friend, you are very rude. I just want to know what country you are from." As a whole, the Egyptian and other Arabic people I have met are very hospitable, but the Egyptians hanging out at the base of the Pyramids are not there to make friends—they are there to extract money from tourists using any trick imaginable.

"LET GO OF MY ARM NOW!" I yelled, as I stood as tall, imposing and angry as possible. My glaring eyes said I would fight him if he didn't let go immediately. He let go of my arm, mumbled some incomprehensible insult, and then looked at me with sad, puppy-dog eyes, as if I had hurt his feelings! While I have been taught courtesy by my parents and teachers, courtesy doesn't extend to being bullied, and the riffraff making a living exploiting travelers around the Pyramids are intimidating, rude bullies. If I approached tourists at the rim of the Grand Canyon and asked where they are from, solely to extract money from their pockets, I would rightfully deserve the same rejection the rude conmen loitering around the Pyramids received from me.

The experience of basking in the Pyramids was so intense that I almost immediately let go of my anger, even as I continued to fend off more obnoxious touts while enjoying standing in the intoxicating presence of man's oldest tourist attraction.

We returned to the bus and drove to a bluff where we could take photos of all three Pyramids. The perspective is the same as most of the postcards and photographs I have seen; the sense of déjà vu was uncanny. Although hundreds of people were simultaneously taking pictures, the Pyramids are large enough, and the distance is great enough, that without too much effort everyone got the perfect Pyramid photo to take home. I was trying to get a picture of my mom, dad and me, with the three Pyramids behind us, but an Egyptian man kept inserting himself in the photo to earn some money. I kept making a go-away gesture with my hand, but like an obsessed fly he kept returning. Finally in frustration I blurted out, "Here is a dollar. I am giving this to you to GO AWAY!" He accepted the dollar, stayed 10 feet back, and the Italian and German tourists next to us all laughed. Although he acted as if is feelings were hurt, he kept my money. I think he was all smiles inside.

Our last stop was the Sphinx. Frank and I leaped out of the bus. Birds were nesting all around the Sphinx's head. "I'd like to get a shotgun and get rid of all the birds," Frank volunteered. We both gave our best David Letterman pose, and my parents snapped away. My mom and dad tried to replicate Frank's and my zany picture, but neither of them have Frank's talent for hilarious goofy pictures. I took a few more photos of Frank and Becka, then left with my parents to see the Sphinx up close.

As we were leaving, I wanted to take a few more pictures of my mom, dad, the Sphinx and me. We had the perfect pose, but unfortunately no photographer. An Egyptian postcard salesman offered to take the picture.

"I don't want any money friend," he assured me. I didn't trust him. I have a $2,000 Nikon, the bus was leaving in a few minutes, and though I knew he would probably return the camera, tourist horror stories abound of cameras being held ransom. I told him no thank you, and asked a French tourist to help. The Egyptian man gave me a disgusted look. I genuinely felt bad I had offended him, as I believe he probably would have returned the camera promptly, but in the same circumstances I would do it again.

As we left the last stop, I turned around and stole one last view of the immortal Sphinx prominently seated in front of all three Giza Pyramids.

"Look, Mom, we have been seeing this picture all our lives," I said. It was the perfect view of the Egyptian mystery I have imagined since childhood. We both turned for a moment and took in our last perfect view of the Sphinx flanked by the three Giza Pyramids.

Most everyone fell asleep on the bus. It had been an early morning, and a hot, stimulating day, and a long ride home lay ahead. My mom had carried a small travel pillow and was sleeping on it across the aisle from my dad. My dad was sleeping in the seat in front of me, his head leaned against the hot window glass. I should take a nap too, I thought. I had brought my black Patagonia fleece to use as a pillow, and I stood in the aisle to remove it from the overhead shelf. As I was rolling it into a comfortable pillow ball, I noticed my father again. He was asleep, his head resting on the glass as the bus bounced down the highway

"Dad," I whispered. He didn't move. "Dad," I said a little louder.

He looked up at me with a startled expression. "Here. Use this," I said as I handed him the rolled-up fleece pillow I'd intended to use for myself. "It will be a lot more comfortable then the bus glass."

He nodded his thanks, placed the pillow between his head and the bus window, and nodded back to sleep.

Things are changing, I thought. Every shore excursion my 75-year-old father takes care of my mom and me by carrying a collapsible cooler stocked with water and Diet Coke, distributing little Dutch coffee candies as pick-me-ups, and generously offering to carry our purchases. My mother offers antibacterial gel when I leave germ-infested, foul-smelling lavatories; she has braved Nautica's laundry room to wash my socks and underwear; she offers clean towels when I am sweating, and cool water, granola bars, fruit or candy when I am thirsty and hungry. The ingrained habit of caring for their son runs deep in both of them, and I was pleased that today, for the first time I can recall, instead of taking the pillow I brought for my comfort, I instinctively offered my pillow to my dad for his comfort. My parents and I are in that short, natural span of time when they can still take care of me, and I am just beginning to instinctively take care of them. I hope our balance continues for a long time—I think it will last longer than average, as both of them are in good health and work hard to have alert minds and healthy bodies—as the next evolution is too painful to think about.

When we arrived at the ship, the band greeted us with a resounding version of "When the Saints Come Marching In," and many familiar faces warmly greeted us as we walked up the plank one last time. I turned to Kirk and asked, "Wasn't that the best $139 you ever spent on any shore excursion anywhere in the world?" He nodded in agreement, a smile on his face as he enthusiastically gave me two thumbs up.

Tonight I am having dinner with Sukey, and later I plan to drink too much caffeine and stay up late, wandering Nautica's silent corridors as we make our final approach into Athens. The last day of a cruise is always bittersweet, none more so than this one, as after 35 days I feel like I belong on Nautica. But I have another home beckoning me too. I miss Ty, I miss my friends at home, and I can't wait to walk in the front door, have my dog attack me with his unbounded joy, and hug Ty. It is better to leave the ship while part of me still wants to remain aboard.

Thanks for reading.

*****

Rob & Beckys mom   May 4th, 2007, 08:11 AM
Thanks, Jack
I will miss you and your writings that I look for first thing each morning after signing on to my computer. Have safe flights home and please let us all know that you all made it home safe and sound. Keeping Ty in our thoughts and prayers.

I have enjoyed your cruise so much, and I wanted you to know that I appreciate your taking the time to share it with us all.

Best to you and yours,

Jan

Jack, Ray Solaire and Sukey

Dad winning the Country Faire geography contest

Jack, Carol, Bob and Dave in the Horizons lounge

Most of our trivia team in the Grand Dining Room

A tranquil corner on Nautica

Swimming pool on Nautica

Jack at the entrance to the Temple of Karnak in Luxor, Egypt

Jack, Mom and Dad at King Tut's tomb in the Valley of the Kings

Jack, Mom and Dad at the Treasury in Petra, Jordan

Jack trying to ride a camel in Petra

Sunset at Wadi Rum

Jack, Mom and Dad on the jeep in Wadi Rum

Jack and Frank at the Giza Pyramids

Jack and Frank at the Sphinx

Dad, Mom and Jack at the Sphinx

Mom, Dad and Jack at the Temple of Poseidon near Athens

orchestrapal   ***May 4th, 2007, 08:56 AM***
    Thanks so much for a wonderful account of your trip.
*You made each port and activity so real for those of us waiting to go
on our own journeys.*
    *We leave Sunday for 27 days on Regatta and can't wait to
chronicle our own experiences.*
    *Enjoy all your memories of a great trip, and thank you for
sharing them with us.*

Emdee   ***May 4th, 2007, 02:12 PM***
Letter to FDR
Dear Frank,
    *Like many readers of this wonderful travelogue I think that you
should do something special for Jack. A lot of us have been so
inspired by his journeys that we will be traveling on Oceania—in
fact I have myself booked two cruises. A wonderful cruise or two for
Jack and Ty with the promise of a another travelogue…Travels with
Jack…would be a nice treat for both Jack and Ty as well as a
rewarding read for his many fans.*
    *Alternatively, I am sure you can arrange for one of the travel
magazines to buy his slightly rewritten episodes complete with
pictures of the journey as well maybe as a series.*
    *For any writer the reward of writing is the enjoyment of his
readers, and I know Jack has had plenty of that…something more
tangible would be nice as well.*
                                        Miriam

Saga Ruby   ***May 4th, 2007, 02:14 PM***
My two-cents' worth about Egypt
    *Several people have talked about their upcoming repo cruises on
the itinerary of what we all now think of as "Jack's Trip." Herewith
are my personal experiences with the vendors at the Giza Plateau,
which were similar to Jack's encounters.*
    *Last December at the Pyramids, my guide and I were talking
about the history of the Great Pyramid when a postcard vendor
walked up to us. I bought a set of 12 cards and was turning away
when the man "gave" me a tiny foil-wrapped pyramid and an Arab
headdress wrapped in plastic. "Free gift for you! Free gift for you!"
I was prepared mentally for these tactics before I ever got to the
Giza Plateau, so I shook my head and walked away.*
    The vendor pursued me, taking the cheap headdress out of the

plastic, assembling it, and then suddenly jamming it onto my head. I was silently furious that a Muslim male would touch a woman like that when it is contrary to every cultural tenet in Islam and a telling sign of disrespect.

I whirled around, took off the headdress, and told the vendor I would give him one American dollar to leave me alone. He agreed. Throughout this entire episode, my female guide was saying, "Shukrun, shukrun," which is "Thank you." It was her sole defense against the male hawker's aggressive tactics. In Giza, it was money before courtesy, greed above all.

I could guess that the hawkers and vendors have a quota to fill each day, which goes to their managers who own the sales permits at the Pyramids. The local attitude must be that we tourists are there for a few hours; the vendors are there for eternity.

As Jack put it so well, one is overwhelmed just to be walking amongst the sands of ancient history, even if only for a brief moment in time. I can tell you that in December there was no heat at all and I was surprised at the sparse numbers of international tourists, although there were busloads of Egyptian schoolchildren visiting the Plateau. Fortunately, I never had problems with aggressive tour guides or bus drivers pushing their personal agendas for sales commissions.

Back onboard Nautica, a couple mentioned that they had bought a camel ride at the Pyramids and wore Santa hats to have photos made for their Christmas cards back home. I asked how much the ride cost and they said it was $10 to ride, then "$150 to get back down!"

I now know that I'm glad I sailed on the eastbound repo. Those first few days in Cairo and then Luxor overnight were thrilling for me, yet exhausting. What a treat it was later onboard Nautica to sit front and center in Horizons and watch in complete comfort as we transited the Suez Canal. That transit was a good "R&R" break that made me eager for Muscat, Dubai, and the many wonders to follow.

Jack's empathy, humor, gentility, sense of adventure, and finely detailed, personal reports have brought us all such great pleasure. Reading his posts was like watching those cliffhanger serials at the Saturday matinee. We are sad for "our" journey to end but happy for Jack as he turns westward toward home and his loved ones.

Thanks, Jack.

Ruby

SeaCCruiser   *May 4th, 2007, 03:20 PM*

Jack, Eddie Haskell (Ken Osmond) was just on television a few nights ago talking about his ongoing friendship with Frank, and I think he said Frank is his stockbroker. It was so nice of you to replace their lost photos.

Thank you so much for regaling us with your insightful and entertaining posts!

Hondorner   *May 4th, 2007, 03:50 PM*

Thanks, Jack. I enjoyed every report. I'll think of you often when we follow in your footsteps next year. I always thought of myself as introspective, but your sensitivity to deeper meanings will be an inspiration for me.

Lauren Spray   *May 5th, 2007, 12:11 AM*
Thank You

Jack, thank you for sharing your wonderful journal. I enjoyed seeing the ports through your eyes. Best of all, you shared a part of yourself. That is what made reading your writing so memorable. I will be traveling on the same cruise as "lahore" and "molomare." I was excited before, but now I can't wait for the experience.

I hope Ty gets a good report from his biopsy. He is in my thoughts and prayers.

Lauri

carolhardy   *May 5th, 2007, 05:32 AM*
Many thanks

Hi, JackfromWA,

Just a quick note from CarolfromUK

I just have to write to thank you so much for all your wonderful posts from your trip. I have eagerly switched on my machine every morning and read all your reports and enjoyed them so much. I felt that I was there too on the trip. We were in Luxor just three weeks ago, and your power of description is so good that I felt I was there again.

We are booked on Oceania in October. I was a bit nervous about the cruise line as it's not that well known here in the U.K., but now I just can't wait and from your descriptions I know we are going to have a wonderful time.

Jack, thank you so much for taking the time to share your travels here on this board. You have given so many people a great deal of pleasure, and I for one will miss my morning read. Have a safe journey home.

Kind regards,
Carol

merryecho   **May 5th, 2007, 12:51 PM**
Jack, if you don't post those photos of you and Lumpy at the Sphinx I will never forgive you.

cathi   **May 5th, 2007, 01:09 PM**
Jack, I just have to tell you that I love your writing. When you get home and put together the journal with your photos you will have an amazing memory of this fantastic journey. Just think when you finally end up in that "rest" home you can pull out that book and relive it all over again!! I sincerely hope you have several more trips with your parents, and I do understand your mention of the changing over from child to parent, from their looking after you to your looking after them. So glad you can enjoy and recognize the significance of all this. It is what makes your writing so meaningful to so many of us. THANKS and please may we have one last page!
Cathi

Twiga   **May 5th, 2007, 01:13 PM**
Jack, I loved your description of seeing the Pyramids. Your words brought back the feelings of wonder and amazement that I felt when I saw them many years ago. I loved reading about taking funny photographs with Frank. I hope you will post them when you return home.

Reading about giving your father your fleece on the bus was touching. I will miss reading about your wonderful parents.

I had tears in my eyes as I read about your last day on the cruise. I hate to see it end. I have enjoyed reading your journal these past weeks. Please write and let us know how Ty is doing. He is in our hearts and prayers.

Thanks for such an enjoyable journey.
Nancy

Chapter 18

ATHENS AND HOME

JackfromWA   *May 6th, 2007, 12:15 PM*
Walking the plank

I made plans to enjoy my last supper with my first Cruise Critic friend, Sukey. Since I despise packing up my cabin and can't bear to imagine the interlopers who will shortly occupy my stateroom, I packed early so I didn't feel I was under an impending deadline. I completed one suitcase the day before Cairo—after 33 days I easily filled it with exactly 70 pounds of souvenirs, clothes I wouldn't wear till I got home, and dirty laundry. My parents are staying in London for a few nights, followed by a week in Holland before arriving back to Seattle in 10 days. I am flying directly home from Athens. The baggage weight limitations are confusing, as I cashed in a little over 400,000 American Airline miles (Christmas came early for Mom and Dad) and got all three of us first-class One World alliance plane tickets. International first class is great, but unfortunately we are on American Airlines home instead of British Air. American allows only two bags in first class, BA allows three bags, and since I am flying BA from Athens to London and AA from London to Chicago to Seattle, I was hoping the BA allowance would apply. Both AA and BA reservation agents said that I could take only two, and I was limited to 50 pounds each, but I could pay an extra $25 per bag to increase the weight of each suitcase from 50 to 70 pounds.

Since I was flying into London Heathrow from Athens on Saturday, however, and didn't leave for the United States until early Sunday morning, I am required to claim my bags in London and pay both BA and AA for the extra weight. If I were transferring the same day, I would pay only once. I was annoyed by the airlines' seemingly unfair and inconsistent policies. I stressed about the luggage before the trip, I stressed about this as my souvenirs piled up under my bed, above my closet, and in the cabin drawers during the early days of the cruise, but I quit worrying about it by mentally budgeting several hundred dollars toward luggage. Since the tickets were paid by miles instead of cash, my total cash outlay wasn't too much, and I wanted to end my anxiety about getting my luggage home. I weighed my bags on the last sea day, as they can't exceed 70 pounds each. I carried my suitcases in the elevator up to the Nautica gym where a set of doctor's scales is located. I wasn't alone—at least six other passengers were weighing their bags too. It was almost certainly the most use the oft-ignored scales received the entire cruise. Coming down in the elevator, a fellow passenger and his wife noted my luggage.

"Are you moving out today?" he asked with a smile. He thought it was funny since today is a sea day.

"No, I can't swim with this. It is too heavy. We'd both sink. I was up using the scales in the gym," I replied.

"Were you weighing yourself there then?" he asked in a further vain attempt to be humorous.

With a look of amused shock I replied, "Are you kidding! I am not going anywhere near any scales until I am off this boat at least two weeks. I was weighing the suitcase."

"I know, I know. I was kidding," he answered.

His slightly rotund wife lightly punched him on the arm, looked me in the eye and said, "I am with you, honey, except I am waiting two months before I step on a scale. You keep waiting, and I will too," she said as she hustled her husband off the elevator.

When I mentioned my luggage anxiety to Sukey, she told me she doesn't worry about it. She uses a luggage service and has her luggage waiting for her when she arrives. It's expensive, but the ease and reduced stress is worth it to her. We enjoyed a wonderful dinner, swapped stories, laughed, gossiped, shared memories, made genuine plans to keep in touch and, far too soon, our ice cream bowls and my coffee cup were empty and it was time to leave the Grand Dining Room.

"I really want to get a picture of you and your parents," Sukey said. They were sitting close by, so we went to their table—they were having their last dinner with Nancy, Sandy and Bill—and Sukey took a few pictures. As she hugged my mom good-bye, I saw tears welling in Sukey's eyes. "You have a wonderful son," she told my mom and dad. I felt a lump in my throat, I hugged her, and she left.

Until now I have never felt sadness from abandoning friends at the end of a cruise. I have felt a sense of sorrow for the loss of fine dining, attentive service and free time, but not from having to say good-bye to my fellow passengers. The difference on this cruise is that after a month, bonds form, friendships develop and too soon— 35 days isn't long—our memorable time together ends. Because we had so much time to choose what we wanted to do, and who we wanted to share experiences with, I spent more time over 35 days with a few new friends than I spend at home with some of my friends over the course of a year. My mom went to a lecture about future Oceania cruises, and toward the end a video of crewmembers was shown. "I actually had a few tears," she said, surprised by the depth of her feelings. "That's never happened to me at the end of a cruise before." My mom wasn't the only one. I heard that several passengers cried during the video, and all during our last day I witnessed and shared in hugs, kisses, tears and heartfelt farewells.

After dinner I went to the lounge to check my e-mail but couldn't get a thing done. The Warsaw String Quartet kept repeating "Time to Say Good-Bye" on the balcony above our heads, and fellow passengers I barely knew kissed me or shook hands good-bye. Friends and acquaintances I did know kept stopping by for one last visit. Even though I couldn't get anything done, I didn't mind. Frank wandered by, and he gave me his business card as we exchanged good-byes; he had generously given me a personally autographed photo earlier in the day in thanks for the photos. Eventually I decided to go to the computer room, thinking it would be quiet, as I needed to look up something on the British Air site, and the reception area was too emotional and busy. Even there I ran into a friend—the only other person in the room—and on the last night of the cruise we talked and said good-bye.

I called Ty; his biopsy has been rescheduled for next week. I tried to let go of my anger and frustration about that, then I wandered the halls, bid as many crew and passengers as I could good-bye, and finally went to bed. When I woke at 7 a.m. my cabin was bare. The suitcase elves had worked tirelessly through the night, and the ship corridors were free of luggage. After showering and dressing, I looked around my constant cabin. It has been a cozy sanctuary for what felt longer than 35 nights, but with my silver elephant from Goa, computer, travel books, hiking shoes, Prickly Heat Powder and clothes gone, it was time for me to vacate too. I walked out and went upstairs with my parents for breakfast at Terraces before leaving. Stu and Jan were there, so I was able to say good-bye to both of them one last time. Our need to depart was loudly announced over the ship P.A. system. Our cruise was over, and it was time to walk the plank.

Feeling melancholy, I handed the security guard my white room-key card so he could record my final exit. As he handed it back, he smiled and said, "Hope to see you again soon, Mr. Jacob," (my legal first name is Jacob; my nickname is Jack). I smiled back, feeling slightly better due to his friendly gesture, and walked outside.

To my great surprise, the captain, Jurica Brajcic, was standing at the bottom of the gangway, wearing a light windbreaker and a smile—at least when Nautica forces you to walk the plank, her captain greets you on the way down. When I stepped off the gangplank and on to Greek soil for the first time, he looked me in the eye, firmly gripped my hand and said, "Thank you for sailing with us. It was a pleasure to have you aboard. We hope to see you again soon." What a nice gesture, I thought. So often it is the little things that matter. If a fantasy genie gave me a choice between a free week on Oceania's Nautica and a free week on Regent's Mariner, I would choose Nautica—even though Nautica is less expensive and has much smaller standard cabins. The little things have made all the difference; Mariner offers a great vacation, but Nautica now feels like coming home.

We were directed to the port, and I saw the Silver Cloud again. She arrived in Athens today too. We went to retrieve our luggage, and I noticed some port baggage carts near them. I grabbed one, and a Silversea crewperson approached me.

"Excuse me, were you on Silversea?" she asked—knowing full well I wasn't, as they have only a few hundred passengers and she would have recognized me if I had been one of their guests.

"No, I am from the Nautica," I replied. It would have been hard to attempt lying to her as I was wearing a navy blue golf shirt with OCEANIA CRUISES/NAUTICA proudly embroidered above my heart.

"These carts are reserved for Silversea guests," she scolded me. I wanted to kick her ass. I am a past Silversea guest and know she shouldn't be treating any passenger from any ship with a condescending attitude.

"Actually, they aren't. They belong to the port, you just decided to move them here, and then attempted to control them. Since they don't belong to you or Silversea any more than they belong to Oceania or me, I am taking this one. You can complain to the port if you like, but I think you are on shaky ground and I don't believe they'll care."

Her mouth hung open in surprise as I wheeled the cart away. How stupid, I thought. Does Silversea really want to alienate potential customers? An Oceania crewperson would have helped a struggling disembarking Silversea passenger load their luggage on a cart. Frank Del Rio, CEO of Oceania, knows how to earn customer loyalty and he makes sure his crew help maintain the line's well-deserved reputation for unfailing service.

Our driver was holding our last name on a sign as we exited the secure area. My brother was in Greece a few weeks ago. He will be at the U.S. Embassy for three years, beginning in August. He had tracked down a good company to pick up our parents and me and take us on a tour before dropping us off at the airport for our 7 p.m. flight to London. Jeff warned the tour company that we had been traveling for more than a month and had six large suitcases, three carry-ons and possibly a few other items. He specifically told them not to send a standard limousine or sedan. They believed him, as our driver pulled up in a 17-passenger Mercedes bus. It was so big that all our luggage comfortably fit in the gargantuan trunk. It was expensive (we paid a little over 400 euros), but it included an all-day tour and guaranteed arriving at the airport on time, luggage intact, with no transportation hassles.

My enthusiasm for the shore excursion was subdued. I didn't want to go to the airport after an all-day tour; I wanted to return to my cabin. Despite having never been to Athens, I felt too glum to enjoy the excitement of more stimulating new sights. In the past seven days, I had visited Luxor, Petra, the Sphinx and the Giza Pyramids, all for the first time. Athens deserved better than my morose attitude. I attempted to put on a happy face, but taking a tour immediately after leaving Nautica felt like attending a wedding the day after a funeral for a friend. The sadness of the end of the cruise weighed too heavily on me, and my parents' cheerful banter annoyed me—I knew it was my problem, not theirs—so I put on my iPod and tried to work through my feelings. Looking at it now—from 30,000 feet en route to London, both my parents sleeping across the aisle—I have a bit more perspective.

My sadness wasn't rooted in the end of a vacation, saying good-bye to new acquaintances and friends, or the loss of fine dining and egregious pampering. My sadness stems from ending this time with my mom and dad. From here, I go back to my life, they go back to theirs, and though we live in the same town, have dinner at least every week or two, and frequently talk on the phone, we don't live together the way we have for the past 35 days. We haven't lived together like that in decades.

"We haven't eaten so many meals together consecutively since I moved away from home," I told my mom at breakfast this morning. Having this time together was a chance to go home again, to live with my parents in a world constructed from our combined hopes, desires, foibles and dreams. It was a nostalgic happy time. Today it ended. Soon I will feel good again, I'll appreciate the time with them as they appreciate the time they spent with each other and me, but I don't let go of grief and loss too quickly.

I spent my later childhood, teenage and early adult years trying not to feel anything—the emotion-suppressing, half-human, half-Vulcan Spock from the original *Star Trek* series was my role model, Pink Floyd's *The Wall* was my favorite album—but today I savor my feelings. I learned the hard way that working through them is one of the healthiest ways to take care of myself—it connects me with my loved ones, as well as the acquaintances whose lives brush mine. No matter how rich, painful, overwhelming or joyous the emotions, they eventually pass. In their wake I consistently find I have learned, grown and become a healthier, wiser, emotionally balanced content soul.

It is a reality of human emotion that my feelings about the loss of the familiar lifestyle I enjoyed with my mom and dad on Nautica motivated me to briefly withdraw from them, when their regular behavior—that I've mostly enjoyed the entire trip—annoyed me today. It's silly to miss someone before they are gone, yet unavoidable separations usually cut the deepest. It is hard to start healing until the person you love goes away.

Our guide Dmitri was superb. He drove us to the Olympics Stadium, safely and efficiently negotiated our 17-passenger bus through Athens traffic, and offered to stop whenever a photo opportunity arose. Since my brother is going to work at the Athens embassy, we wanted to drive by. As we drew near, I noticed a large American flag waving in the cool Mediterranean breeze. Just to the right of the flagpole was a 10-foot-diameter seal featuring the familiar, imposing eagle, identifying the building as the Embassy of the United States of America. I wanted to take a better picture than I could get through the bus window—I thought it would be fun to e-mail my brother and show him we had taken the time to go there—so I asked the guide to stop.

I pulled out my camera and quickly snapped five or six photos of the flag, seal and embassy. My photography instantly caused a small commotion. The Greek policeman stationed outside the building frantically motioned us over in a no-nonsense manner.

"Mom, you'd better hand me my passport," I said. The driver, following the policeman's hand gestures, made an illegal U-turn so the security guards could question me. Putting on my best American-in-Greece face, I exited our bus with a smile, handed the policeman my passport and politely explained I was an American citizen visiting Greece and wanted a picture of the U.S. flag and seal. They copied my name, passport number and birth date and asked me to retrieve my camera to delete all the photos. While they looked over my shoulder I removed all my pictures of Old Glory waving in the breeze and the Seal of the United States of America attached to my homeland's embassy. I wasn't angry. With all the terrorist threats in the world, I understand they are trying to protect people like my brother who bravely work in overseas embassies, but I am sad that the violence in the world makes taking a picture of my flag at an embassy a security risk.

Our next stop was the residence of the Greek prime minister and the Greek Parliament. We were encouraged to take all the photos we wanted. A major tourist attraction and photo opportunity is a military ceremonial guard stationed directly in front of the Parliament building who stands still as a Foot Guard outside Buckingham Palace and rotates hourly.

We went to the Temple of Zeus, a pleasant, grassy stop where I snapped photos of the tall, imposing Greek columns, then made our way to the Acropolis and roamed around at the top. It is impressive, drenched in history and imagination, but the thousands of teeming, pushy fellow tourists, the effort required to get good photos, the detracting scaffolds surrounding the Parthenon and my improving but still despondent mood, made the visit less than I expect it to be when Ty and I come visit my brother and his family here.

We ate lunch at a restaurant in a trendy beach area where Starbucks, Marks & Spencer, Armani and Benetton Stores intersect with style-conscious locals and tourists. Dad, Mom and I all wanted to have Greek food, so we passed by the Applebee's, Pizza Hut, Starbucks and hamburger joints and found a promising little Greek restaurant. The proprietor was friendly, the menus were in Greek and English, and soon we had ordered chicken gyros and kebabs. To avoid any confusion, we pointed directly to the items we wanted on the menu, and when they arrived the servings were large and the food well prepared. We had to meet the guide at 12:30, so at 12:15 I signaled for the bill.

"How much do you think it will be?" my mom asked.

"It should be about 15 euros, three apiece for the meals, three for the Coke Light, and there could be a table or service charge," my dad said.

When the bill arrived, it was 25 euros. The proprietor deceitfully charged us for chicken gyro and kebab *plates*—which are each an additional four euros apiece and were listed on a different page than the selections we made. We clearly identified through finger pointing exactly what we wanted. I confronted him with his dishonest culinary upgrade. His friendly personality disappeared and he shrugged his shoulders, blandly turned his back on us, and walked away. We decided to pay for the meal. Time was short, and a 10-euro fight didn't feel like it was worth the effort to any of us that day, but we left no tip.

The next two hours were the best of the day. My brother had instructed the tour company to drive us outside of Athens along the coastline. The Mediterranean scenery was sublime; blue oceans, traditional and modern Greek homes, lush vegetation. After the coastline of Egypt it looked like Eden. We drove about an hour and eventually arrived at our destination, the Temple of Poseidon. The entry charge was four euros each with a two-euro discount for senior citizens. Since both my parents are over 65, my dad wanted his discount.

"Two senior citizens and one adult, please," my dad told the old woman at the small ticket stand.

She looked at him skeptically. "Where do you come from?" she asked in halting English.

"The Netherlands," Dad answered. Since he was born in Holland, his answer was accurate enough to deserve the senior-citizen discount that he quickly ascertained was granted only to travelers from other European Union countries. I was proud of his sharp response. The ticket seller grudgingly handed him two discounted senior-citizens' tickets, along with the standard adult ticket for me.

The temple had a few—maybe 30—tourists visiting. It sits atop a colorful rocky promontory with a generous 180-degree view of the surrounding sea. If Poseidon had chosen it himself, I can't imagine choosing a better site. The actual temple looked similar to the columns at the Temple of Zeus or those at the Acropolis, but the isolated, picturesque location and relative lack of crowds made it a much more memorable stop. I saw a young couple kissing near the temple, the ocean waves crashing on the shores below the hill behind them, and I envied their young, passionate love. It was a good place to be romantic, a natural place to kiss. Their Greek ancestors would approve, I thought. I felt good again—I wanted someone to kiss me in the shadow of Poseidon's Temple, so I could feel more of the romance pouring from the sky, ocean and Grecian columns. My slight depression had passed, and I was glad my brother had sent us to Poseidon's Temple. After spending 35 fair, sunny, calm days on and over the world's oceans, the least I owed Poseidon was a brief visit. Now that I had thanked the God of the Seas, I was ready to fly home.

The drive to the airport took a little over an hour. Despite all the consistent information to the contrary, from both British Air and American Airlines, when I checked in, the pleasant woman from British Air didn't charge me anything for extra weight, and to my unexpected and delighted surprise, she successfully checked my two 70-pound suitcases all the way to Seattle. I won't see them again until I clear U.S. Customs in Chicago, sometime tomorrow afternoon. I completed the U.S. Customs Clearance Form, and Question 8 asked what countries I visited since I left the U.S. I suppressed a burst of laughter. Chuckling inside, I wrote down the following in chronological order: Hong Kong (SAR), China, Vietnam, Thailand, Singapore, India, Oman, Egypt, Jordan, Greece and the U.K. The list didn't fit on the two lines provided, so Greece and the U.K. ended up in the margin.

So the trip is over. New guests now occupy Stateroom 4024. New passengers are enjoying their first meals in Toscana, Polo Grill and the Grand Dining Room. The crew are trying to adapt to a new group of travelers—they'll be successful, they are a well-oiled and polished machine—sometime tonight I'll say good-bye to my mom and dad until I pick them up at Seattle Tacoma International Airport in a little over a week, and sometime tomorrow I'll walk in my front door, embrace Ty, deal with Rusty's unbridled canine enthusiasm at our reunion, and Stewart will eventually come sit in my lap and greet me in his feline fashion.

Of course, that leaves each of you. I don't want to say good-bye to any of you any more than you want to say good-bye to me. It has been a journey for all of us, and on some level none of us traveling together ever wanted it to end. A few of you pioneered this trip on Oceania before me, many more of you will follow in my footsteps, and some of you will simply enjoy it through the magic of the written word.

I have always wanted to be a writer. Now I am. If I never write another word, I will always carry the unanticipated joy of knowing that with practice, inspiration, good teachers, wonderful reader feedback and the unmerited favor of a little talent, I was able to help some of you, my unmet friends across cyberspace, laugh, cry, feel joy and nostalgia and through our shared thoughts and feelings communicate some of what I have learned,

One of my favorite authors, Richard Bach, sent me a postcard in 1982. I had interviewed him for the Whatcom Community College newspaper. In part the postcard—which still hangs on a special place in my home—reads, "Your article captured the spirit of our time together beautifully. We are guided through difficult times for a reason, and yours we'd guess is to communicate what you've learned." I have moved many times since his postcard reached me at a 28-day treatment center for drug addiction and alcoholism, and after 17 years of continuous abstinence, many years of learning to live as a person of integrity, and 44 years of waking up each day on our shared planet, I believe that I have finally learned some lessons worth sharing.

I have developed the self-esteem necessary to open myself to the criticism that often comes from sharing the Truths that I've discovered. I have learned that someone else's is not necessarily mine, nor is mine always theirs. Some are deeply personal, and though sometimes we get to share them—which is especially nice when it is with someone we love—other times we live with and love people whose Truths are different than ours.

I believe love and tolerance allow us to bridge the gap when our deep personal Truths threaten to separate us from those we choose to be close to. I know that is how my mom, dad and I try to negotiate our own different beliefs—which, like many other children and parents, at times have threatened to irreparably separate us.

I still make lots of mistakes, false assumptions and bad conclusions—just look at how I initially judged Frank a.k.a. Lumpy—but that doesn't negate the Truth that I finally have learned a few things worth passing on. I hope that in the many pages I wrote about this journey on Nautica with my parents that you discovered something that made your life a little happier, your time spent reading a little more pleasant. And whether it was an insightful Truth, or just some ideas of how to make your own travels better, I feel privileged to have shared this time and space with you. For those of you reading this who were on the trip with me (I know some of you are out there), I hope it brings back some of the wonderful memories of our trip together on Nautica. Everyone's heartfelt words for Ty's good health, encouragement to keep writing, and the hundreds of loving, friendly comments you posted have brought great joy and new wisdom to me—and I wish the same rewards to each one of you.

I will write a follow-up—and I'll reply to everyone who has recently posted questions or comments since I last did so—when I am settled home in Bellingham, Washington. Despite an incredibly competent and loyal staff, I have several feet of mail stacked on or around my desk, hundreds of work-related e-mails, numerous phone calls, and over 3,000 photos from this trip to look through. Like all of us who traveled from Hong Kong to Athens on Nautica, I'll be busy for a few days. I'll update everyone on Ty's tongue biopsy as soon as we have the results. That's a promise. We both appreciate your prayers and thoughts. I'll get a few pictures up soon, along with a link; that's a promise too. Until then I want to leave you with the words of Robert Frost, which I unexpectedly discovered in Whatcom Middle School's library many years ago while reading S.E. Hinton's *The Outsiders*. It captures the brief time on Nautica with my parents perfectly.

> Nature's first green is gold
> Her hardest hue to hold.
> Her early leaf's a flower;
> But only so an hour.
> Then leaf subsides to leaf.
> So Eden sank to grief,
> So dawn goes down to day.
> Nothing gold can stay.
> > —Robert Frost, "Nothing Gold Can Stay"

Thanks for reading. God bless.

*****

Marebear   **May 6th, 2007, 05:36 PM**
I am totally amazed by the marvelous insights you shared with all of us and the fantastic trip you took us through! Thank you seems so insignificant—I will never forget the voyage—Dankeshoen, merci and gracias!

merryecho   **May 6th, 2007, 06:01 PM**
Can somebody get me a Kleenex?

Magicnelly   **May 6th, 2007, 08:43 PM**
"Don't be dismayed at good-byes. A farewell is necessary before you can meet again. And meeting again, after moments or lifetimes, is certain for those who are friends."
> *—Richard Bach*

Rob & Beckys mom   **May 6th, 2007, 09:42 PM**
WOW!
That was a great ending, Jack. Thanks so much for taking so much of your time to keep us entertained. So much of yourself can be felt and seen through your words. Our son has 3½ years clean and

sober; he now works at the treatment center where he spent four months. God really does work miracles.

Jan

scdreamer   ***May 7th, 2007, 01:07 AM***

You have conveyed your feelings so clearly that I am feeling them, too. Thank you so much for taking the time to share your experiences and your impressions with us.

Because our upcoming October cruise begins in Athens, I was gratified to read what you had written about your short time there.

And you have definitely inspired us to dream of future journeys to so many other destinations with your lovely portraits in words.

Yes, you are *a writer. And a damn good one at that!*

Thank you so very much!

Leslie & Wayne

(P.S. We are sending positive thoughts for Ty's biopsy—all the best to both of you)

Twiga   ***May 7th, 2007, 01:33 AM***

Wow, Jack! What an amazing end to your journey. I had tears in my eyes reading your previous posting. This one really had me choked up! I could feel how hard it was for you to leave the Nautica. But I know that you left some good energy onboard, though, that I will feel when I board the Nautica in September. This will be my first cruise on Oceania, and you have already made the Nautica feel like home to me.

My husband and I have planned to visit the Temple of Poseidon when we are in Athens. Now it will be even more special knowing how it affected you. I will remember what you said about the kiss at the Temple!

Thank you for your wonderful writing. You have touched so many of us readers. The end of your journey was also the end of ours—no more installments of Jack's cruise to look forward to. Reading your last posting was like reluctantly having to finish an especially enjoyable book. Keep up the writing!

I am looking forward to hearing about your homecoming and also hearing how Ty is doing.

From a fellow back-of-the-bus traveler,

Nancy

PennyAgain   *May 7th, 2007, 01:48 AM*
It comes down to this…
>   *BRAVO!*
>   *Blessings for a long, healthy and happy life!*
>   *My sincere thanks.*

esther e   *May 7th, 2007, 03:27 AM*
>   *Once again I have to thank you, Jack, for the seat I shared next to you on your voyage. Oh, yes, you never saw me, but after reading your wonderful posts I realized I was right there, experiencing everything you did.*
>   *My best wishes to you and Ty, and I pray his biopsy goes well. I look forward to being on a trip with you again in the future.*
>   *Thank you for such a wonderful adventure.*
>   *Esther*

CruisingSerenity   *May 7th, 2007, 02:45 PM*
Thank you, Jack
>   *Thank you for sharing so much with all of us, Jack. I like reading Cruise Critic, but it's just not going to be the same without a new installment of your adventures.*
>   *Man, what a read!*
>   *I still root for you to get a blog.*

Decebal   *May 7th, 2007, 04:36 PM*
Welcome home
>   *Welcome home, Jack. I still can't believe we've been reading your wonderful adventures for a whole month. It went by as fast for us as it passed for you. Looking forward to the pictures, and thanks for sharing your experiences.*
>   *Thanks to you, I know now, that as mad as I am to see Luxor, sit my bottom on a Pyramid block, and blow a kiss at the Sphinx, I will not do it through a rushed two-day ship excursion.*

jckvpa0   *May 7th, 2007, 07:40 PM*
>   *Thanks for a great thread!!! I just happened to stumble onto it because my sister and DH boarded your ship on Saturday and I thought by some off chance maybe someone would be posting from onboard. Actually I never did look to see if someone was posting because I just couldn't stop reading after I found your thread.*

Once again thank you so much for taking the time to post. Your great description of the beautiful places you have visited has made me rethink my travel plans for the future.

Aussie Gal **May 7th, 2007, 10:10 PM**

Jack, my mornings are not going to be the same again. I have enjoyed waking up and printing out your wonderful posts for the past five weeks, and now that the posts and the journey have come to an end, I feel I have lost a very good friend.

Thanks so much for taking us along with you and letting us see the world through your eyes. My thoughts are with you and Ty and hope everything goes well.

Jennie

cathi **May 8th, 2007, 12:53 AM**

Simply thanks, Jack. It's been wonderful, and words cannot express how I feel after reading your words. I know Ty will be just fine with you by his side. Keep the faith. I only hope my recovering-addict son will grow into as nice a human as you have.

Please keep in touch on this board, as we would love to know what you are going to be doing next.

We have flown first class from Melbourne to the U.S. and back, and it is a wonderful way to travel. We also used frequent-flier points. I wouldn't pay out the money for first class but would for business, which is not that much of a difference, or it isn't on the airlines we fly with, e.g., Qantas, Singapore and Cathay. They also have the lie-down beds, pajamas and good food plus the legroom and width in the seats.

Your parents sound delightful, and you have all been blessed with each other. I have always felt that what you put into your children does come back threefold and more, and you have proved that.

Toranut97 **May 8th, 2007, 02:00 AM**
Vaya con Dios!

Blessings, Jack, to you, Ty and your beloved furry kids in the future! You have so generously shared of yourself during your trip. I have saved all your posts in a file so I can re-read in the future. Thanks for your kindness, sharp vision and insight!

Donna

monina01   *May 8th, 2007, 07:10 AM*

Thanks once again...I already miss your (almost daily) contributions...It was a great way for me to start the day, in the early morning with a cup of tea and this wonderful thread.

I am looking forward to seeing some of the photos you promised you would post.

Isla Gal   *May 8th, 2007, 08:27 PM*

Jack, I've been lurking here for some time reading your travel log, and I just wanted to thank you for sharing your experiences and insights with us. Someday I hope I will get to see the places you visited but, if not, you gave such vivid descriptions in some ways I feel I have already been! And what a gift to spend this time with your parents; my father died young, and I regret not having more quality time with him.

Being a U2 fan myself ("Joshua Tree" is one of my three desert-island disks!) I especially loved how you related "In God's Country" into your journey. If you ever choose to, I think you could give Rick Steves a run for his money!!

*****

JackfromWA   *May 9th, 2007, 03:19 AM*

A FEW (belated-so-I-could-finish-the-story) RESPONSES:

fjdelrio: If you are still reading, I need to thank you. I wasn't expecting my entire Internet to be paid, and your incredible staff removed every charge. I also received another gift you are probably aware of, so thank you. Your generous gestures were above and beyond...just like the service on Nautica. I had a wonderful time on the cruise—of course you know that since you have been reading this—in your last post you asked for more details, and I hope you are pleased with the end result. I know I am. If in some small way, my writing has helped your business I am pleased—Oceania deserves it.

CruisingSerenity: I am touched that you found something in my works that goes beyond the entertainment or thoughts about traveling. Thank you so much for sharing your feelings with me. I don't think I'll start a blog anytime soon, but if I ever do I'll let you know. Thanks again for all your encouragement…It made a difference.

scdreamer: Thanks for the reading suggestion. I am going to get *The Red Tent* from the library. Also, thanks for the well wishes for Ty and the assurance that I can write.

zutalors: Enjoy your trip! I hope you enjoy the Pyramids as much as I did.

ChatKat in Ca.: I am happily ensconced at home. My wheaten was absolutely beside himself when I walked in the door. It was almost worth leaving for the enthusiastic reception! Enjoy Nautica next month.

Lagunaman: I loved meeting your brother and sister-in-law. They are both wonderful people, and I wish I had more time to get to know them better.

esther e: If there is a higher compliment to a writer than staying up way past your bedtime to read, I don't know what it is…thank you! (P.S. I hope you got the much-needed sleep finally), and I was glad you were sitting on the vacant seat to my side. Maybe we can do it again sometime.

monina01: I know…I didn't want it to end either. You are welcome. I miss it too!

lahore: I will always feel honored that I impressed an Australian. I will miss our frequent interactions here. You have been a wonderful inspiration…Please stay open-minded about going to Luxor. I don't think you will regret it if you go…at least the one-day excursion.

aneka: The pictures are up. I will write again in a week or so, after Ty has his biopsy.

PennyAgain: Thanks for the encouragement. I hope you get to Petra someday, and thanks for the Bravo. I wish it could have lasted longer too.

Wendy The Wanderer: I am trying to compile it and clean it up a bit. The stream-of-consciousness style didn't lend itself to improving the grammar as much as I would like.

molomare: I wish I could join you, I hope you have a wonderful time…I know you will.

merryecho: You cracked me up. That is exactly what we would say at Stack III in Fairhaven. Thanks for the happy memories and for the voice from home, and thanks for the genuine encouragement to find my voice and keep writing. Photos are up!

cathi: Glad you enjoyed it. I hope you decide to do the Luxor and Cairo things. As strenuous as they can be, I can't help but encourage you to go. The trials are well worth the reward. I will put the journal together, and it will be a keep-for-life personal treasure. I wish all the best for your son and your family.

Rob & Beckys mom: You are welcome, and fortunately the flight home was fine. So happy to hear about your son. He is lucky to have your support, and I am glad he has been clean so long.

Emdee: Thanks for your support. Actually, FDR already did quite a bit for me, and I hope that in some small way my writing contributes to their success. Oceania deserves it—they are a first-class company.

orchestrapal: I look forward to hearing about your experience on Regatta. Have a wonderful trip.

Saga Ruby: As always, I love reading your eloquent writing. Thanks for sharing your experience.

SeaCCruiser: You are welcome; glad you liked the stories.

Hondorner: I look forward to hearing about your trip.

meow!: My mom does exactly what you suggest. She keeps a large bottle of sanitizer and frequently fills the small bottle. Great tip! Yes, Bellingham is literally at the Canadian border. The photos are up.

Lauren Spray: Thank you for the well wishes for Ty. I am starting to wish I were on that cruise with you, "lahore" and "molomare." Have fun!

carolhardy: I hadn't heard much about Oceania either. You have nothing to worry about. They've earned the accolades others and I have given them.

Twiga: You are welcome. Thanks for mentioning the fleece. My mom enjoyed reading that too—they really are wonderful parents. Have a good kiss in Athens, and enjoy the back of the bus...I'll be there in spirit.

Marebear: You are welcome many times over.

Magicnelly: Hmmm...quoting the Messiah's handbook to me...very tricky and very clever. Thank you. It was perfect.

Decebal: Glad you enjoyed it. I am sorry it went so fast too.

jckvpa0: Glad you liked it. Hope your travel plans someday take you to some of the great places I visited.

Toranut97: You are welcome. I am honored you deem the threads worth saving.

Isla Gal: You are my neighbor! I love Whidbey. I am sorry about your father, and I know I am fortunate. Ty's mother died when he was only 20, so he was very supportive about letting me do this with my parents. Thanks for the compliment—that is high praise indeed. Glad someone liked the U2 reference. "In God's Country" forever took on a new meaning to me after Wadi Rum.

Aussie Gal: I don't want to say good-bye to you, so I saved you for last. Have a great trip. We will always have April 4th, won't we? I hope someday our paths cross in the "real" world.

Chapter 19

AFTER NAUTICA

JackfromWA   *May 9th, 2007, 03:19 AM*
Photos and replies

Hello, everyone. I made it home. Life is slowly taking on its usual form. My laundry is washed and folded and the jetlag is slipping away. Ty told me tonight that he learned, "absence makes the heart grow fonder" in a deeper sense…so the trip gave both of us deeper insight about our relationship. I know if I take a trip this long again, Ty is coming. I posted about 90 photos tonight. For those of you who have read since the beginning, you will recognize many of the scenes. I tried to include those pictures that are most interesting to readers of the entire account of our trip. The link to the photos:

http://web.mac.com/jhovenier/iWeb/Site/NAUTON.html

I will post again after I pick up my parents next week and when I have news about Ty's health. Thank you all so much for all the encouragement, kind words and support.

*****

Aussie Gal   *May 9th, 2007, 04:13 AM*
     Jack, have just been viewing your wonderful photos. They are terrific and now we can put names to all the faces. Your mum and dad look terrific, and you are just as I imagined, thanks to your excellent description of yourself.
     So glad that you arrived home safely. You are very efficient to have managed to organize the photos so quickly.
     We will have our fingers crossed for you and Ty next week.
                                      Jennie

Lagunaman   *May 9th, 2007, 06:07 AM*
Thanks, Jack!

I really appreciate your very kind words; I am sending your thread to LA for them to add to their already extensive collection of "Jack's" compositions.

I will reiterate what many others have already expressed, THANK YOU. It has been such a treat to read your extremely entertaining and very talented storytelling, such an amazing giving of your time and effort during your vacation.

Nice to know that your return to reality has been such a pleasant one and should you both ever consider visiting Phuket again (AGAIN for you) or Marbella, please contact me...

I shall be really delighted to offer you a VERY nice break on accommodation—subject to your providing daily travel updates!!!

Marbella is actually a good base for seeing Andalusia, including places such as Granada/ Sevilla; also Gibraltar is only a 40-minute car ride away, and from there you have a speedy hydrofoil to Tangier, the gateway to Morocco.

You can see more on Marbella rentals link on www.phuketmarbella.com and if you do decide (HOPEFULLY) to take me up on this, contact me through info@phuketmarbella.com

Finally, trust that Ty will receive a very positive medical report and that you will enjoy a great future together

John

ChatKat in Ca.   *May 9th, 2007, 07:05 AM*
The best part of coming home

Is the greeting from the Wagging Tail brigade and defenders of the castle.

Welcome Home, Jack, and thank you for the Bon Voyage. We head up to Vancouver on HAL and a visit to dear friends on Camano Island next week. Then we head out on Nautica.

I will try to post some here from onboard—but I promise that it will be nowhere as entertaining as this thread has been. We will all be waiting for a report about Ty.

lahore   *May 9th, 2007, 10:13 AM*
G'day

Hi, Jack (whoops, that's not a very politically correct greeting is it...urghh sorry, bet you've had it a thousand times).

This little Aussie is more than impressed. As if your writing wasn't cool enough, now you're an ace photographer as well! I am so excited by your photos; it's such a vicarious thrill because we will be there soon and it's excellent to see all the things you described. I can't tell you how much more excited I am about our upcoming trip having lived through it with you. Also, now I can see what Salalah port looks like, so I know how much I need to make sure my taxi driver turns up! I will keep an open mind about Luxor—do you recall what the cost of the one-day trip was? And I can see that I was worried about camel riding with good reason (I am scared of heights)—but fair dinkum, I cracked up at that photo of you on the camel, what a hoot. And "Moonrise at Wadi Rum" should go into a photo competition...gorgeous.

esther e   ***May 9th, 2007, 10:16 AM***
Jack, thank you for sharing your wonderful photos and finally getting to meet you and Mom and Dad. This is definitely the best I've ever read or seen on CC. Thanks again.
Esther

mk0520   ***May 9th, 2007, 11:17 AM***
I am another fan of yours although I haven't posted before now. Thank you so much for all of the wonderful information and photos of your trip. The photos really made your journal complete. We are leaving on May 22nd on Insignia (Rome to Athens). This is our first Oceania cruise, and one of our stops will be Cairo, where we will be spending two days. We will be celebrating our 40th wedding anniversary. It has always been my DH dream to visit the Pyramids.
Our prayers are with you and Ty. Please keep us posted as to Ty's health.

scdreamer   ***May 9th, 2007, 03:06 PM***
Lovely photographs, Jack! Thank you for sharing your trip...seeing the photos after having read the journal was just perfect. Great to put faces to all the traveling companions we felt we had come to know, and seeing the sites you visited was wonderful.
Sending along our best to you and the ones you love.
Leslie & Wayne

Decebal   ***May 10th, 2007, 04:38 PM***
More pics...

Excellent photos, Jack. Loved the Christmas-card one in Egypt. Your parents are adorable.

I am showing the pics to my mom, as I've been telling her about the trip, and it's something that we talk about, er, rather dream about, doing ourselves.

Jack, when you have settled and have some time, could you also post some photos of the ship and the cabin, if you have any? Thanks.

seasoned   ***May 10th, 2007, 05:47 PM***
Knowing Jack...

I had the extraordinary pleasure of being on the ship with Jack, so I got to experience the cruise with him in person and then again as I read his posts here. We met on Cruise Critic and bonded by e-mail even before we left home. It was a treat to meet Jack and his lovely parents once we boarded the Nautica in Hong Kong. I second every positive thing he said about the ship and our time together on it. This was my third Oceania cruise. I don't think I'll ever try another line, as all the rest have disappointed me.

Jack and I did different excursions and thus had different experiences in the ports. Salalah, in particular, varied from his day. Friends and I hired a taxi and visited the picturesque towns of Toqah and Mirbat, occasionally stopping on the highway to wait for camels to cross; we also had a wonderful lunch of local food.

By anyone's account, the journey from Hong Kong to Athens was an incredible adventure, both on the ship and off. Since my gentleman friend wasn't able to join me on the 35-day trip this year, he has booked us for the 35-day itinerary for 2008! I'll have no problem repeating the experience, and it will be my pleasure to meet some of you then.

It's a special treat to know Jack, as all of you have realized on these boards. Thank you all for encouraging him in his writing. Indeed, he has The Gift.

                                                        Sukey

shedevil   ***May 11th, 2007, 01:36 AM***
Thank you

One complaint, Jack. Where is the photo of the family reunion when you got home to the furry children and Ty? Thank you for taking the time to share your trip, your insights, and those great photos that made the trip really come to life.

I have logged in every day of your cruise hoping for a new

*installment of Jack. We have cruised on Oceania and have traveled
all over the globe, but it always seems like I don't have time to keep
a journal, make a photo album, take the time to jot a few notes about
my impression of new places and people. Confession—the digital
photos from our June 2006 Insignia trip to the Baltic and the March
2007 Transatlantic to Marseille are all still on the memory
chip...nary a photo printed.*

*Thank you also for helping me realize that part of the joy of
traveling is the tale, the journey and by keeping a journal—
electronic or paper—I can relive the memories and share with my
loved ones.*

*You have inspired me to drag out the leather journals given to
me by my father—which have sat empty in a closet—and make a
commitment to journaling my journeys, short and long. My first task
will be to get some of those travel photos printed.*

Thank you again for sharing and inspiring.

Sharon

wildduck　　　**May 11th, 2007, 12:44 PM**

*Thank you, Jack, for sharing your wonderful photos and your
amazing journey. I was especially interested in the photos of the
Pyramids at Giza, as my dad fought in Egypt in 1939-45 war. I look
forward to seeing them on our trip next year.*

I wish all the best to you, Ty and your mum and dad.

mvmag　　　**May 13th, 2007, 04:11 AM**
I'm jealous

*Having read through your cruise experiences, I'm a wee bit
jealous. I was on the Silver Cloud, the Silversea ship you kept
running into. My husband and I had an excellent cruise. But now
that I've read your experiences, I'm chagrined to know that the
extremely expensive Silversea cruise had a lesser itinerary than what
seems to be a much-better-value Oceania cruise. It looks like we had
the same experiences in Luxor/Valley of the Kings. But in Jordan,
you were able to do Petra plus Wadi Rum; our choice was one or the
other, and the only couple I know who hired a private company to
allow them to do both almost missed our departure from Aqaba.
Even worse, we went from Petra to Sharm al Sheik, basically a waste
of a day, while you were cruising on up to Cairo/Port Said. We
didn't get a chance to get to the Pyramids; you did. Finally, when we
all got off our cruises about the same time in Greece, I saw all you*

229

people in your T-shirts and I thought: Well, either they ran out of
clean clothes (which, given the laundry facilities, could have been
the case—and trust me, the Silversea laundry facilities were only
marginally better) OR they really, really loved Oceania and want
everyone to know. Now that I've read your blog, I'm thinking it's the
latter. Long story shorter: I'm looking at Oceania for our next
cruise, and it's all due to this blog.

*****

JackfromWA   May 13th, 2007, 05:34 AM
Silversea vs. Oceania and Happy Mother's Day

Hi, everyone. Life is slowly returning to the patterns I am accustomed to. As I type this, Rusty is sleeping on the living-room floor, Stewart is laying on Ty and annoyingly flicking his tail, and Ty is on the couch watching last Sunday's *60 Minutes*. I answered most of my e-mails, paid the few bills I didn't properly anticipate, finished opening all the mail, experienced shock at the gas pump (Bellingham has the most expensive gas in Washington State, and there are three gas refineries within 20 miles...go figure), and in two days I pick up my mom and dad at the airport. After all the time together, it is ironic that I can't wish my mom a Happy Mother's Day tomorrow!

I was prompted to write tonight after reading the post from "mvmag," who was on the Silver Cloud, the ship that was often in close proximity to Nautica. She mentioned that inexplicably the Silversea itinerary wasn't as good as Oceania's. Since she didn't get to the Pyramids and went to Sharm al Sheik instead, I am inclined to agree. Rather than bash Silversea, though, I wanted to reiterate a theme from my posts. To me, more important than the itinerary are the people you travel with. I would much rather have skipped the Pyramids and spent the time with my mother and father than having seen the Pyramids and traveled without them. So, I am delighted that "mvmag" assured us she and her husband had an excellent cruise. I think that is the most important thing—when you take a cruise, you have a good time. For me, having a good time is a combination of the people I travel with and the ship I sail on. Having been on both Oceania and Silversea, I would almost always choose Oceania—I prefer to save some money, and the better cabins on Silversea don't justify the extra expense for me. I am glad that my reports have a Silversea customer considering cruising on Oceania. I don't want Silversea to lose customers but, after my 35-day experience, I am an unapologetic fan of Oceania, and I certainly believe they are worthy of a trial cruise from passengers usually loyal to Regent, Crystal, Silversea, etc. ("mvmag," you hit the nail on the head. The reason I wore an Oceania shirt is that I was proud of it and wanted everyone to know that Nautica was my tribe. It is the same reason that I bought and once wore a Silver Wind shirt.)

To all of you, I miss our travel dialogue, but I still have one more surprise up my sleeve, thanks to Sukey ("seasoned") so you aren't quite done with me yet.

Glad so many of you enjoyed the pictures.

Happy Mother's Day to everyone. See you again soon.

*****

TenerifeSharon   May 13th, 2007, 02:27 PM
May I please add my humble thanks? This is one of the most beautiful postings I have ever read.

Amazingly enough, I discovered your "Journal" about four hours ago and, once started, have read it from beginning to end. Absolutely beautiful.

Thank you again. Wishing you and Ty a wonderful lifetime together and am keeping my fingers crossed that the result of Ty's biopsy is negative and that you have many more years of wonderful experiences with your parents that you can all treasure.

Jancruz1   May 13th, 2007, 03:32 PM
Hi, Jack, After one week at home and looking back…I believe our cruise was the best we have ever taken out of 55 (we started when I was 10) lol…my children told me "you walked in the footsteps of history" and it is true!!!!

Thanks for the wonderful pictures…(ours are still in the camera…) it was so much fun reliving the cruise…your haircutting picture reminded me of the courage I had to have a wash, cut and blow-dry in the hotel in Luxor for $15.

It was great meeting you and your folks…and we look forward to traveling with you again one day...

Fair seas and calm waters to you and your family (of course Ty included) in the future...a big Hello to your parents...
> *Regards, Jan*
> *CruzUnlimited*

dancingpaula   May 13th, 2007, 04:36 PM

Jack, thank you so much for your wonderful reports and your precious time...you have had me in fits of laughter and an occasional tear in the eye...I could even imagine the smells and colors in the cities as you described them.

Wishing you every happiness for the future.
> *Paula xx*

mvmag   May 13th, 2007, 08:50 PM
I'm jealous

Jack, I absolutely agree with you and with other posters. Each of us chooses a cruise for many different reasons, and my husband and I will always cherish the fabulous trip and wonderful friends we made on the Silversea cruise we took. I would never bash Silversea...or Crystal...or Celebrity...all of which we have cruised and enjoyed for different reasons. I'm just saying that based on your blog and what I have read since and people to whom I have spoken, I look forward greatly to an Oceania cruise.

As to the other reply re the cabin size—just not a problem for us—I'd rather have the destinations!

Twiga   May 13th, 2007, 10:56 PM

Thanks for sharing your photos, Jack! The moonrise over Wadi Rum is a masterpiece. The sunset with your footprints is also fantastic. The photos of you and Frank are hilarious! Best of all is seeing you and your parents at the Pyramids. I've come to know you and like you through your journal, and I must say that I love your parents! I think they are wonderful people. I am so happy that you got the chance to take this cruise with them. It was a very special opportunity for you all. I was happy to read that FDR paid for your Internet charges and beyond. That is good business! You have convinced a lot of people to sail with Oceania. You definitely convinced me that I made the perfect choice in choosing to sail on the Nautica. Now if September 14th will just get here quickly!

I wish you well and hope to read more from you in the future.

232

Nancy

TenerifeSharon   May 13th, 2007, 11:43 PM
    Thanks again for sharing! The pictures are all wonderful, but the moonrise over Wadi Rum is absolutely breathtaking (cover photo for the book maybe??).

CruisingSerenity   May 14th, 2007, 01:57 PM
    Heehee! I love TenerifeSharon's hinting suggestion…I second it.
    And I'm also yelling, "Hurray!!!" in my mind with your statement about something special "up your sleeve."
    I don't have a printer at home…I wonder if I can sneakily print your posts at work so I can read them again and again.
    Welcome home, Jack.

aneka   May 14th, 2007, 04:13 PM
Thank you, Jack
    Thanks so much for posting the great pictures. They complement your excellent travel journal perfectly. I think the sun-setting picture is wonderful. It was great to finally "meet" you, your parents, and even the famous "Lumpy." Thanks for recording this fabulous trip for all of us to read and dream about. I know we will all be looking forward to your surprise!
    Thanks for your time and talents,
                                      Annette

Daw6id   May 14th, 2007, 07:24 PM
    As one who has not commented all through this cruise—let me add my thanks, now that it's over. FDR should be grateful for all the people who are now interested in this itinerary, like me. I am curious as to why the east coast of India [Kolkata, Chennai] are ignored. This series has been delightful—from the powder to the Pyramids, and I thank you for sharing with us.

merryecho   May 14th, 2007, 08:18 PM
    The picture of Jack and Lumpy at the Pyramids is now on my bulletin board. DH asked who it was, but it was just too hard to explain—well, it's a guy who went to the same college I did but I have never met, who went to the Pyramids with his parents and had a wonderful time, along with the Lumpy from Leave It to Beaver, *and they both are making funny faces—why do you ask?*

233

KatWag   ***May 19th, 2007, 12:48 AM***

Jack, this has been such a treat. I happened to see a post on another board suggesting that folks check out your thread. I enjoyed it so much that I read it straight through.

I'm more in Ty's vacation situation right now (can't get six weeks off, darn it.) But you've completely convinced me that we need to try Oceania.

Thanks so much for sharing your amazing adventure.

And I completely agree with the other posters' recommendations that you continue with your writing. The writer of Marley and Me, *John Grogan, was our local columnist for a number of years. He has an amazing ability to bring the reader right into the story. You have the same gift. Thanks for the smiles, the laughs and a few teary moments. Best to you and Ty always.*

                 Kathy

*****

JackfromWA   ***May 23rd, 2007, 04:14 AM***

A FEW RESPONSES:

Aussie Gal: So glad you loved the photos. Make sure you meet Sukey ("seasoned") on the 2008 Hong Kong to Athens Nautica cruise. If you enjoy trivia, I strongly suggest you recruit her early for your team.

meow!: Yes, I am shooting with a digital Nikon D80 SLR. I think it holds about 250 photos shot in large format, but since I downloaded frequently to my laptop, I am not sure how many it would have held before the card was full.

Lagunaman: I enjoyed meeting your family. Glad you enjoyed the story, and I truly appreciate your magnanimous offer of hospitality. When I get to your part of the world, I will contact you and try to enjoy your generosity. Thank you.

ChatKat in Ca.: You are right. The best part of coming home was the greeting from the wagging-tail brigade (Rusty) and defenders of the castle (Ty & Stewart). When I walked in the door, Rusty came running up to me. But instead of leaping up and down, licking my arms and barking, he hesitated. He sniffed, looked at me, sniffed again, and some olfactory canine sense verified to him it was really me. At that point, all hell broke loose. He was beside himself and didn't let me out of his sight for a day.

lahore: Glad you enjoyed the photos and really glad you are keeping an open mind about Luxor. While a ship shore excursion isn't the ideal way to tour there, it would be a shame in my mind to avoid it. The hassles, inconveniences and limited time can't eclipse the intense feeling of personally stepping in the cradle of history. I hope you go. Let me know.

esther e: Thanks for the compliments. Glad you enjoyed reading it and seeing the photos.

mk0520: You left today on Oceania. You may not read this for quite some time, so I hope you had a wonderful trip and enjoyed Cairo as much as I did. Thank you for your encouragement and kind words about Ty.

scdreamer: Glad you enjoyed the writing and photos. Hope you have a wonderful trip on Insignia.

PennyAgain: Glad the photos clarified the cabanas.

Rob & Beckys mom: I gave my mom and dad a big hug from you, and my mom hugged me back—so your hugs got passed on. I just read your note to Ty, and he said, "I appreciate everyone's thoughts and prayers, even though I won't know anything for a little longer. I am glad so many people are concerned."

Decebal: Glad you enjoyed the photos. I will try to add a few more photos from the ship in the next week or two.

seasoned: I am writing to you here because you posted, so now you are fair game. You are the person I imagined reading when I sat alone in the cabin and wrote everything. When I left the new installments on your cabin door, I was nervous. It was your favorable opinion I was seeking. I knew you would be kind if you didn't like it, but I also knew you wouldn't give me false hope—you are too straight a shooter for that. Your publicly writing I have The Gift is the greatest motivation I could receive. Thank you. I don't think it was coincidence we met. I believe when the student is ready, the teacher appears, and I am grateful, and feel very fortunate, to learn from you.

shedevil: Glad you found some positive motivation through reading this account. An unanticipated byproduct of writing this has been my newfound appreciation of the joy of traveling with people I love. Like all the best stories, the joy is in the journey, not the destination.

wildduck: I can't wait to read about your visit to the Pyramids. Have a great time next year. If you play trivia try to recruit "seasoned" (Sukey) before "Aussie Gal" does, or better yet, form a team online with "Aussie Gal" and "seasoned" before the cruise on your Roll Call board.

TenerifeSharon: Thank you for writing. I showed Ty your words of encouragement and it made him smile. One of the nicest features of the Internet is it allows friends you haven't met in person to send you positive thoughts and advice. I am thrilled you invested four hours of your life to read everything from beginning to end. Glad you enjoyed it.

Jancruz1: One of the highlights of the cruise was meeting you and Stu—now I always have a personal connection to one of the best-informed people on the planet about Oceania. For those of you reading who don't know it, Jan knows her stuff and is extraordinarily well connected with Oceania. I feel fortunate she and Stu are friends.

dancingpaula: You are welcome. The gift of the time it took to write was my pleasure to give, and since it brought you fits of laughter and an occasional tear, it was all worth it. Thanks for reading.

mvmag: Glad you are considering Oceania. Silversea can be amazing—I have nothing bad to say about them—but I don't think you'll ever regret trying Oceania. You know my feelings about Oceania, and I love the money I saved by choosing Nautica over Silversea or Regent.

Twiga: My parents are wonderful. Too bad it took me so long to figure that out. Glad you liked the photos—it does bring some of the events to life.

CruisingSerenity: Thanks for your encouragement. I think you'll like what "I had up my sleeve" when you read the following chapter.

aneka: You are welcome. Glad you enjoyed the photos and the writing. Enjoy your upcoming cruise on Insignia.

Daw6id: Thanks for posting. Glad I was able to share with you something you enjoyed.

merryecho: I will be in Portland later this week, and I'll think of you when I cross the bridge. Your conversation, trying to explain the story of the photo of Lumpy and me on your wall, made me laugh out loud. Some things are too hard to explain!

KatWag: To mention me in the same paragraph as John Grogan is humbling. I read *Marley and Me* on Nautica. I missed my dog terribly as I read the book, and I cried when I thought of how sad and painful his death will be for me. My wheaten terrier is eight. He has made a difference in my life, made me a better person and unknowingly saved me from making some serious mistakes. Reading *Marley and Me* made me appreciate Rusty even more than I ever did before. Thank you for your kind words, encouragement and high praise.

Chapter 20

EPILOGUE

JackfromWA   May 23rd, 2007, 04:14 AM
Books and biopsies (follow-up No. 1)

"Look, Jack! You have a package from Lumpy!" Kay said as I arrived in my office. Kay is my extremely competent office manager. She and my co-worker Eric's valiant efforts made my extended absence possible. She has read some of the posts of my trip and knows the history of my relationship with Frank.

A few days ago, Frank called to thank me for some light-up Dodgers hats I sent him, and when Kay answered the phone she was in the middle of reading my account of the 35-day trip on Nautica.

"It's Frank on the phone," she excitedly said. Having him call as she was reading my posts made the story even more real. Frank generously sent me an autographed copy of his autobiography "Call Me LUMPY." I plan to read it over the weekend. He also invited me to come to the Peppermill Hotel in Reno this summer. Frank and his friend, Kenny Osmond, more commonly known as Eddie Haskell, will be featured as part of the Hot August Nights celebration. In my wildest dreams, I never imagined cruising on Nautica would result in an invitation to hang out with Lumpy and Eddie Haskell in Reno this summer. I would love to go, but my brothers and their families are coming to visit Bellingham in early August, and I want to stay home to spend time with them.

After hanging up with Frank, I called Ty.

"When is your biopsy? Did they finally call with a date?"

"Yes, it is Wednesday, May 23rd at 2:15," Ty said.

"OK, can I go with you?" I wanted to make sure there were no more delays.

"Sure, it would be great if you could take me," he replied.

So, tomorrow afternoon, I will drive to Ty's office, pick him up, take him to the doctor's office and sit in the waiting room while they carve up his tongue. I don't know why it has taken this long. Sometime in the next week his test results will come back and we will know if he has early-stage tongue cancer. The doctors have assured him that if he has cancer, it is early and treatable. So, in the long run, he will be fine. In the short run, we need to know the facts, because fear and uncertainly are almost as malignant as cancer. It feels like our lives are on hold until we know the results. It is time for answers.

No matter how great the journey, life patterns, both good and bad, have a habit of quickly resurfacing after I am home. After a week of taking out the garbage, going to work, doing laundry, answering the phone, eating mediocre (compared to Nautica) food and watching TV, the trip feels further and further away. Fortunately, I can look at my pictures, call Sukey, talk to my parents, or read my posts. This cruise was special, and I don't want to let it get too far away from me. As I wrote while traveling, I want to apply to some of the wisdom I learned to my life. Some I have applied, some I haven't. Yet. Writing to all of you helps me remember my intentions.

Yesterday my dad came to my office to mail some Dutch cheese to my sister and brother.

"Here is a card for you. You better open it," he told me. The envelope was addressed to me in my mother's handwriting. When I opened the card a large check fell out. I had charged the purchases in Goa to my American Express card, and my dad inserted a check to pay for the exquisite Indian silk rug he and my mom purchased.

I smiled at him. "Thanks, Dad. You know I love checks."

The card had no printed greeting, but it was completely filled with my dad and mom's neat, cursive script. I began to read:

May 17, 2007

Dear Jack,

I'm not sure how to begin to thank you for all that you have done to make our cruise to Asia the most wonderful trip in my life. As I unpack and put things away, I catch myself smiling, remembering where we were the day we bought the carpet, or the vendors in Goa, or the Gandhi house. These are memories I'll treasure forever. As wonderful as the cruise was, it was not the best part. Spending so much quality time with you was the highlight of the trip. It is a rare privilege for a parent to have so much uninterrupted time with a grown child. You were and are a joy to be with. I know it wasn't always easy for you, but I do appreciate your consideration and thoughtfulness. Your insights and comments on your online journal were wonderful. You do have writing talent! Thank you for taking the time to share this wonderful experience with us.

Love, Mom

P.S. Thanks for letting me use your camera.

Dear Jack,

Being in second place to write a two-person "thank you" note is not easy. I agree with all your mother has written. I only hope that the trip was equally enjoyable for you. I am also grateful for your generosity with air miles and frequent contributions. You did much more than your fair share. It was a bit humbling to be known as Jack's dad/parents. I am sure that you were the best-known passenger on the Nautica, or at least it seemed so to me, and the best thing was that your notoriety was all related to positive behavior. I will always remember the many new and wonderful things we saw for the first time. We would never have made this voyage without your encouragement and help. Thank you!

Love, Dad

Some things are priceless. When the day comes that health or death make a trip like the one I just took with my parents impossible, I will have no regrets. We already took it.

Two songs have always haunted me. "Cat's in the Cradle" by Harry Chapin and "In the Living Years" by Mike and the Mechanics. Both speak to missed opportunities and sadly realizing the mistake when it is too late to do things differently. I think the men who wrote those songs would be pleased to know that I listened. I learned from their sage lyrics, and while I continue to make some mistakes, I won't make the mistake of procrastinating spending time with my dad and mom and family and friends I love until it is too late. I tell the people important to me that I love them, and more important than telling them, I show them. I know the value of spending time with people I love. To me, it is the most precious thing in life. My greatest possessions can't be stolen—they are my memories, my character, the love I have for others, and the love others have for me.

In my last post I promised a surprise. Thanks to Sukey (known on Cruise Critic boards as "seasoned"), I will have a neatly formatted, professionally copyedited manuscript of our journey. Sukey spent more than 30 years working for Time Inc. as a copy editor. Her effort is a labor of love. I probably couldn't afford her. She has completed about half of the posts, and I suspect she will finish the rest in the next few weeks. If not, I will happily, gratefully, wait until she is done. Many of your posts will be included, as the story isn't just my story; it is our dialogue that makes the story what it is. Since I am not a professional writer, don't have a publisher, don't know all the legal intricacies involved, etc., I am not going to sell the books to people on Cruise Critic. I am going to give them away. Of course, there is one condition. The cost to print and send you a copy is about $10. If you'd like to receive a copy, I request that you please make a $10 donation to the Red Cross, or to any other charity you choose that helps people in time of crisis. The link to donate to the Red Cross is here:

http://www.redcross.org/donate/donate.html

I plan to print 100 of these manuscripts. I am keeping a few myself, so if you want one, please send an e-mail to nautica@gumball.com and be sure to include your name, number of copies and your mailing address. I will ship "first come, first served" and will try to fill every request. Please don't make a donation until after you receive your book, as I don't know if I will have enough books to fill every request. It will probably be a few months before this is ready to ship, so please be patient. I will post on the thread when the copies are done.

This is a cruise board, and though I'll eventually run out of cruise-related things to write about, I think there is still a little left. I'll post again soon when I know the results of Ty's biopsy. I appreciate all your well wishes, encouragement and most of all your taking this journey with me.

Thanks for reading.

*****

Aussie Gal   ***May 23rd, 2007, 06:07 AM***
Jack, I have just read your wonderful post. I had tears in my eyes when I read what your parents had written in their card. Having two wonderful children aged 39 and 37, I could relate immediately to how your parents feel about you.

I am going to e-mail you immediately to order a copy of your journal. Can I send my donation to the Australian Red Cross instead of the U.S. based one?

Thanks also for the tip of asking Sukey if we can be in her trivia team. We have a lot of knowledge about the wider world, but nothing about U.S. sport or U.S. TV shows and need someone who is an expert in that field. We are looking forward to belonging to a team and playing that whilst on board.

Please keep in touch; we are all waiting to hear that Ty's health is back on track.

Jennie

*****

JackfromWA   ***May 23rd, 2007, 06:13 AM***
Any Red Cross is fine

Jennie, any Red Cross, or any charity of your choice that helps anyone in time of crisis, is fine with me. As amazing, inspiring and

243

exciting as the cruise was, the poverty was difficult to see, so I am happy to print the books and send them out, as long as the actual cost goes toward helping those in need. I know the amount we will send is a pittance, given the scope of extreme poverty, but if everybody did what we are doing…

Always good to hear from you. Recruit Sukey early. I hope to have Ty's results by early next week.

G'day
Jack

*****

lahore   ***May 23rd, 2007, 09:50 AM***

Hey, Jack, thanks so much for everything you have done on the Cruise Critic board.

I really can't write a lot at the moment but just wanted to say thanks again; you have done a wonderful thing. You have taken a personal experience that would be wonderful in any circumstance, and you have converted it into something even more: a wonderful treasured experience with your parents and on top of that you also made a lot of unknown people very happy/excited/pleased.

As some say here in Australia "On ya, mate!" (That means "Well done, friend!")

seasoned   ***May 23rd, 2007, 09:59 PM***
To everyone, but especially Jack

I must thank Jack for his very kind words.

When the work is done, it will be Jack's writing that deserves the continued praise. As he knows, I am on a necessary road trip right now and online when I can spare time from various obligations with my family. I am waiting for my own quiet zone when I can dig into the last half of his journal. I hope it will be this weekend. Till then I hope everyone will remain patient for the finished product, which will still, no doubt, be a work in progress.

Sukey

JoePDX   ***May 24th, 2007, 02:45 AM***
Dear Jack,

I can't begin to tell you how impressed and touched I have been by your travel journals. I've laughed, I've cried, and I've been in awe of your experiences and the talented way in which you wrote

244

about them. You made it easy for me to close my eyes and envision that I was there too. I've been sharing snippets of your tales with my partner Jeff since I came across the post last Friday. I guess in some ways I was lucky to be able to read the entries from start to finish, without having to wait for the daily installments. Although, as many pointed out, that may have been the highlight of several weeks to log onto Cruise Critic and hope for another entry from you describing your adventures with your parents and the others who by sheer chance just happened to share the journey with you.

I am thankful every day for the travels that Jeff and I have been able to share together, along with a wonderful cast of characters, some who entered our lives for one cruise only, but also a big group that we've been able to travel with numerous times. Travel has enriched our lives and provided us with education beyond expectation. This particular cruise has long been on my wish list, so I send a thousand thank-yous to you for sharing it with all of us, but also selfishly with me, in your own personal way. One day I'll be the one taking this journey—I know it.

I'm sending to Ty a "Lucky Dollar" through the Internet since I don't have your address. Stu received one that Jan told me she taped above his hospital bed in Florida during that very dark time. It sure worked for Stu, and I send every belief and best wish that it will do the same for Ty. Peace to you both.

> *With great respect,*
> *Joe & Jeff*

Jancruz1 **May 24th, 2007, 02:59 AM**
Joe, I cant tell you how much I appreciated all the good wishes and the lucky dollar at that time…I do believe in my heart it was all the prayers from everyone on this board and friends that helped Stu recover, and I'm sure that we all can help Ty also with our prayers…

> *Jan*
> *CruzUnlimited*

*****

JackfromWA **May 24th, 2007, 03:58 AM**
Thanks, everyone

Ty and I are home from his biopsy. The season finale of

245

American Idol is on in the background, and Ty is eating some of the Popsicles I got him—he loves Popsicles when he isn't feeling well, and tonight there are stitches in his tongue. We are in the waiting-for-the-results place in the cancer game—one of my least favorite places to be. We both thank everyone for the prayers and good thoughts.

Reading Jan's and Joe's posts prompted me to write tonight. I do believe all the prayers and wishes for good health, many from people I've met only here, make a huge difference. I don't have a logical reason why I believe that; I just do. When I was a cancer caregiver for my best friend, I spent months posting in the oral-cancer message boards. The love, support, encouragement and advice there was unimaginable. Online communities can make a difference.

We will have his results soon, and I will let everyone know. I am hopeful, but either way I know things will be all right. I am glad I am not on Nautica this weekend—I need to be home with Ty. I learned today the reason the biopsy kept getting postponed is the doctor was hoping the unusual bumps on his tongue would just go away. Most eventually do. His did not, so he finally got the test.

I have received about 50 requests for books, at least six were from Australia. Wow! There should still be plenty left for anyone else that wants one, and I think I can print a few more if necessary. So, if you want one I'll do my best to make sure you get it. A few people have asked if they can give to other charities. Absolutely! Some of my favorites are the Red Cross and American Cancer Society. Any charity you choose that helps people in need is perfectly fine. A few people have asked if I need a receipt. NO! I trust you. My brother mentioned today he was willing to start a charity for his kid's college fund (next week I go to Washington D.C. to watch my oldest niece graduate from high school), and I should ask everyone to donate to that, but I told him his need wasn't significant enough. It did make me laugh, especially since I think he would have taken the money!

I hope everyone in the United States has a great Memorial Day weekend.

246

*****

Saga Ruby   **May 24th, 2007, 07:06 PM**
To Jack

In today's mail is my new issue of Smithsonian, *and the cover story is Petra with the cover photo being that magnificent slot in the rocks leading toward the Treasury building.*

I was gobsmacked with the "finest kind" of photography that you shot on your trip—the Wadi Rum and Petra photos are top-notch. I'll enjoy reading the article because, thanks to your writing skills, I feel like I've already been there.

Happy sails!

Ruby

molomare   **May 26th, 2007, 04:09 AM**
To Jack

Jack, You never cease to amaze me with your sensitivity and understanding. Your description of your relationship to your parents on this trip just hit a very tender spot in my heart. You really hit the nail on the head—my married children live in St. Paul, MN and I do not get to see them very much. They, like many children today, are caught up in the frenzy of life, and I am constantly aching to see them and talk to them. My daughter has not grown up, at the age of 51, to understand that I am in the winter of my years and like your parents, won't be around forever. I love your description of how you treasured your moments with them on this trip. It did bring a tear to my eye. I guess if I offered them a trip just to be with them, I might get a positive response, but I can't, and they would not have the free time. So, Jack, having just come back from three days with my children in Binghamton, NY for one of their three kids' college graduation, I have to take my pleasure in small doses when I can. It was all too hectic and not really quality time. I just love you to pieces, Jack, and I don't even know you. You are a treasure! My DH and I look forward to our cruise along with "lahore" in November, and I thank you so much for your wonderful insight into some of the places we will have shared on our trip. My best to you and Ty and your wonderful parents.

Sincerely,
Marcia

247

meow!   ***May 26th, 2007, 05:21 AM***

*On the last count, this thread is very close to 20,000 "views"!
Let's keep reading and posting on this thread, to make it the first on
this Oceania column to surpass 20,000.*

Roselieb   ***May 26th, 2007, 07:32 PM***
Thank you, thank you, thank you

*Jack, Thank you so much for sharing this amazing journey with
us. I was on the Insignia's April 28th sailing (Rome-Venice) when
another Cruise Critic member mentioned this post to me. It took me
until this week to find the time to read it. I have been at my computer
for hours since I've discovered it, reading your posts, sharing in
your adventures, rejoicing at the wonderful bonds you have with
your family, anticipating Ty's biopsy results, and living vicariously
through your incredible memoir. My family (four kids) have
wondered why dinner is late, and my husband wanders in frequently
asking who I am talking to. I explain I not talking to anyone, just
feeling, learning and sharing a trip to many places I will probably
never get to but feel now I've experienced. Thank you for taking the
time to write so eloquently and with so many insightful thoughts. I
laughed at your descriptions of the trivia teams…it brought back
fond memories of the wonderful people who were part of our trivia
team onboard (Ah, what we'll do for an Oceania workout towel or
hat). I too love Oceania after my first cruise with them last month. I
came home immediately and wanted to book another cruise with
them but instead encouraged a good friend to experience sailing
with Oceania. One day I hope to be lucky enough to sail Oceania
again. My thoughts are with Ty and you as he awaits his results (I
know how scary this time can be). I hope when my children grow up
we can share a journey similar to yours and your parents. I wish you
only the best and look forward to reading about your adventures and
travels in the future.*

heinzweiser   ***May 29th, 2007, 04:51 PM***

*Jack, thank you for your postings! I just found this thread
yesterday.*

*Your words describing the Nautica cruise my wife and I were on
in 2006 are truly magnificent and deserve to be preserved in the
book I requested today.*

Heinz

JackfromWA   ***June 1st, 2007, 02:50 AM***

A FEW RESPONSES:

<u>Saga Ruby:</u> A friend brought the recent *Smithsonian* magazine and said the cover of Petra looked just like the picture I showed her. I read the article with much greater interest than I would have two months ago!

<u>molomare:</u> I shared your comments with my mom and dad. Your words really touched me. Have a wonderful time on your cruise in November.

<u>meow!:</u> It did…Wow! Over 20,000 "views." Seems like a lot to me—I sure didn't anticipate that the first night I sat in my cabin and wrote about boarding Nautica.

<u>Roselieb:</u> I am glad you enjoyed it and dinner is back to the table on time. Please extend my apologies for the tardy dinners to your family. I hope you get to enjoy a journey like this with your kids someday.

<u>heinzweiser:</u> Glad reading the thread brought back some memories of your time on Oceania.

*****

BENIGN!

"I finally got hold of the doctors," Ty said. We were just finishing dinner and watching the 6:30 evening news.

"Did they call you? What did they say?" I asked.

"I called them just before five. My test came back negative. The growth is benign."

I was so relieved I didn't even ask why he waited almost two hours to tell me. Sometimes I think Ty thinks it is his role to teach

249

me patience. Maybe it is. I had called him frequently at work every day since the biopsy to see if he had heard anything. I know he got tired of my asking if he had heard anything yet.

"Do you feel relieved?" I asked.

"What do you think! Of course I feel relieved."

"Do they know what it is? Do they know when it will go away?"

"Nope, it isn't cancer and it doesn't appear serious."

With that, it was done. I am so grateful Ty isn't adding "cancer patient" to his life résumé. He is only in his late twenties and has already experienced more than his share of trauma, cancer and death. He deserves better than cancer, but that is true of every cancer sufferer I know.

With Ty's news behind me it feels like the last thread in this story is complete. My mom is working on sorting our pictures—between us we had 3,500. I whittled it down to 1,200, and now she is trying to choose the best to share with friends. My dad is getting his yard in shape for the summer, and I am already lost in the pressures, twists and turns of my job.

I miss Nautica.

Even though life looks the same on the outside, I feel different since returning home. The people, cities and poverty I saw gave me a newfound appreciation for my life. Being away from Ty—my partner of seven years—for almost six weeks, put how much I love him and value our relationship in perspective. The compliments and encouragement from all of you online was overwhelming and humbling. I have made some writing goals, some fitness goals and some family and spiritual goals.

I received some luggage tags from Oceania a week ago. They are monogrammed with a metal Oceania Club logo set in a tan leather circle. I brought them home from my office today to attach to my suitcase. Ty and I are talking about taking an Oceania cruise together. The Amazon and Caribbean sound great, but the

November date won't work for either of us. Maybe the Panama Canal in January. We'll find something—I am going to share Oceania with him.

It's hard to write this last paragraph. This thread is my last tangible connection to the cruise—and the cruise was the best journey of my life. All good things must come to an end, and it is time to say good-bye, move on, and look forward to meeting you again on another journey on another ship. Until then, I wish you fair skies, calm seas and happy sailing.

Thanks for reading.

ACKNOWLEDGMENTS

First and foremost I want to thank Sukey Rosenbaum. I first met Sukey online before the cruise. Throughout the cruise our friendship blossomed, but I never suspected she would encourage me to turn my online posts into the book in your hand today. Without her meticulous copyediting, formatting, editing, encouragement and friendship, this book would not be a reality—the original posts would be words in cyberspace inexorably fading as time passed and servers crashed. Because of her generous and dedicated effort, people who don't read online bulletin boards can enjoy this story in much better shape than it was online. Words aren't enough to thank her for her countless hours, skill and advice.

I also want to thank the following:

Frank Del Rio, CEO of Oceania, for his encouragement, motivation and free onboard Internet.

The crew of Nautica, particularly her captain, Jurica Brajcic, for commanding one of the finest ships at sea; general manager Michael Coghlan, who always took time from his busy day to make sure my parents and I were having a great vacation; cruise director Ray Solaire for wonderful entertainment; concierge Robert Kinkhorst for his impeccable advice; destinations manager Cinthya Pavan for making our port visits so memorable; and executive chef Wolfgang Maier for his extraordinary culinary accomplishments.

Frank Bank, a.k.a. Lumpy, for reminding me not to judge a book by its cover, and for his friendship.

My trivia team: Mom, Dad, Ann, Jerry, Kirk, Tony, Gary, Neddra, Sandy, Nancy and Bob. You made me look forward to every afternoon at sea.

Carol, Bob and Dave for our time together in the Horizons lounge.

Jan Fishbein, founder of CruzUnlimited travel and Oceania's most knowledgeable travel agent; www.cruzunlimited.com

253

The following for posting on my Cruise Critic thread, "Nautica Impressions: Hong Kong to Athens": aneka, Aussie Gal, bdmagee, benfield, Big Julie, carolhardy, cathi, ChatKat in Ca., china addict, CruisingSerenity, dancingpaula, Daw6id, Decebal, dianancolin, Druke I, Emdee, esther e, Fetchpeople, fjdelrio, heinzweiser, herenthere, Hibiscuss, Hondorner, Isla Gal, Jancruz1, jckvpa0, JoePDX, KatWag, KIWP, Lagunaman, lahore, Lane40, Lauren Spray, LHT28, Magicnelly, Marebear, meow!, merryecho, mikebrill, mk0520, molomare, monina01, mvmag, OnboardNautica3-16-07, orchestrapal, Patty Cruiser, PennyAgain, pmcgsan, potterhill, raffeer, ricktalcott, Rob & Beckys mom, Roselieb, rrett, Saga Ruby, scdreamer, seasoned, SeaCCruiser, Sharicruz6, shedevil, shesgoneagain, Sweeterpea, tak2, tallship, TenerifeSharon, tgg, Toranut97, Twiga, TyrelJ, Wadadli1, Wendy The Wanderer, wildduck, zutalors and zu zu's petals.

Eric, Kay, Bernie, Elliot and Susan for covering for me at work during the trip—I couldn't have done it without you.

Jerry T. for encouraging me to take the trip. Without your advice, I wouldn't have gone.

Sharon Socherman, my friend and travel agent. Thanks for many years of expert cruise advice; travelwithsharon.com

Mom and Dad for making our dream a reality.

Tyrel, you encouraged me to go with my parents, you kept the home fires burning, you advised me in my editing, and you taught me that absence make the heart grow fonder. I love you.

ABOUT THE AUTHOR

Jack Hovenier is a successful entrepreneur. His occupations include paperboy, waiter, magician, pitchman, and founder and president of United Wholesale Gumball (www.gumball.com) and Lightwear (www.lightwear.com).

He enjoys reading, card games, oceans, good food and spending time with his family and friends. He dislikes exercise, income tax and speeding tickets.

Jack has lived most of his life in Bellingham, Washington, where he and his partner Tyrel Jackson currently live. They share their home with Rusty, a wheaten terrier, and Stewart, a gray cat.